BAD
MOMS

BAD MOMS
THE NOVEL

NORA
McINERNY

BASED ON THE MOVIE WRITTEN BY
JON LUCAS & SCOTT MOORE

DEY ST.
An Imprint of WILLIAM MORROW

DEY ST.

BAD MOMS. Copyright © 2020 by STX Financing, LLC. All rights reserved. Printed in the United States of America. No part of this book may be used or reproduced in any manner whatsoever without written permission except in the case of brief quotations embodied in critical articles and reviews. For information, address HarperCollins Publishers, 195 Broadway, New York, NY 10007.

HarperCollins books may be purchased for educational, business, or sales promotional use. For information, please email the Special Markets Department at SPsales@harpercollins.com.

FIRST EDITION

Designed by Renata De Oliveira

Library of Congress Cataloging-in-Publication Data has been applied for.

ISBN 978-0-06-290915-2

20 21 22 23 24   LSC   10 9 8 7 6 5 4 3 2 1

For Madge,
the Original Bad Mom

CONTENTS

PART I
SUMMER

WELCOME TO HELL

To: McKinley Mom Squad
From: Gwendolyn James
CC: Principal Burr; McKinley Staff
BCC: Gwendolyn James
Subject: MCKINLEY MOM SQUAD 2019!!!

Hello Mamas,

For those of you who don't know me, I'm the leader of the McKinley Mom Squad, more commonly known as the PTA. I'm a mompreneur who runs the lifestyle blog that Reese Witherspoon called a "must read" (link here). I'm passionate about empowering all moms to step into the fullness of the motherhood journey. My girls, Blair and Gandhi, are proud McKinley Mustangs, and I've loved every minute of our time at this award-winning institution of learning.

I hope you're all having a restful summer. You know the girls and I have been squeezing every drop of joy out of these past two months (if you've missed any of my daily posts, you can click here to sign up for my weekly newsletter, and here to follow me on Instagram). But no matter how many puppies we save from being put down, or visits we make to the homebound elderly, there is nothing that makes us happier than knowing the first day of school is just around the corner! In fact, it's just 33 days away (click here to download my back-to-school checklist and get 10% off your next order from Amazon!).

Attached please find the McKinley Mom Squad Contract. It's not just for new moms—we've had some significant changes to our programming since our last meeting, which were outlined in our weekly podcast, on our website, and in our email newsletter.

Our 100% involvement rate doesn't happen by accident. It happens because all McKinley Moms take the below contract seriously. Please note that this is not a legally binding document, but that signing it binds you to something greater: the sisterhood of mothers in your community, who are raising their children alongside yours. Please make sure you sign and return this to me within 24 hours or you will be placed on immediate probation.

Looking forward to getting to know all of you this coming school year.

In Love and Style,
Gwendolyn James
AKA @GwendolynJamesStyle

McKinley Mom Squad Contract

I, _____, being of sound mind and hot body, hereby dedicate myself to the betterment of McKinley School, and to the achievement of my child.

By signing this document, I agree to the following:

- To attend all PTA meetings within this school year. This includes our regularly scheduled bi-monthly (that means twice a month, not every other month) meetings, any and all emergency meetings, additional committee meetings for events I have committed to, and any other meeting that should arise at the behest of our leader.
- To serve on a minimum of two (2) committees for this school year, knowing that two is the absolute minimum, and I'll likely have so much fun I'll want to do even more.
- To ensure that any and all food I provide for the children of McKinley follow our dietary guidelines (link here).
- To ensure that any and all items I bring into our school are free of BPA, phthalates, parabens, GMOs, plastic of any kind, latex, soy, corn, or any corn by-products.
- To do my best to put forth an attitude of gratitude, and to be the change I wish to see in McKinley.

Xo,

Print and Sign Name/Date

PART II
FALL

2

AMY

6:00–7:00: Gym

7:00–7:30: Wake up kids, shower, start breakfast

7:30–8:00: Feed kids, walk dog, get dressed

8:00: Wake up Mike

8:00–8:30: Morning Huddle: Call In

8:15–8:30: School drop-off

8:30–9:30: Weekly Team Meeting

9:30–10:30: Sales meeting

10:30–11:30: Marketing status meeting

11:30–12:30: Performance Review, Tessa

12:30–1:30: Lunch

12:30–1:30: Meeting with Dale

12:30–1:30: Product tasting

1:30–3:00: BLOCK TO DO ACTUAL WORK

3:00–4:00: Proposed: Meeting with Dale

3:30–4:00: School pickup
4:00–5:00: Proposed: Supply Chain Update
5:30–6:00: DINNER!!
6:00–7:00: Email catch-up
6:00–7:00: Proposed: West Coast Sales Update

Remember when you were a kid, and summer seemed like it was full of wonder and possibility? The days would be hot enough to go swimming and drink lemonade and the nights cool enough for roasting marshmallows and catching fireflies. Perfectly sliced watermelon would appear before you even knew you were hungry, and you'd be carted to and from enough camps and sporting events to keep you from ever feeling bored. At night, you'd tumble into bed perfectly satisfied and exhausted, into a deep and dream-filled sleep. In the morning, you'd leap from bed, fully rested and ready for a new day filled with new adventures.

Well, behind all that joy and wonder was probably a mother wondering how the hell she was going to manage to keep you entertained and alive for three months. A mother counting down the days until the first day of school. A mother like me.

Summer is freedom for children, and a prison sentence for mothers. At least during the school year, you can count on your kids being in one place for eight hours. Summer requires us to fill sixty to eighty days with a variety of activities that are somehow all scheduled to be as inconvenient as possible for anyone who may have a job outside of chauffeuring their children around. Every year since Dylan was born, I've sworn that *this* summer I would take it slow. This summer I would enjoy my life and my kids. Have you seen that meme about only having eighteen summers with our children? Just eighteen summers before they grow up and leave forever, to repeat the cycle of wasted summers with children of their own? Well, I've wasted twelve of my eighteen summers with Dylan so far. I wasted them working to support our family and driving the kids from activity to activity in a minivan whose interior is coated in a fine dust of Cheerio residue and melted ice cream. That meme can go to hell and take all the mom guilt with it.

Every New Year's Eve, I'd take the time to envision the three of us enjoying picnic lunches and riding roller coasters and taking our dog, Roscoe, on long, leisurely walks every afternoon. I'd resolve to only work part-time, and not "part-time plus constantly being available on my phone at all hours of the night for my incompetent boss and his team of adult infants." I'd see myself making intricate salads with the mysterious vegetables in the CSA box I pick up every Friday at the school parking lot. That's how specific my vision was: that I'd actually know how to use a kohlrabi, *and* the kids would like it.

But, like the twelve summers before it, this was not the summer for enjoying myself. But you'd never know it looking at our end-of-summer assignments. By *our* assignments, I mean Dylan's and Jane's projects, which of course I helped with. I may have failed at summer, but my kids are going to start the school year with an A+ on their summer reports. I haven't spent ten years working in sales and marketing to let my kids turn in some handwritten essay on dirty loose-leaf paper. Instead, I tapped the interns at work to help me create two beautifully crafted, cinematic recap videos, which are already up on You-Tube and ready to show off to the class. Tonight, we'd watched them as a family after dinner, gathered around Mike's phone while our summer slid by our eyes, set to music that sounded enough like Top-40 pop to be enjoyable, but not enough like any specific artist to be flagged by YouTube. See? I'm a pro.

Jane's video is a recap of her accomplishments. It's the summer that she:

Read thirty-three books
Attended seven soccer camps
Was named Most Intense by her club soccer team, the
    Northern Mites
Ran her first 5K (and won her age group!)

It does not include that, of Jane's seven soccer camps, none started before the workday or ended at the lunch hour, and all required me to get to work late and leave early every day for seven consecutive weeks.

Her club soccer team members, who just last year were more like a collection of girls in matching outfits aimlessly chasing a soccer ball, suddenly gained full control of all their appendages and shot to the top of their league. They won game after game after game, and with every congratulatory trip to the Dairy Queen for twist cones, we watched our hope for any relaxing summer weekends dissolve into a series of weekend soccer tournaments in far-flung suburbs where the dads seem to be legally required to wear cargo shorts.

The video montage includes Jane triumphantly scoring

goal after game-winning goal. Our real-life montage would include that, and the rest of us baking in the hot Midwestern sun for seven hours on a Saturday, so desperate for shade that Mike and I became the parents who started bringing a pop-up "sun shelter" with us to every game so we could at least see our phone screens without straining our eyes. One day, as the temperature hovered in the mid-nineties, with no cloud in the sky, I prayed for the first time in years.

"Dear God," I whispered, "please let her team lose." The Lord refused to hear my prayer and punished me with an undefeated season and a child who was now officially addicted to winning.

While I was trying to plot with God against my daughter, I should have been thanking him for Dylan. Sweet, sweet Dylan. His video was a challenge, because it's hard to make dynamic content for someone whose summer was like one extremely long weekend. He slept late. He stayed up late. He wore a small groove into our couch, just the size of his skinny little butt. He will go back to school with a skin tone that's lighter than it was before summer started, and with a possible Vitamin D deficiency. The only clear memory I have of him from this entire summer was the day after he started coding camp, which I'd signed him up for thinking it would be a creative and productive way for him to explore his love of video games. "Tell us about camp," I said excitedly that night at the dinner table, sure he would absolutely ooze with enthusiasm over how I'd found the perfect activity for him. In so many ways, Dylan is an exact replica of his father. Of course, an actual boy child is supposed to look boyish, but looking at

Dylan and Mike together you can see that Dylan's future face will have the same charm it does now, even when it's lined with light wrinkles and his hair sprouts a few strands of silver.

"Well, I wanted to talk to you about that," Dylan said, leaning back in his chair the same way that Mike does when he is about to say something particularly annoying.

"I resigned today."

Resigning isn't usually something one does from a fully voluntary activity that one's parents paid two hundred dollars for, but Dylan seemed undeterred when I questioned him about his word choice.

Dylan continued. "I think that with the limited resources we have for the summer—namely, time—it would be a better use of those resources for me to just stay home with my Xbox. Plus . . . it's free."

"Good thinking, bud," Mike agreed. "*Plus*, if you get good enough at this shit, you can make a Twitch account, and livestream your little game thing, and actually *make* us money." Mike winked at me, though I know him well enough to know when he's serious. "Think about it, Amy. This kid could go from a cost center to a profit center for us. By doing *this shit*!"

I know that I'm supposed to be limiting the kid's screen time. And you know what? I did limit his screen time, by taking the Xbox controllers to work with me, which meant that he downloaded his favorite game to the iPad, which I then limited with a special app that he was somehow able to circumvent, which is when I gave up. That explains why Dylan's video is three minutes of Dylan spooning on the couch with

Roscoe, Dylan conked out in the backseat of the car on the way home from one of Jane's tournaments, or photos of Dylan staring slack-jawed at the TV with Roscoe tucked in next to him. I did the best with what I had and titled the video "Dylan's Summer of Snooze." Not bad, right?

Is that the bar I'm trying to meet? Not bad? I know from Instagram just how much summer the other mothers have squeezed from these past few months. I know whose kids went to language immersion camp (the Koehlers), and whose kids spent time learning to program their own video games (the Wenners), and I'm pretty sure one of the eighth graders gave a friggin' TED Talk about climate change.

It's late, and I should sleep, but I've been watching these videos over and over on my iPad, and with every view it's clearer that I need to be better. Be more present. Be more organized. I need to do what all those old ladies in the grocery store checkout line would pressure me to do when Dylan and Jane were tiny monsters, squawking and screaming in the cart. "Enjoy every minute," these women would say, blinking their watery eyes at me. "It goes so fast." I would smile and bite my tongue, because those days refused to go by. A single Monday could take three years to get through.

Tonight, while the crickets are singing their end-of-summer song outside our windows, our kids are sleeping down the hall and Mike is burning the midnight oil in his home office. I feel like he needs to take a productivity workshop, because even I don't work that much after hours, and I'm at a startup.

I'm way too tired to wait up for him, so I iMessage him the links to the video, waiting for his thumbs-up emoji before putting on my sleep mask, my hand cream, and my mouth-guard. Mike calls my nighttime routine the Boner Killer.

It's just cool enough for the breeze to feel like autumn to-night, and I sense that changing of the seasons more sharply than I used to. As of this evening, my thirteenth summer as a mother is officially over. How did I do? Not bad. And not great.

The CSA vegetables have all turned into a rotting soup in our fridge.

Dylan is not yet a profit center for our family but *has* prob-ably developed a repetitive stress injury from pushing control-ler buttons all summer.

I'm already late for everything on my calendar tomorrow, and tomorrow isn't even here yet.

I HAD EVERY INTENTION OF BEING EARLY FOR THE FIRST DAY of school.

I left Mike snoring gently, his phone still in his hand from the night before, and snuck downstairs, letting Roscoe out for his morning pee, filling his water dish, and grabbing my keys and one of the million reusable water bottles the kids always leave on the counter.

I suppose men can attend my gym, but it's marketed di-rectly to moms. The lobby encourages you to remove your shoes and "center yourself" before entering, but since most of us are running five minutes late and want to get to "our spot" in class, it's really just a pile of ballet flats and flip-flops cast off on the way to class. The windows of each classroom are covered in sheer drapes that diffuse the outside light into a warm glow. The overhead lights are strictly prohibited, but the teachers pretend to light the flameless LED votive candles before each class.

The class is always filled with other McKinley Moms, the kind who wear coordinating lululemon outfits and seem to never break a sweat. I tend to wear whatever I can pick up off the floor without turning on a light, which today is a shirt of Mike's that reads "Fill to here with margaritas." Squaring myself to the wall of mirrors, I noticed that the "fill line" cuts right across my boobs, adding a touch of class to my ensemble.

Class lasts forty minutes, which gives all of us enough time to get home and get our kids ready for school. Our instructor starts with some Sanskrit words, which seems slightly wrong coming from a white woman named Kelsey. Then, before she presses play on her Work, Bitch! playlist, she asks us to silently dedicate our practice to someone. "Send them your sacred energy," she whispers, handing each of us a small, blue inflatable ball, which we dutifully tuck between our legs. For forty minutes, we listen to Nicki Minaj and Ariana Grande and scoop our butts, carve our thighs, and pulse along to the instructions shouted at us from our instructor, who narrates and participates in the entire class. She has four children and absolutely no body fat, possibly because she spends three hours a day pulsing and scooping and carving, and possibly because I have never seen her eat a bite of food, even at the all-school picnic.

This is "my time," so I spend most of the class mentally going over my agenda during the day, and a fair amount pondering the fact that at least 60 percent of these women are married to dudes who consistently look as though they're eight months pregnant, and who have never pulsed, scooped, or sculpted any part of their body, and definitely not at six AM. Mike still has the body he had in college: not totally ripped, but fit enough that my mom still showers him with compliments. "Mikey!" she purrs to him every time she stops over, "I can't believe you have TWO KIDS!" She says this like Dylan and Jane came out of *his* body, and then ate from *his* nipples for ten months each.

This morning's class is too intense for my mind to wander far. "I want you to pull up on those vaginal muscles," Kelsey screams over a late-nineties rap song. "Pretend like this ball said something terrible about your child!"

I squeeze as hard as I can. Until my thighs burn and my legs shake.

"Squeeze! Squeeze like you're trying to suck that ball right into you, using nothing but your legs and your vagina!"

I had dedicated this practice to my children.

ANY ZEN I HAD LEFT FROM TRYING TO SUCK AN INFLATABLE ball into my vaginal canal was gone by the time we left for school. Jane was *not* happy with her summer recap video. "The teacher asked for a REPORT," she cried, as if I'd betrayed her deepest confidence. "This is a VIDEO. It's totally wrong!"

Dylan had looked at his sister sympathetically. "I thought you'd be upset because all those photos make you look like a brontosaurus."

Jane had responded by locking herself in the bathroom.

Dylan had responded to *that* by telling her if she didn't open the door, he would pee in her dresser drawer. He'd done that once in his sleep, so the threat was credible.

Mike had wandered into the hallway, eyes glued to his phone, just as I was attempting to pick the lock with a bobby pin, which is only possible on TV and in real life is just a good way to waste a bobby pin and damage your bathroom door handle. "What's going on?" he'd asked none of us specifically, and the tension had dissipated immediately. Jane unlocked the bathroom door and slipped into Mike's arms for a hug. Dylan apologized to his sister without being asked and used the toilet instead of her dresser drawer. Mike pulled me into his arms for a group hug with Jane, who tried to wriggle away.

"No way, Janer!" He laughed, pulling her face into his armpit. Jane screamed, and Dylan snuck out from the bathroom and jumped on Mike's back, shouting, "Unhand her, fiend!" Our house filled with my favorite sound: the laughter of my three favorite people.

I love Mike for that—how quickly he can defuse the chaos, even if it's him who caused it. But I hate that Mike's only real attempt at parenting is just making everything a joke. I hate that he always swoops in for the fun stuff and conveniently misses the hard stuff. And I really, really hate Mike for waiting until 7:48 to pull his Fun Dad card. And now we were most certainly going to be late for the first day of school.

THE SPEED LIMIT ON OUR CITY STREETS IS TWENTY-FIVE. Which means you can reasonably drive thirty and make the case that you're just keeping up with traffic. Which means I am driving extremely unreasonably—closer to forty, if I'm being honest—when our van pulls up to McKinley. We are *not* late. We could have actually been early if there wasn't a pointless one-way meant to "calm traffic" that forces us to zigzag our way to the front of the school. I'm tempted every day to just take the left on Sycamore, but Jane loves rules too much. Anyway, we are *not* late. School begins promptly at 8:10 and it's 8:07, and besides, there are plenty of other cars pulling up behind me. Or, at least one. A Trans Am, maybe? The kind of car you typically only see people driving ironically or in music videos from the early nineties.

Jane activates the sliding door the moment I put the van in park, and she and Dylan tumble out of the car. They both had told me all summer that this year I was to stay in the car at drop-off. Or, as Jane put it, "Under no circumstances should you exit your vehicle during school drop-off. Do you understand?" I had nodded yes every time; I had agreed to the terms of service. But on the very first day of school, when I'd always, always jumped out to hug them goodbye? It's muscle memory that compels me to undo my seatbelt. To run around the front of my idling minivan. To pull them both close to me and smell their heads. Those first few years, I'd have to pry them off me, wipe their tears, and lovingly shove them toward the front door. But not this year. This year, before I can gather them into my arms, they've already merged into the stream of kids wearing too-large backpacks, no doubt containing the standard "How I Spent My Summer" report, a dull recap of their summer printed on 8.5" × 11" paper and stapled in the upper-left-hand corner, the way Jane would have liked.

My throat aches. Am I going to cry? Are they really not going to glance back at me?

"WAIT!" I shout, and I see their little bodies freeze in horror. I am addressing them. In public. I have broken our verbal contract. They turn toward me, slowly and wordlessly. Their eyes say, "If you say another word, we will both scream for help." Their mouths shout, "WHAT?!"

There are moments in life when you have to lean into the awkwardness you've created. This is one of them.

"I love you guys so much!" I scream, holding my hands up in a heart shape. "I love my babies!"

Jane and Dylan blanch, more horrified than I've seen them since the day they walked in on Mike and me watching *Fifty Shades of Grey* on a Saturday morning. They both turn coolly away from me and walk toward the first day of sixth and eighth grades.

"Hey, Amy," a crisp voice calls out.

I turn to see Gwendolyn James, standing with her posse, wearing what I'm sure she believes is a sincere-looking smile. Gwendolyn is waving at me with perfectly manicured fingers (nontoxic, small-batch polish), her giant diamond ring—#conflictfree, I knew—dazzling in the morning light. This is my punishment for embarrassing my children: I will now be forced to interact with this woman.

"Hey guys." I smile back, and find myself drifting over, drawn by the irresistible gravity of social etiquette.

"I don't know how you do it." Gwendolyn sighs. "You leave your kids all day and go to work? You're so strong."

I hesitate, startled by the brazen backhanded compliment and unsure how to respond. Gwendolyn frowns, mistaking my silence. "You do work still, right?" I catch her eyeing my blazer, which . . . yes, does have a little bit of cream cheese on the lapel.

"Yes," I say, trying to smile, "I work."

"Well," she says, "that's probably why I haven't heard back from you about this year's Mom Squad Fiscal Plan."

FUCK. Maybe forty-nine hours had passed since she sent her last email, and no, of course I hadn't replied. I'd *intended* to reply, but I barely have time to read my emails, let alone reply to them. I'm sure, somewhere in my millions of drafts of unsent emails, there are at least thirty replies to Gwendolyn, each attempting to say as *positively* as possible, "Please just assign me a committee or push me off a cliff. Your choice!"

"You didn't get my reply? Hm," I say, playing dumb as I scroll through my phone. "I'll resend it. I bet it got caught up in your SPAM filter."

Gwendolyn smiles charitably, her teeth so white they look nearly iridescent. She has a face so pretty you really have to hate her, and a personality to match.

IT'S NOT THAT I DON'T LIKE GWENDOLYN. EVERYONE LIKES Gwendolyn. Everyone likes Gwendolyn, because they have to like Gwendolyn. She's @GwendolynJamesStyle, the authority on motherhood for our school, our neighborhood, and for her 144,000 Instagram followers, who shower her with praise for things like a photo of her coffee cup placed in the perfect light of her perfectly white kitchen, or her inspirational phrases, like: Mom all day, then rosé.

I don't get it, but I do get it. Like everyone else at McKinley, I follow everything that Gwendolyn does. It's a form of digital self-harm, comparing my mothering to hers. Comparing my children to hers. Comparing my house, my clothes, my car, my life to hers. I've seen every blog post, every Instagram story. It's a great way to make sure you avoid running into her, actually.

Seeing Gwendolyn is like being hit by a sniper: you don't know what's happened until she's already taken her shot, and your guts are spilling out on the concrete in front of you. Dramatic? Maybe. Or maybe not. Maybe, if you look closely enough at something shiny and beautiful, you start to see that it's made mostly of Instagram filters and clever angles.

When Dylan started at McKinley, one of Gwendolyn's friends had complimented my dress. We were all volunteering at one of the many "special days" McKinley has for its students, a series of carnivals and farmer's markets and artisanal craft fairs where the children sell their own handmade wares and donate the money to charity. That compliment had meant a lot to me. It had eased some of the anxiety I had about being so much younger and so much poorer than the other moms. They had arrived in outfits made by brands I hadn't even heard of, bought in stores I never thought of walking into. I was shopping in the clearance section of Old Navy (still do, always will), and before I could blurt out "It only cost $8.97!," Gwendolyn had filled the momentary silence.

"She's in great shape because running late is her cardio," she said breezily, and we'd all exploded in laughter. Even me. Laughing seemed easier than saying, "Wait, what do you mean? Is this about the time I tried to sneak into kindergarten orientation late—and on a conference call—and the principal called me out? Are you talking about the time that Dylan refused to perform in the holiday concert until I arrived, but my boss had called an all-hands meeting for six PM on a Thursday, so I didn't walk in the door until the last song, which meant that Dylan spent forty-seven minutes lying on the floor of the stage?"

For months I replayed the interaction, over and over in my head, trying to decipher her secret code.

Eventually, I realized the message was loud and clear: Gwendolyn James is an asshat.

3

CARLA

First day of school!!! STARTS AT 8:10 AM.
Vag waxes: 10–3
Jeopardy: 4
Karate: 5

What I Did on My Summer Vacation

By Jaxon Dunkler

This summer ruled. I heard the weather was beautiful, but I can't confirm that, since I slept until about 3pm every day, and then spent the rest of the daylight hours sitting in a cloud of my own farts and playing Fortnite.

Every evening, I took a break from my gaming to go to baseball practice for 3 hours. My mom, who is super cool and takes Karate, drove me in her awesome car. The only bad thing about my mom is that she's so hot that my team-mate's dads get uncomfortable around her, so she can't come to a lot of the games.

The hottest thing about my mom is her brain. Not many people know that my mom has read the entire Harry Potter series, or that she was voted "raddest" by her high school class. She has gotten the Final Jeopardy question right twice. She loves Sudoku. She can also change the oil in a car and drive a stick. Surprising, right? Nobody expects a lady who looks like her to have it all.

This year, I'm looking forward to playing more baseball, and to having the coolest, hottest mom at McKinley.

Jaxon's handwriting looks like a chimp got hold of a ballpoint pen. Seriously, one time a guy at the strip mall had a chimp he had taught to use a pen and if you paid him ten dollars the chimp would write your name on an index card for you. Looked just like Jaxon's handwriting, but I still got a chimp card. I used that chimp card as an inspiration for this report. I also held the pen in my left hand, which made it look halfway believable. This year, Jaxon's finally got a good teacher. And by a good teacher I just mean a hot dude teacher. I think any teacher is a good teacher, because anyone who can handle being around more than one kid for more than an hour at a time clearly has a gift. But none of Jaxon's teachers have been anything near bangable. Mrs. Weaver was pretty hot, but she was stone cold. You could just tell her vagina had formed a layer of ice over it years ago.

This year, Jaxon has Mr. Nolan, the only male teacher

who wasn't alive during the Vietnam War. He's tallish, has most of his hair, and one time when he was wearing short sleeves, I saw a little bit of a tattoo peeking out from under his sleeve. And it wasn't one of those dopey floral tattoos that guys have now. This was a straight-up barbed-wire armband. Hot stuff, and not what you'd expect from a man with a deep side part and a collection of pastel polo shirts. Mr. Nolan is a solid six even in his pleated khakis, and you only get one chance to make a first impression. I wasted that first impression by threatening to run him over in the crosswalk last year, but I doubt he remembers every confrontation he has in the school parking lot, and this way, he'll be able to get to know the real me through a trusted source: my dumb son who forgot to do his own summer report.

Nobody can call Jaxon dumb but me. He's dumb in a cute way, like a puppy chasing its tail, or a baby trying to play with itself in the mirror. Nothing gets Jaxon down, and the only thing he ever worries about is baseball. I have no idea how he got into baseball, but he's freakishly good at it. I would love to take credit for that, but I did my best to keep him out of sports. Signing a kid up for sports is just signing away your free time as a parent, and I love my Carla Time. It's hard to even tell who is good at baseball, there's so much standing around, but I've heard from a lot of coaches and a lot of parents that Jaxon is good.

But more importantly, he's a *good kid*. He may not be the sharpest bulb in the pack, but unlike a lot of the kids at McKinley, my kid isn't an entitled brat. I handed him his report in the car, and he grunted out "thanks" between bites of his breakfast. The paper looked suspiciously clean, but luckily that lovable doofus hasn't figured out how napkins work, and his report was instantly smudged with grease stains. Most Arby's don't open until ten AM, but the cashier at the Marshall Street location is an old "friend" of mine, and since he sleeps in the parking lot, he doesn't mind making my boy a couple beef and cheddars before school.

McKinley is a circus when we arrive. There are dozens of vans idling in the street in front of the school, and the traffic cop, whose only job is to keep things moving, has given up entirely. He stands there, dejected, in the middle of the street, not even bothering to direct the moms who refuse to even notice his orange traffic flag. The whole drop-off line is dumb as hell. They expect you to just inch forward in the right-hand lane until your car reaches the front of the school. They even marked the left lane as "NO DROP OFFS," painted repeatedly in giant yellow letters right on the road. But fuck that. We're late, and there's still a whole line of mom-mobiles moving so slowly they're probably in reverse. I whip up the left lane, ready to plead illiteracy to anyone who gives me shit and slam the car into park. "Love you," Jaxon mumbles, kissing me on the cheek with his greasy mouth. Jaxon lumbers away from the car with his bag of Arby's and a backpack that will probably never see an actual book. I don't bother trying to take a photo, they do those at school anyway.

I swear, Back to School is like a drug for these moms. And I say "moms" only because the pickup and drop-off and PTA and volunteers are a solid 95 percent female. And not single moms, either. I'm a weirdo here, a complete outlier. Most of these broads have perfectly able-bodied husbands who all seem to have a disability that prevents them from doing jack shit for their kids.

McKinley is known for the smoking-hot moms, and I say that *absolutely* including myself. Now, for my taste, most of the McKinley moms are a little uptight. Nobody who runs without an assailant behind them can possibly be very good in the sack, but the men in our suburb seem to get the appeal of a skeleton cased in a very slender, very tan meat sack and wrapped in lululemon.

The McKinley dads, though? They don't get enough credit. I know because I spend forty hours a week waxing their wives' labia and trimming their cuticles, and all these bitches do is complain about their husbands. Keith is too fat. Jonathan is distant. All thirty-seven Matts seem to be unable to tell the difference between Real Housewives of Orange County and Real Housewives of Beverly Hills. Kevin's bonus wasn't as big as they'd expected, and now Tabby has to break it to the kids that they won't be going to Nantucket for the summer. Instead, they'll be slumming it in Door County, Wisconsin. It's going to be *humbling*.

None of these dads are Vin Diesel, but the men of Mc-Kinley have their charms. And even though I definitely *could*, I don't sleep with married men. And I don't have sex with them, either. Dom Toretto said it best: a man's gotta have a code. Dom Toretto is Vin Diesel's most popular character—from the *Fast & Furious* filmography, obviously. He's why I bought my car. I met Vin at a bar in the city one night, and he was selling his favorite street-racing car because he just had too many, and wanted to spread the love of racing. He had me pay him in cash, so he could protect his privacy. All I have to remember him by is this car, and the four hours we spent in the backseat together. Oh, and a selfie I took with him right before we banged the first five times. I wish I hadn't been so drunk, because it's too blurry to really tell that it's Vin. And I'm 90 percent sure it was him. 70 percent sure. People act like he'd have no reason to be in the Midwest on a Tuesday in February, but people are dumb as hell.

But back to dads.

A Jock Dad *looks* great but is usually too insecure to have any fun. Jonathan spent the entire ten minutes we were together looking at his own abs in the mirror.

A Boring Dad is kind of perfect if you just want a warm body on top of you, and someone who agrees to bring a tray of take-out nachos with him when he comes over.

My personal favorite is a Sad Dad, one whose divorce is fresh, like Keith. Keith *is* a little chunky, but since the divorce, I've seen him at the karate studio nearly every day, working out his rage issues. He's still got a potbelly, but what's not to like about a guy who makes *you* look fitter the moment he takes off his shirt? A Sad Dad's standards are low enough that anything you do will be considered off the charts hot. They've been poking around in the same vagina for at least a decade, so you don't even need to *do* anything. You can just lie there, bite your lip, and say a few curse words and they'll think you're a sex goddess.

And then there's the holy grail: the Widowed Dad. You get all the benefits of a divorced dad, but without a crazy ex-wife to deal with! We only have one at this school. So far, at least. I mean, anything can happen. Jesse would be the hottest dad at McKinley even if his wife were alive, but the fact that he's grief-stricken *and* hot just makes his stock soar. I swear, when he walks into a room, you can hear the other moms wishing their husbands would die. Not painfully, just . . . in their sleep, maybe? And I don't blame them. I'm not usually into extremely handsome men with flawless bodies—aside from Vin, of course—but Jesse releases a special pheromone that makes all the moms want to heal his broken heart with sex. Nobody, to my knowledge, has accomplished this yet.

Once, Jesse was wearing his daughter's *Frozen* backpack at drop-off, and the moms lost their shit over her two perfect French braids. They were good braids, but these bitches acted like they'd never seen a braid before. They wanted to know everything: What hair products did he use, and did he watch a YouTube tutorial or was he just a natural? Even their compliments sounded like questions. And the giggling. It was nonstop. You'd think Jesse was doing a stand-up set and not just . . . standing up. Jesse makes all these women completely insane. I don't see them tripping all over each other like "Jennifer, that braid! Amanda, you packed a lunch!" I'm not saying that Jesse isn't a good dad. I'm just saying that Jesse is treated like a living saint for *just doing shit a parent is supposed to do.* The same women who look down on me and Jaxon, who I know whisper about how I dress and why I don't have a ring on my finger, think that Jesse is some kind of hero for doing the same shit we all do every single day.

The mom groups are breaking up, and the traffic cop is

showing new signs of life, attempting to guide the minivans into my personal fast lane. I rev the engine of my Trans Am and peel out, watching in the rearview mirror as each mom's head snaps in my direction.

Show's over, ladies.

4

KIKI

7:00: Wake up

7:05: Start coffee

7:10: Shower

7:20: Wake up Kent and kids

7:25: Feed kids

7:30: Get dressed

7:30–7:45: Get kids dressed

7:50: Leave for school!

8:00: Drop-off/first-day photos

8:05: Talk to Gwendolyn

8:15: Special coffee date with Gwendolyn??

9:30: Kids' morning nap: clean kitchen, fold laundry

11:00: Check the mail!

11:05: Leave for library

11:15–12:00: Story time

12:05: Drive home

12:30: Lunch

1:00: Kids' afternoon nap: start laundry, clean living
   room, check email

3:00: Leave for pickup

3:05: Catch up with Gwendolyn//text??

3:20: After-school snacks

3:30–4:00: Grocery store

5:00: Start dinner

5:30: End dinner

6:00: Clean kitchen

6:30: Baths

7:30: Bedtime routine

8:00: Special time with Kent

8:45: Lights out!!!

It's 7:07, and I am awake, showered, *and* have started the coffee. Kent doesn't need to be awake for thirteen more minutes,
so I'm *very* ahead of schedule, according to my new planner. I
draw a clean black line through each of those items. It's *satisfy-
ing.* Is this me time? Gwendolyn James is always talking about
me time, the importance of having "an essential self-care routine for all mamas." Her Instagram, @GwendolynJamesStyle,
is full of wisdom and inspiration. Gwendolyn says that we
should start each day with an attitude of gratitude and that
our thoughts become things. So, if I think, *The twins are going
to be really difficult if they don't nap for at least ninety minutes
this afternoon*, well, guess what? They will be really difficult
if they don't nap for at least ninety minutes this afternoon! She

says that if we aren't happy with our lives, that has nothing to do with anything or anyone but *us*. Gwendolyn says that daily meditation is the key to a balanced life. Even her *kids* meditate!

I have exactly eleven minutes left until Kent and the kids wake up.

Gwendolyn says to find a quiet, peaceful place where you can sit uninterrupted. I choose the kitchen table, which is still clean from the wipe-down I gave it last night. *Thanks for that, Past Kiki*, I think. *You're welcome*, I reply. My attitude of gratitude is already working!

Thoughts become things. Thoughts become things. Today, I will talk to Gwendolyn. I will meet a new mom friend. I'll have a special coffee date. I will not be weird and awkward, and nobody will regret talking to me.

I breathe in. I breathe out.

"KIKI? KIKI!" KENT IS SHAKING MY SHOULDERS. WHERE AM I? What happened?

"KIKI. It's seven thirty! Why are you asleep?" Kent's face is crisscrossed by the crease lines from the pillowcase. He has the adorable habit of sleeping facedown, like a hibernating frog. Behind him, the kids are standing, confused, hungry, still in their pajamas.

Did he say seven thirty?! No. No. No. NO. NO.

Seven thirty is not good. Seven thirty is when the kids and I should be dressed and getting in formation to load into the van. "I was meditating," I blurt out, but Kent is already halfway out the kitchen, probably on his way to take the shower he should have taken five minutes ago.

"Kiki," he says, sighing tenderly, "this is why I got you a planner, honey bunny."

I flip my planner back open to today.

Today will be a good day, I tell myself. *Thoughts become things.*

BERNARD REFUSED TO WEAR THE OUTFIT I PICKED OUT FOR him today. I bought it through one of Gwendolyn's affiliate links. It was a cute little pair of shorts that had an attached set of suspenders, with coordinating knee socks and saddle shoes. It's *exactly* what Blair and Gandhi are wearing. They could have matched! Then I could have talked to Gwendolyn about clothes and shopping! Wait, did I buy Bernard a girls' outfit? No. It's unisex. Gwendolyn doesn't believe in gender, gender is over! It doesn't matter, because Bernard refused to wear it anyway. Instead, he's wearing a University of North Dakota T-shirt that he took from his little sister's drawer, and one of Kent's neckties, which he insisted on tying himself. It looks like a DIY bolo tie or something a drunk party clown would wear.

BEFORE BERNARD WAS BORN, I HAD THOUGHT OF MOTHER- hood as a club I'd join the moment I gave birth. My baby would be the equivalent of receiving a Mom card: I could present Bernard to any other mother to instantly form the bonds of friendship. Instead, I found out that there were lots of different *kinds* of moms, and you could only befriend the moms who completely subscribed to the exact same list of beliefs and practices that you did. This was determined swiftly, and often without a conversation. Once, when Bernard was very little and I was pregnant with Clara and he was absolutely losing his mind in the grocery store checkout line, I handed him my phone just to get him to stop fussing. It wasn't even unlocked, I *knew* screen time was bad, it was just the phone itself he wanted. Just holding it got him to stop screaming. In that silence, I heard a gasp behind me, and a mom reached across my cart to snatch the phone from Bernard's chubby little hands. He screamed, and I stood there, dumbfounded, while this stranger explained to me that my phone was absolutely crawling in germs, that it was dirtier than a toilet seat! I have never gone back to that grocery store. Motherhood for me has been a series of interactions like this: of mothers sizing me up and then gently or not-so-gently closing their circle.

I tried the Crunchy Moms, whose kids have never eaten sugar and who only play with nontoxic, recycled, handmade toys cobbled by local artisans. They're the moms who told me that LEGOs are an assault on our ecosystem and that soy is going to give Bernard cancer.

Then I tried the Attachment Moms, whose kids can breastfeed until they decide not to. They all seem to like harem pants? Kent said harem pants made it look like I was wearing a full diaper. The Attachment Moms were nice, but when they found out that Bernard slept in a crib they started sending me links about co-sleeping, and then stopped posting their meet-ups in the Facebook group.

There are Tiger Moms, but they scare me. I wasn't intense enough to keep up, and Bernard refused to participate in any extracurriculars, even as an infant.

I tried the Fit Moms, but I couldn't keep up with them either. The Strollercize classes were hard enough, but I can't train for a 5K while pushing four kids in a stroller. Their motto was "STRONG AS A MOTHER," but *my* mother smoked throughout my pregnancy so that I'd be a smaller baby, and I don't think my lung capacity is as good as it would have been if she'd at least cut back to two or three cigs a day.

There are Cool Moms, of course, but they terrify me. How are you supposed to keep up with all the new memes and novelty tees with punny phrases on motherhood *and* wine? How do you make your hair messy on purpose?

I still don't know what kind of a mom I am, but I am determined that this year will be different. A new start for me. I won't just be a stay-at-home mom with four kids. I'll be a stay-at-home mom with a kid who is in *school*. I'll be a part of the Mom Squad. I'm going to be friends with *Gwendolyn*.

GWENDOLYN JAMES IS EVEN MORE BEAUTIFUL IN REAL LIFE. I know she gets highlights (she did an Instagram live from the salon just to #keepitreal with her followers), but they look like they were painted on by God himself.

Today she's wearing an outfit I haven't seen her wear yet: they aren't sweatpants, but they're sort of sweatpants? But not like my University of North Dakota sweatpants that Kent gave me when I was pregnant with Bernard. These are . . . sexy sweatpants? And they show off her smooth, tan calves. Does she shave every day? No way. She doesn't shave at all. I bet she doesn't even *have* leg hair.

Bernard has already run ahead, but Clara is walking unsteadily in front of the stroller, where the twins are giggling. I paid a lot of money for a stroller that has a special platform for her to stand on, but she refuses to use it. She's a "strong-willed child," which my mom would have called "a problem child."

"Claraaaaa!" I sing to her. "Let's play a game called walk in a straight line!"

Clara changes direction again, and the front wheel of the stroller clips the back of her leg. We've got a toddler down.

Bernard doesn't mind that his sister is yowling in pain in front of his school, but the twins are both parrots, and even though they are not even a little bit hurt, they join their sister in creating a full-on a cappella chorus of screaming children. For a moment, I consider just leaving them all there, getting in my van, and driving away. Maybe all the way to North Dakota. Maybe South Dakota. Maybe even Kansas, depending on traffic. I'd throw the Kidz Bop CD out the window on the freeway and stop at the McDonald's drive-thru just for myself. I'd eat my fries one at a time instead of trying to pour them down my throat while they're still boiling hot just so I can have enough calories in my body to survive wrestling the twins in and out of their car seats.

My daydream is interrupted by a mom. A mom! She's clearly already done with drop-off, and she's on the way to her car. "Hope your morning gets a little better." She winks at me. "We've all been there."

Be normal. Be normal. Be normal.

"Great, how are you?" I say, and she graciously pretends that makes sense. I want to say more, I want to ask her if she has time to get a coffee, or if she wants to meet up before pickup. But I can tell from her outfit and her car that she's on her way to the office. That she takes her coffee like she takes her meetings: standing up at an ergonomically designed desk.

Parents aren't allowed past the front door of McKinley on the first day of school, owing to some "misunderstandings" between staff and parents that have only been alluded to vaguely in the daily emails that Gwendolyn sends from the Mom Squad. Instead, all the moms have congregated in groups on the front lawn. They look so *natural*, like this is something they do every day: just stand around with their friends in cute outfits having regular conversations.

Be normal. Be normal. Be normal.

Today, I know, my thoughts will become things. Today, I will meet Gwendolyn. I'll give her the gift I made for her—a throw pillow that's printed with some of her best Instagram photos—and tell her how much her account has inspired me. She'll be so flattered, but also humble. "You inspire *me*," she'll say, bringing me in for a hug. "I *love* this." Then we'll have a special coffee date. Then we'll be friends; and next year, she'll be posting photos of all our kids on the yearly spirit quest through Joshua Tree, which I learned on Wikipedia is *not* just a U2 album that my parents forbade me from listening to because they believed that secular rock music was the work of the Devil but is *also* a place where Gwendolyn takes her family each year just to revive their spirits and renew their sense of purpose in the world.

Gwendolyn is standing with her closest friends. I don't know them, but I know *of* them. She tags them in her photos. One of them makes jewelry and the other one has shoulder muscles that make me slightly scared and a little tingly in my swimsuit zone. Neither of them has as many Instagram followers as Gwendolyn, but they are definitely Cool Moms.

"Hi, Gwendolyn!" I say. I was hoping it would sound normal, but my voice catches in my throat, and what comes out is more of a gurgly whisper, like I'm a troll hiding under a bridge that Gwendolyn James is walking across in her eco-friendly, fair trade shoes.

"Hi, Gwendolyn!" I try again. The conversation pauses, and for a moment, the sun that is Gwendolyn shines upon me.

"Hiiiiiiii," she coos back to me.

I don't know what comes out of my mouth next. It's a collection of every thought I've ever had but cut up and rearranged like the verbal equivalent of a ransom note made from magazine cutouts. I watch as Gwendolyn's smile turns to a pained grimace, and then as her eyes shift to meet those of her friends.

I'm blowing it. NO. THOUGHTS BECOME THINGS. I am doing great!?!

I thrust the gift bag forward, suddenly embarrassed by how childish it looks, how cheesy my bubble letters must look to a woman who taught Gwyneth Paltrow brush calligraphy. Gwendolyn smiles, but there's a hint of something else there, like the smile the woman at the grocery store gave me when she took my phone from my screaming toddler. I'm imagining that, of course. My meditation app would tell me that I am letting my thoughts wash me away in the tide of anxiety. I sweep away that anxious thought and struggle for the next thing to say.

"Would you like to have coffee?" I croak, but the moment is over. Gwendolyn's voice, clear and confident, eclipses my own little whisper. "Thanks *so* much," she says to me, and turns back to her friends, closing the circle behind her.

5

AMY

Sometimes, when I'm sleeping, the actual dream will be interrupted by an email notification. It's like my dream is the computer screen and whatever is happening in my subconscious—I'm running through my high school trying to make it to my math final, or I'm trying to swim away from a shark but the ocean has turned into nacho cheese—will be interrupted by a soft *ping* and a small window, bearing only the first part of an email that is always, *always* marked as urgent.

> **Subject: 911 !!! Call-in info for 8am conf??**
> **Subject: URGENT where tf is our packaging copy??**

It's like having a nightmare within a nightmare, and after a night like that, I always feel cheated, like those eight (okay, six and a half) hours I spent being interrupted by imaginary emails should count as work hours.

The reality of my day isn't much different from that nightmare. I'm the Sales and Marketing Director of Coffee Collective, a forward-thinking curator of highly crafted coffees that disrupts the traditional bean-to-cup coffee model by reimagining your morning routine. If that's hard for you to comprehend, let me put it this way: we sell coffee.

I'm good at my job. No, I'm great at my job. In the past eight years, I've single-handedly built us from a hobby company founded by a bored rich kid named Dale, who Mike calls the Child Executive Officer (not fair, Dale was twenty when he started the company, which is legally an adult), to a legitimate business enterprise that supplies overpriced coffee that is most definitely the same stuff you can buy at Costco, but in a folksy craft paper bag with a "hand-stamped" logo across the front.

My boss, Dale, is a mostly-well-intentioned rich kid who will tell you and anyone who asks that he dropped out of college to pursue his dream of building a business on his own. The thing is, anyone with Facebook, Twitter, or Instagram and a little time on their hands can scroll through his posts and see that, really, he failed out of three different state schools before his parents gave him a large chunk of money to keep him busy and out of the family business.

I was Employee #1 at Coffee Collective. I met Dale when Dylan and Jane were still little, and I was working crazy hours at an ad agency downtown. I dropped Jane and Dylan off at daycare before the sun was even up and picked them up when it was dark. I saw them for maybe forty-five minutes a night before they fell asleep, and I spent most of those forty-five minutes on my laptop, anxiously replying to client emails. On Saturdays, we tried to explore farmer's markets and pop-up shops in the city, to spend as much time as a family as we could. One sunny spring day, while Mike and I argued over whether a thirty-dollar jar of local honey was in the budget, I saw him: a dopey loner standing awkwardly at a folding table with a cheap vinyl banner duct-taped along the front. He made eye contact with me, and my motherly heart swelled in pity for this doofus. Two cups of coffee later, I was buzzing with ideas and too much caffeine. He needed branding—actual branding, not just the default font in Microsoft Paint. He needed a sales rep and a marketing director. He needed a point of view and some confidence. Dale nodded along with everything I said, a mixture of awe and fear on his face.

"So," he said awkwardly, "can I just hire you to do that for me?" Mike and I looked at each other. *Could he?* Our negotiation took place at the farmer's market, that same day. I'd be a part-time Sales and Marketing Director. I'd get phantom shares in the company and a board seat. I'd work between twenty and thirty hours a week, doing three days in the office, so I could be more present with our kids. I left the farmer's market that day with five pounds of squash I had no idea how to cook, and a new job.

That Monday, I put in my two-weeks' notice at the agency and was immediately escorted from the building. I was free.

That first year at Coffee Collective was electric. I arrived every day ready to create something incredible, and we did. Dale was grateful for my expertise and valued my input. We tested every roast, named every coffee, and approved every design choice, together.

And then it happened. Dale's parents, finally feeling that swell of parental pride in their third child, used some of their social capital to get the local business journal to come and interview their son. Dale was a nervous wreck, but I prepped him for days beforehand, filling his head with perfect pull quotes and impressive statistics. I bought him a new outfit just for the occasion: a fresh black hoodie and a crisp button-down to go under it, the perfect combination of professional and casual.

It worked.

Three months later, Dale's face was on the cover, smirking boyishly from the magazine rack of every local grocery store. The writer had been charmed by Dale, by his work ethic and ethos. By me, via Dale.

Investors outside of Dale's family showed up with buckets of money for him. The college "buddies" who had ditched him long before he failed out showed up "ready to help," and pretty soon our little duo became five and ten and fifteen and twenty people, hired impulsively by a person who just wanted to be *liked*.

Someone had to be a grown-up, and that someone was me. I became more than just part-time sales and marketing. I became the COO. The CFO. The CMO. HR. Not officially—there was no title or salary change—but by default, the same way I became the who knows where the fire extinguisher is, and the person who had to explain to actual adult males why you cannot light fireworks indoors. Someone had to do it, so I did. I do. Every single day, for way more than four hours a day.

What we sell is five times more expensive than anything your parents ever drank, and we sell fuck-tons of it. We sell it to unnamed restaurants, to "general stores," to anywhere there may be a piece of reclaimed wood and a man who was born a Chad but reinvented himself after college as a Silas. You know exactly who I'm talking about. Last year, we became the exclusive coffee partner for America's third-leading airline. The year before, we got onto the shelves of two of the nation's top discount retailers, which meant we were fast becoming the coffee of choice for the most powerful financial demographic in the US: moms.

My anxiety starts the moment I see our building. It took three architects and two "vibe experts" to create what Dale envisioned as "the chillest work zone ever." Most of our space is devoted to "co-working zones," areas that are free from individual workstations and "designed to foster cross-functional collaboration across departments." Walking by, you might assume that it's an adult daycare: oversize beanbags (really) cluster around a gas fireplace, a large kitchen fully stocked with sugary snacks, and ping-pong tables that are always in use. In one corner, individual "nap pods" are set up for our employees to "recharge." My office, up a flight of industrial chic stairs, overlooks this entire scene. It's like a terrarium of young millennials.

"Where have you been, Mama?" Tessa asks me the moment I walk in the door. She's in the middle of a ping-pong game but has the courtesy to set down her paddle and pretend to be working when she sees me.

I'm the oldest person in our office by only five years, but that five years must seem like a lifetime, because they all call me some variation of "mom." "I'm twenty minutes early!" I clip back to her, and she falls into step, pulling up my schedule.

"There's no such thing as on time for you," she says, and I know she's right. It doesn't matter when I walk in the door because I'm always booked to be in at least two meetings at once. I like Tessa. She's smart as hell, and completely unafraid. She practices what she calls a "growth mind-set," which I think just means she is open to trying new things and isn't too upset when she's not automatically good at them. I wish that mind-set had existed when I was younger. Tessa has been with me for a year now—the longest she's been at any job, she keeps reminding me—and I want to help her develop into the professional I know she can be. I also want her to stop reading me her sex horoscopes and asking me to diagnose her rashes.

Tessa is in the middle of giving me the download on our weekly sales data when she stops suddenly and turns white as a sheet.

"Tessa?" I ask. "Are you okay?"

She shakes her head.

"I'm . . . really hungover. Can I have your trash can?"

I open my laptop and watch my unread emails pour into my inbox while Tessa heaves up last night's mistakes.

To: McKinley Mom Squad
From: Gwendolyn James
CC: Principal Burr; McKinley Staff
BCC: Gwendolyn James
Subject: RE: RE: RE: RE: RE: MCKINLEY MOM SQUAD
2019!!!

Hi Mamas,

If you're reading this, it's because we haven't heard from you about our McKinley Mom Squad Fiscal Plan. We have big plans for this year, and we can only accomplish our dreams for our children's future if we have you on board! Please reply to this email within 15 minutes to indicate your preference for committees or fundraisers, or a duty will be assigned to you.

In Love,
Gwendolyn James
@GwendolynJamesStyle
Click here for my latest blog post
Click here to shop my Amazon affiliate links
Click here to download my free eBook: *Rich Mom, Loser Mom*
"The greatest victory is that which requires no battle."
—Sun Tzu, *The Art of War*

"I had the weirdest dream last night."

I didn't even see Dale come into my office, but he's circling a scooter around my coffee table like he owns the place.

Which, fine, he does. But does he have to scoot everywhere? My kids are the actual target demographic for the exact scooter that Dale insists on riding, and even *they* have moved on from the need to glide through the house on what is basically a two-wheeled skateboard with a handle. At least when Dale walks, with the heavy, unathletic gait of a man whose main sport growing up was playing NBA Jam on his PlayStation, I can hear him coming.

I have no idea what Dale is saying. Something about a dream? As I always do in these moments, I reply with my default Dale response.

"Oh yeah?"

The question leads him to say more and indicates that I'm taking a small amount of interest in whatever he is saying. It placates him just enough that while he's expounding on his latest brilliant idea, I can actually get my work done. I did the same thing with Dylan and Jane when they were little, and I was working from home. It worked until they realized that "Oh yeah?" meant that I wasn't actually paying attention and they could go climb up on the counter to the cabinet where I "hid" their Halloween candy. Dale, bless him, hasn't realized that yet. I thought that phase in my life was the most stressed I'd ever be. Agency life meant working sixty-hour weeks, screaming into the daycare parking lot at 5:58 and ignoring the glares from the teachers, who already had Dylan and Jane bundled up in their coats and ready to go. The center imposed a fee of five dollars per minute for late pickups, but as long as I crossed that threshold before the clock struck six, I was golden. Those years are a blur of cortisol and caffeine, and I was so sure that I had left them behind when I met Dale. Instead, I'm basically right back where I started, only with more children in my care.

Dale's ability to get lost in his recounting of his own dreams is amazing to me. He's absorbed enough in his own voice that I can grab my phone and tap out a text to Mike without getting busted.

ME: Work sucks today. Can you be on after-school duty?

Three dots flicker next to his name, then disappear.

My brain feels like my computer: like too many windows are open, and too many programs are running at once. From the moment I wake up, I'm operating at full capacity, trying to shift my attention from the kids to Mike to work to the million other tasks that seem to always, always, fall onto my to-do list. I have to buy Mike's mom a birthday present. I have to find a venue for the company retreat. I have to schedule the kids' yearly checkups and make sure Roscoe gets his flea and tick medication sometime this week.

Still no response from Mike.

ME: Mike. Answer me.

The three dots flicker again and then disappear.

"It's like, there I am, butt naked . . ."

Dale is still talking about his stupid dream, but my computer is beeping at me. I'm supposed to dial in to a conference call with our sales team.

"Amy Mitchell," I say, overenunciating when the robo-operator asks for my name.

"Huh?" says Dale.

I hold up my finger to indicate that he should be quiet, but apparently Dale's real mom never used that move with him, because he does the exact opposite and pulls his scooter right up to my desk, where he plops his scrawny little butt right next to my laptop.

Oh. Right. It's a video call. On my screen, our sales reps are popping up in little squares like members of the Brady Bunch, dialing in from their homes and hotel rooms. Does everyone else have better lighting? Get better sleep? Have better genes? Because my camera has picked up on the dark circles under my eyes. They're somehow casting a shadow upward, making me look like the business-lady version of Skeletor.

"So, what do you think? End of quarter?" Dale says as he jumps up and scoots behind my desk to show off for all his salespeople.

They cheer and wave to him, and I mute my microphone and switch off my camera, turning my chair and my focus to the man-child in charge of my income and my daily schedule.

"What do you think?" he repeats, with the excitement of someone completely unencumbered by reality.

In the corner of my eye, I can see my email notifications rolling in, just like they do in my nightmares: Jane, Tessa, GAP, Tessa, Mike, Gwendolyn, Gwendolyn, Gwendolyn . . .

"Well, what do *you* think?" I ask. Another trick I use on Dylan and Jane when I haven't been listening to a word they're saying.

"I think . . . that if anyone can roll out a brand-new sales program to hotels, it's you. Our team mom."

My blood pressure rises.

My phone dings. Mike has finally responded. It's . . . a gif. Of a dog wearing sunglasses. The word "COOL" wiggles beneath it. Is this a yes? Is he picking up the kids after school . . . ?

More email notifications pop up in my peripheral vision, rolling in like a tide of bullshit threatening to pull me under . . .

The conference call beckons, a half dozen people waiting for guidance. I turn around, switch the camera back on, smile, and signal that I need a sec. Somehow I look *more* tired when I smile?

It's all too much. There is no way I can juggle all this bullshit. I feel like I'm going to scream. Instead, I spin back to my boss.

"And just when would I do this, Dale?" I ask, gesturing to the piles of work on my desk. "I'm already running sales for supermarkets, restaurants, and airlines. I'm already running basically everything."

He's back on my desk, kicking his feet against the legs the same way Dylan used to kick the back of my seat from his car seat. He nods, and for a moment, I think that he might be considering the position I'm in. That he might look at my overflowing plate and think, *Wow. This woman is doing a lot. She's going so far above and beyond that there is no way I could add yet another ball to the circus act she is currently juggling.*

"You know, Amy?" he finally says. "I can't remember if it was Dr. Martin Luther King or Dr. Oz who said it, but it's true . . . we make time for the things that are important to us."

————————

To: carladunkler69@hotmail.com; Amy Mitchell;
kikiloveskent@gmail.com
From: Gwendolyn James
CC: Principal Burr; McKinley Staff
BCC: Gwendolyn James
Subject: McKinley Mom Squad Assignments

Hi Mamas,

Thanks for being a part of our McKinley Mom Squad. We're looking forward to this year being the best year yet. Your assignments are as follows:

> Lice Task Force
> Landscaping

In Love,
Gwendolyn James
@GwendolynJamesStyle
Click here to see why Oprah called my blog "a must-read"
Click here to download my free eBook: *It All Comes Down to Mom: 1,000 Reasons Why Motherhood Is Your Most Important Job*

To: Amy Mitchell
From: Jane Mitchell
Subject: Emergency!!!!

Mom,

I have an emergency. Soccer tryouts aren't next week. They're THIS WEEK. I haven't had any time to work on my first touch, and Blair and Gandhi said they spent the summer training with Abby Wambach??? Please tell me you know a professional athlete who can get me up to speed ASAP.

PS—who is picking us up from school?

To: Mike Mitchell
From: Amy Mitchell
Subject: ARE YOU PICKING UP THE KIDS FROM SCHOOL

To: Amy Mitchell
From: Mike Mitchell
Subject: RE: ARE YOU PICKING UP THE KIDS FROM SCHOOL

What? Babe. I have a job. I can't do pickup! I'm taking our EVP out for drinks to celebrate his promotion. See you at home?

6

KIKI

To: kikiloveskent@gmail.com
From: Deck Warehouse Dot Com
Subject: 40% off all-weather decking!

Dear {Name},

As a valued member of our community of contractors, we'd
like to offer you 40% off the essentials that will cut your costs
AND keep your customers happy. Your 40% off coupon code
is BIGDECKENERGY and is good for the next 48 hours.

To: noreply@deckwarehouse.com
From: kikiloveskent@gmail.com
Subject: RE: 40% off all-weather decking!

Hello!

My name is Kiki, and I got the email below this morning. I wanted to reply to thank you for the generous offer, and to let you know that I am afraid there must have been a mistake. I am not a decking contractor, and therefore am probably unqualified to use this coupon. I apologize if I misled anyone, but I wanted to correct this to ensure your very generous offer could be extended to a person who truly deserves it.

Thank you so much for the kind offer and keep up the good work!

Best wishes,
Kiki

To: noreply@deckwarehouse.com
From: kikiloveskent@gmail.com
Subject: RE: RE: 40% off all-weather decking!

STATUS: UNDELIVERABLE.

———————————

My life revolves around poop.

When Clara eats too many blueberries, her poop looks like it's made of kinetic sand. When the twins have peanut butter, their poops look like peanut butter. Bernard poops exactly five minutes before we leave for school. Last month, Clara didn't poop for four days straight, and when she finally did, it was like she was delivering a baby. I'm not kidding. I had to help her deliver her poop baby. I had to actually put my finger in her butt and break the poop apart so it could come out of her tiny little butt without ripping her apart. It wasn't even disgusting to me. It was *exciting*.

It was exciting because it was *different*. Most days blend together. Monday is the same as Tuesday and Wednesday and Thursday and Friday. Saturday and Sunday aren't even all that different, aside from the fact that Kent is home more and we go to church for a few hours. That should feel nice and helpful, but it's more of a disruption to our routine. Clara's poop baby was like when breaking news interrupts *Dancing with the Stars*. It's a little annoying at first, but then you realize, wow, I'm glad I knew a tornado was heading for our house. Kent being at home is like when they try to introduce a new coach on *The Voice*, and the chemistry is off, and you just think, *Why couldn't Gwen Stefani stay out of this?!!*

One morning this summer, Bernard stabbed me in the leg with a fork while I was making lunch. I think it was an accident— people get stabbed every day in America!—but it sure was an exciting afternoon. The urgent care doctor said that next time I get stabbed, I could feel free to go right to the emergency room.

THERE'S A REASON MY MOM AND DAD CALLED ME MISSUS Peepers growing up. Two reasons, I guess. I have giant blue eyeballs, and I watch people. Only children get used to observing the world around them. As a kid, I saw motherhood as both a duty and a full-time job. All the moms in Minot were the same. They wore the same crewneck sweatshirts, which changed with the seasons. Typically, they were silk-screened with nature scenes, but every mom owned a few special seasonal sweatshirts, fancy ones that were embroidered with Christmas scenes or an Easter bunny. The fanciest ones had a decorative polo collar attached, which would be embroidered with a coordinating pattern. During our summers, the moms would switch to a wardrobe of loose, elastic-waisted pants, cut to land in the least flattering part of their calves, and switch to a palette of pastel tees and tanks. Their wardrobes changed with the seasons, but not with the years. Sometimes, when I'm homesick, I concentrate really hard and try to imagine what my mom is wearing that day before I FaceTime her. My predictions are spot-on.

I don't know what I'm supposed to wear now that I'm a mom. The fancy sweatshirts I have seem out of place here. I would have been fine staying in Fargo, but Kent's job offered him a much better position and a lot more money if we'd just move a short ten-hour drive from everything and everyone we've ever known. I didn't think we *needed* more money, but Kenton wants to be debt-free and retired by fifty-five so we can spend our golden years driving through all forty-eight of our contiguous United States in an RV.

"You'll be fine, Keeks," he promised me. "Everyone always likes you, you're the best person I know!" But I don't think that's true. About everyone liking me, I mean. Last year, I wore my Christmas sweatshirt, the one with a giant teddy bear dressed as Santa Claus, the one with actual *bells* sewn to it? And someone at Target told me that it was *hilarious*. Here, it seems like moms are always dressed like they just went to the gym, but they're never sweaty or dirty in any way. Or they're dressed like sexy teenagers from one of those CW shows.

When I was growing up, a few of the moms in Minot worked part-time jobs at the school, or the dollar store, but otherwise, being a mother was their full-time job. They spent their days making lunches, vacuuming the sitting room, making dinner, and watching *Oprah*. In the winter, they'd snow-blow the driveway and drive us to school on the back of a snowmobile. At night, they'd call one another on their home phones. I remember my mother, sitting at the kitchen table, laughing hysterically with Sharon Mulcahy or Mary Beth Jensen. Motherhood was like a club they'd all joined together. One they all belonged to, as equals. All of them except for Janice Holmes, because she was a real *b*-word.

The moms I knew were all soft and inviting, like worn-in couches. They didn't *moisturize*, they just put on Pond's Cold Cream every night. They didn't run small businesses or have blogs. They weren't influencers, or mompreneurs. They were just . . . moms? I wasn't even aware that there were different food groups until I went to college. Dinner at every house I ever went to growing up was simple: casserole, whole milk, a slice of white bread. For dessert, a bar made from some combination of flour, sugar, butter, chocolate, and caramel. The vegetables we ate came from a can, or from our own gardens. I don't know if our gardens were considered organic, but I once grew a prize-winning zucchini and got a blue ribbon at the county fair because it really did look exactly like a giant question mark.

I love my kids. I *l-o-v-e* my kids. But I don't love being a mom the way I thought I would. I love macaroni necklaces and #1 Mom mugs that Kent buys the day after Mother's Day when they're on clearance. I don't love feeling like Missus Peepers, watching the world from the outside while my daughter gets another piece of pea gravel stuck in her nostril.

Today, Gwendolyn posted a photo of Blair and Gandhi sitting quietly in their Adirondack chairs, finger-knitting chunky scarves from what looks like hand-spun, organic cotton yarn. The caption read: "We are what we love, and I love every minute with these two." I double-tap it immediately.

I want to love motherhood. I want it to be effortless and fulfilling. I want to be a part of whatever club this is.

I want to be like Gwendolyn.

GWENDOLYN JAMES STYLE

"How do you do it all?"

It's the question I hear most often.

"How do you run a successful blog, raise two beautiful children, maintain a happy marriage, find time to train for another marathon, *and* inspire mothers around the world?"

The secret is this: I just do.

Do you want to know what you have in common with Beyoncé and Oprah and me and Gwyneth and Hillary?

We all have 24 hours in a day.

All of us.

24 hours to mother, to run, to train, to inspire.

24 hours to live, laugh, and love.

You can fill that 24 hours with action and accountability, or with excuses and regret.

You can spend that 24 hours wishing you had the life you wanted, or making it happen.

24 hours.

How will you use yours today?

In Love,
Gwendolyn James

Click here to sign up for my "Mega-Mom" eCourse. Just $599 with code GWENJ.

7

CARLA

There's a reason why I use a flip phone. There are lots of reasons, but here are the most important ones:

1. The government has a harder time tracking them. An iPhone is probably real slick, but I don't need the CIA knowing what I look up on the Internet, and that's also why I use my library card when I need to Google something. It's nobody's business what kind of rash I have, and I want to keep that between me and WebMD.
2. Russians will watch you through that stupid camera phone, and if I'm going to be on camera, I want advance warning and I don't want it to be at that weird angle where my neck looks like an elephant leg coated in self-tanner.
3. I don't need all that email shit.

I mean, I *have* an email address, but that's only because I need something to give to salespeople that isn't my phone number. My phone number is a prize to be won, not something I'm handing out at Walgreens so they know what kind of vitamins to give me coupons for. How about no vitamin coupons? How about a coupon for Nyquil or nicotine gum or something actually useful? Giving someone my phone number is like giving them my home address. Giving someone my email address is like telling them, "Good luck finding me."

Not everyone has the luxury to just *not* email. I know. I'm blessed.

I'm lucky to have a career where I'm not sitting at a desk all day, replying to messages from John in Accounting about where the invoices are for the whatever thing. I'm lucky not to be sitting at home wiping nuts and butts nonstop.

When I was in high school, I took a series of tests with my guidance counselor to help me figure out what to do with my life, but I already knew what I wanted to be. I wanted to *be* my guidance counselor. Lisa—she *never* let us call her Ms. McCarthy—was smoking hot. She was the only teacher at our school who wore heels in the winter, when this godforsaken place is covered in feet of snow for months at a time. She'd wear her frumpy winter boots only as far as the lobby, and then change right into a pair of stilettos. The other teachers thumped around like rhinos, but Lisa *click-click-clicked* down the hallway, tight skirt hugging her butt. She reminded me of my mom, only employed, and she had a way of looking into your eyes that made your skin feel hot and your brain feel loose in your head. I found myself saying things to her that I hadn't said to anybody else, spilling my little teenage guts all over her floor and taking a tissue when she gently slid them across her desk toward me. My mom always told me that I should just get a job in a correctional facility so I could find a man, but I wanted to make people feel like Lisa made me feel: like they mattered.

And thanks to all those tests, that's exactly what I do! Every day, I wake up, put on my face, hike up my tits, and make the world a more beautiful place, one vagina wax, one manicure, one facial at a time. I know more about the women of our city than their husbands, their best friends, and their therapists combined. By the time they get to my table, they've spent fifteen minutes sipping cucumber water in the sunroom, ten minutes listening to nature sounds and having an "aroma-therapy experience," and anywhere from thirty to forty-five years saving up their deepest secrets and insecurities.

The rules of my table are the same as a therapist's office: it is a safe space, and I won't tell anyone about the hole your child punched through your labia during childbirth, or about the confusing weekend you spent with your best friend from college where you maybe had sex but does it count as sex if it's mainly hands? (Yes, it does.)

What's funny to me is how my table works like a two-way mirror. These women pour out their secrets to me like they're cheap liquor on Thirsty Thursdays. They tell me the things they haven't told anyone else in their lives, things they probably don't even admit to themselves when they're pay-ing thirty-five dollars to sit in a dark room riding a bike that doesn't even fucking go anywhere. And you know what they know about me? Nothing. They don't know my last name, or my star sign. They don't know that I'm a mom, or that I rely on whatever they choose to write into the tip area when they sign their credit card slip as they go.

These women, who I see every day at the grocery store or at school pickup, don't see me like I saw Lisa. They don't see me at fucking all.

8

AMY

"What I'm about to show you is highly confidential, and intensely personal. Please hold all commentary until the end of the presentation."

Jane is standing next to her desk, her hair brushed and parted neatly in the center. She is, for some reason, wearing one of my blazers over her soccer T-shirt. I thought she'd called me into her room to tuck her in, but instead, she confiscated my phone and seated me in her beanbag chair the moment I crossed her threshold.

"Sixth grade is a critical year for me," she says. "What happens this year can and will impact the rest of my life. Every grade, every goal: it counts. It could be the difference between me having it all . . . or losing it all."

Jane takes a deep breath and hits the spacebar on her laptop, and IN IT TO WIN IT: JANE MITCHELL'S TEN-YEAR PLAN shoots up onscreen with a flourish. When did my kid learn PowerPoint?

Jane's presentation includes her goals for what she called "the three pillars of personal success," broken down by one, three, five, seven, and ten years. She's calculated the amount she would need to save each year to retire comfortably at age sixty-three, and the projected cost of a four-year college with and without an athletic and academic scholarship. My first thought was *Why the hell did I do her summer report if she's apparently a PowerPoint savant?* My second thought was *How does my kid know more about personal finance than I do? And should I hire her to plan the next ten years of my life?* Jane has always been an intense child. As a baby, Mike and I would look into her eyes and say, "She's onto us." She was wiser than us from the start, an old soul who happened to land in the laps of two people who conceived her older brother after a night of keg stands and body shots.

"What do you think she's thinking?" we'd ask each other as her giant brown eyes fixed on us, boring deep into our souls.

"Probably that she was born into the wrong family," Mike would say, and we'd both laugh at this serious little creature, evaluating us with such skepticism.

Jane had every right to be skeptical. We were barely twenty-two when Dylan was born, and not even twenty-five when she joined us on the planet. Most of the parents in our Baby and Me group were closer in age to our own parents than they were to us, and they looked at Mike and me as if we were irresponsible teens, instead of irresponsible legal adults. But Jane did belong in our family. She *does* belong in our family.

I had been just like Jane growing up. I didn't have Power-Point at her age, but I did have a series of journals and a copy of *The 7 Habits of Highly Effective People*, which I had dog-eared and underlined. The book had been a gift from my own mother, and at the time I dreamed of passing it down to my own daughter one day. But I knew from Jane's birth that she would not need any help getting motivated or being a self-starter.

"*MOM*." JANE'S IRRITATED VOICE SNAPS ME BACK TO HER focus group of one. I can tell from her pursed lips that she was annoyed with my lack of participation. "Do you get it? A lot is riding on my making the soccer team this year."

When Jane gets worked up, she can't get her words out fast enough. She is *definitely* worked up, flipping back through her presentation as her voice gets higher and higher. "Soccer is *everything* this year. Making the soccer team will *prove* that I am a well-rounded student-athlete. That will ensure I am admitted into a competitive high school, which will ensure my attendance at a quality university, which will set me up for a good life! If I don't make the team, I'll die alone and on the streets. Is that what you want?!"

I struggle to get up from the squish of the beanbag chair.

"One second, baby."

I'VE MADE IT A POINT TO INTENTIONALLY AVOID OUR BASE-ment. It's a hole in the ground that our house sits on. An oversize storage unit for all the detritus of our life together. Also, there are spiders.

I find the box under our staircase. It's one of many my mother had left on our doorstep when Mike and I had moved in together. Her writing was still on top, scrawled in permanent marker. *Mike! These are Amy's. She's yours now, and so is her mess! Ha!*

There it is: my childhood in a box. I dig through the blue ribbons and the postcards from my friends' trips to Florida until I find it, a blue composition notebook, clearly labeled: AMY MITCHELL. 6TH GRADE. MOM DO NOT READ THIS!

JANE IS BEYOND DISAPPOINTED WHEN I RETURN TO HER room. "Why would I want to read your childhood diary?" she asks, wiping the cover of the notebook with an antibacterial wipe. I forgot that I may have been the last generation to be raised with secrets; Jane and her friends broadcast their feelings and insecurities on social media. My friends and I stuffed them into notebooks we hid from our mothers, and in intricately folded notes we passed to one another in the hallways.

I crack open the notebook and start to read aloud, doing my best to decipher the bubbly cursive.

"September 7. I swear to God I am the only person in my class who has any ambition. The other kids just don't understand me. They're perfectly happy to spend their days paging through the Delia's catalog or Frenching their Jonathan Taylor

Thomas posters. Well, excuse me if I have dreams for myself, Kristen!!!! Excuse me if I know where I'm going in life and what I want! They don't understand the value of having a vision. I know exactly what I want out of life. I'm going to go to Mizzou and major in journalism. Then I will move to New York and live in a fancy apartment. I will not have a husband because I will need to fully focus on my career as a news anchor. I will have two Pomeranians."

I close the notebook, prematurely satisfied with the life lesson I am imparting on my offspring. Jane is already on her laptop, editing her presentation.

"Jane."

"Mom."

"Sound like anyone you know?"

"Not really. Those aren't SMART goals. Those are just dreams. A SMART goal is Specific, Measurable—"

"I know what a SMART goal is, Jane. But do you know how much of my sixth-grade life plan came true?"

Jane gives me the same look I give people when they're trying to force me to answer a rhetorical question.

"None of it," I answer. "No Mizzou. No New York City. No fancy apartment. Two kids. Zero Pomeranians. One husband—and it's not even Leonardo DiCaprio."

Jane rolls her eyes so hard I'm afraid they might dislocate.

"I get it, Mom." She sighs. "*You* didn't achieve your dreams. But that doesn't mean that I won't."

Well. That went poorly.

"The point I was *trying* to make, honey, is that my dreams

changed. I have everything I never dreamed of, because my dreams when I was in sixth grade were just ideas of who I could be, not who I definitely for sure would be."

Jane gives me the same skeptical look she was born with.

"What I'm trying to say, Janer, is that there are many paths you can take in life. And most of them aren't even on your radar yet. If you're too attached to one idea of what a good life looks like, you run the risk of missing out on what a good life is. The things I couldn't imagine—you and Dylan! A dog that is basically the opposite of a Pomeranian! Those are the things I can't imagine living without. Just . . . keep your options open, honey. You don't have to have it all figured out in middle school."

Jane gives me a tight smile and closes out her presentation. It's time for me to tag Mike into this conversation.

LET ME BE CLEAR: I HATE THE PHRASE "MAN CAVE." IT'S proof that toxic masculinity has seeped into every aspect of life: How could a guy possibly have just an *office* or a *room to himself*? Could a den possibly suffice? A study? No. The modern man requires a room that is so manly it can only be described as a cave to which he drags his kill. Or, in Mike's case, takes conference calls and plays Call of Duty with our college friends. His office isn't off-limits to any of us, but there aren't many reasons to go in there unless you like the smell of old coffee and stale farts.

Whatever he prefers to call it, I call it Mike's home office.

But it's more like a dorm room than anything else. Which is why he should have put a fucking sock on the door.

LOOK, WE'VE BEEN MARRIED SINCE BEFORE WE WERE OLD enough to rent a car. I've seen the guy masturbate. But there's something extremely unsexy about seeing your husband sitting in an Aeron chair jerking off in front of a computer screen.

"Oh, shit!" he shouts when I walk into the room. He's pulling up his sweatpants, scrambling to act like nothing is happening.

We're *both* embarrassed. But because I grew up reading women's magazines that beat it into my head that it was my job to keep a man interested in me, I quickly do the mental gymnastics necessary to turn something embarrassing into something . . . sexy and embarrassing?

"Sooooo," I whisper—*why am I whispering??*—"what are you watching?" I'll admit that it's really hard for me to watch porn. I'm not a prude, it's just that there's never enough plot, and I've had enough sex to know that there is never a reason to scream that loud. Also, what happened to pubic hair? It's there for a reason! It's hygienic! It protects your vagina from stuff!

Mike looks like he's witnessing a car wreck. There's no sound coming from his computer, so maybe he's just looking at pictures? Would *that* be weird? I remember my brother always disappearing to his bedroom with the JC Penney catalog, but that's only because we grew up in the dark ages when our family Internet access was limited to the number of free minutes provided by the free AOL CDs that showed up in the mail.

By the time I do my sexiest walk (are walks sexy?) over to Mike's desk, his boner is safely tucked back into his Wisconsin sweatpants, and he is frantically clicking around, trying to close the window.

It didn't work. On the computer, I can see a plain, half-heartedly decorated bedroom and a tall blond woman who exists only in the dreams of straight men and—"Oh my god, that's a huge bush!" I blurt out. Apparently I'm wrong about pubic hair. This woman clearly has Sasquatch in her bloodline.

"What's going on?" the woman responds, leaning into her camera.

Oh my god. Holy shit. "Is this . . . live?"

Mike stammers.

"Hi!" the woman says, running her hands over her body in a way that I have to admit is pretty sexy, "do you want to watch, too?"

The gears in my head click into place, and my rage machine is ON. My head swivels 180 degrees and lasers shoot from my eyeballs.

"*Mike.*"

"Amy, it's not cheating."

"Wow, great opener. It's not cheating. So what is it?"

"We just . . ."

From onscreen, that pleasant voice chimes in, "We just . . . chat. We just . . . we watch each other. We talk."

"You TALK? What the fuck do you talk about?"

Mike is frozen, but his girlfriend isn't. "Oh, everything! Our hopes, our lives, our families . . ."

A gear pops. My head spins. More lasers shoot from my eyes. He talks about his *family* with this woman? His *family*? *Our* family?

"Mike, you need to say something now. I don't know what this is, but it's not okay. Is this . . . do you have feelings for her?"

Mike looks down.

Onscreen, I can see the answer in the way this woman's slight and beautiful shoulders deflate at his nonresponse.

He does have feelings for her.

You know how you always hear about how if her kids are in danger, a mom could easily deadlift a minivan if she needed to? Well, if her marriage is in danger, she can clear a desktop computer, a flat-screen monitor, and piles of paperwork off a desk with her bare hands.

Maybe not as impressive, but it feels damn good.

"MOM? DAD?" I CAN *SENSE* JANE AND DYLAN ON THE OTHER side of the office door. I can see them, like X-ray vision of the heart: they are in their dad's college T-shirts and the matching pajama pants our family gets from my mom every Christmas. They are pressed to the door, waiting for a clue about what they just heard. Are Mom and Dad *fighting*?

Mike projects his hearty, room-filling laugh.

"One second, guys! Your klutzy mom knocked some stuff

over in here trying to clean up this dumpster. Don't come in . . . uh, broken glass!"

Of course he'd make this about me.

"Go to bed, sweeties! I'll be in soon for tuck-in."

I hear them, *sense* them, backing away, making incredulous eye contact at each other.

For someone who is allegedly smart and successful, Mike is a fucking idiot. How hadn't this doofus known what he was doing? How hadn't he realized that he was playing with our family, that he could ruin *everything*? Or had he realized it all along, and just not cared?

I am out of my body, watching Mike on his hands and knees, gathering up files and pens and knickknacks as if this *had* been an accident. As if this *had* just been an act of my physical klutziness, and not his emotional carelessness. As if once all the glass was vacuumed up and the papers re-sorted, I'd go tuck in the kids and put in my retainer, and he'd crawl into bed next to me, warm and familiar.

THE NIGHT MIKE AND I MET, I'D PUKED ABOUT THIRTY OUNCES of half-digested Natural Light on his feet. He'd been wearing flip-flops, and while most college boys would have turned that into a story about a girl they never spoke to again, Mike had held my hand and walked me right back to my dorm room. He'd stayed with me in the kitchen until I'd downed a whole bottle of red Gatorade, and then used my hot plate to make me a cup of instant ramen. He'd been sweet, and I remember thinking to myself, *This boy is special.*

Mike loves our "how we met" story. He loves to be the one to tell it, to repeat it even to people who had heard it before. It's his testament to how much he'd loved me, right away. "This girl," he always says, "is so special I'd let her puke on my bare feet any day."

Where had that boy gone? When and how had he turned into this kind of man? And what the hell is going to happen to my marriage? To my family?!

I roll my head, cracking my neck, and summon the internal power of every mom who had ever come before me. The redness creeping up my neck begins to cool. The tears dry from my eyes. I open the office door.

"Get the fuck out."

———————————

To: Amy Mitchell
From: Dale
Subject: WTF do you not have wifi at home are you not getting my texts

To: Amy Mitchell
From: Dale
Subject: AMY. DUDE.

To: Amy Mitchell
From: Dale
Subject: Okay. I get it. Power move.

To: Amy Mitchell
From: Dale
Subject: What if this were an emergency, you're my
emergency contact

To: Amy Mitchell; Mike Mitchell
From: McKinley Soccer Club
Subject: Welcome to the team

Mr. and Mrs. Mitchell,

We are pleased to announce that your daughter Jane has earned
a spot on the MSC 12 and under team. We are looking forward
to a competitive season, and to bringing home the hardware
this fall in our first state tournament team. Please click here to
accept Jane's spot on the team, and to place your $500 deposit.

9

PRINCIPAL BURR

889.

That's the number of days I have left at McKinley before I retire. Not the days that will pass on a calendar until I retire, but the number of workdays where I am required to show up, wear a suit, and sit behind a desk I have strategically placed to ensure my computer monitor is never visible to anyone but myself.

I've spent twenty-three years at McKinley. Some things are always the same: the toilets on the first floor are clogged by kindergartners who require one roll of toilet paper each to wipe their butts. There's *always* one inter-teacher feud that requires me to mediate an argument that could have been easily resolved by one of them not commenting on the other's haircut or teaching style. There are always a few naughty kids. And a few parents who are much worse.

For the past seven years, that parent has been Gwendolyn James. Her husband is fine. I think. I've never met him, but his donation checks always clear. Gwendolyn, though, is what we used to call "a real piece of work." Gwendolyn James is our PTA president, but she won't call it the PTA because she has anointed herself the Queen of Everything. Gwendolyn James is why our teacher's lounge was replaced by a "feelings room" for the kids. Now our teachers sit on a few couches in the lobby. Which Gwendolyn has renamed the foyer.

Gwendolyn canceled Valentine's Day and Halloween but insists the children celebrate the winter solstice. Last year, she spent the entire school year developing a Study Abroad program. When I mentioned that studying abroad seems to be an inappropriate endeavor for children who can't blow their own noses, she accused me of being a xenophobe. Me! She's the one who insists that every classroom have a "foam in, foam out" hand sanitizer policy, as if the kids are all performing brain surgery.

Gwendolyn is why I've routed every email that even vaguely references Gwendolyn or her Mom Squad to land directly in my trash can.

Because if Gwendolyn really wants to run this school for free, what do I care? If she thinks we should be the first school with a space program, or wants to launch a capital campaign to start a circus school within our school for kids whose bodies learn better than their brains do? Okay! In 889 school days, I'll be done with McKinley, and until then, I'll be playing solitaire.

———————————

To: McKinley Mom Squad
From: Cathy M.
Subject: Screen time

Hi Mamas!

A gentle reminder that many of us at McKinley are practicing a screen-free lifestyle for our children. While not everyone is interested in the research (which I've shared before) that proves that screen time is eroding our children's attention spans, socialization skills, and peace of mind, please do respect that not everyone places their children in front of an iPad after school and do your best to help us provide a consistent childhood experience for our children while they are at your house for a playdate.

Sincerely,
Cathy

To: McKinley Mom Squad
From: Brittany J.
Subject: RE: Screen time

Thanks, Cathy. Might I also add that the squad spent a lot of time preparing a screen time contract for all incoming kindergartners? A contract that we *and* our children signed before they entered the kindergarten room? Please be in touch if you need your copy, Gwendolyn has filed them all alphabetically according to college graduation year in our shared drive.

Best,
Britt

To: McKinley Mom Squad
From: Jessica C.
Subject: RE: RE: Screen time

Is this for real?

To: McKinley Mom Squad
From: Emily P.
Subject: RE: RE: RE: Screen time

Yes, Jessica C., this is for real. It's a for real waste of time trying to police everybody's parenting when the group hasn't even addressed whether or not we're going to ban *Hop on Pop* from our kindergarten reading list for inciting violence against fathers!!

To: McKinley Mom Squad
From: Lindsay W.
Subject: RE: RE: RE: RE: Screen time

A gentle reminder to one another that it's possible to care about two things at once, and a discussion about screen time does not mean we are not passionate about our kids' reading lists!!

To: McKinley Mom Squad
From: Katie T.
Subject: RE: RE: RE: RE: RE: Screen time

As someone who *works* in tech, can I just say that I find it really shortsighted to prevent our children from engaging with technology in a meaningful way? How can we expect our children to be leaders on the world stage if they're so far behind their international peers?

To: McKinley Mom Squad
From: Emily J.
Subject: RE: RE: RE: RE: RE: RE: Screen time

I have no idea how I got on this email chain but please remove me immediately. I'm begging you. You've been clogging up my inbox all summer and just seeing these subject lines gives me anxiety. I'm not even a mom!!!!

10

KIKI

It all happened so fast. I'd dropped Bernard at school and Clara at hip-hop dance class. The twins were with Kent's mom, who flew in just to spend time with them before she gets too old and useless.

There was a dog—a beagle? No. A shih tzu—just sitting in the middle of the street. I swerved the van just in time to spare its life, and then I woke up here.

It's quiet. And calm. The sheets are soft and clean and there is a vase of peonies by the window. My favorite.

"Honey?" I hear his voice before I see him. It's Kent. There are tears in his eyes, and even though he doesn't want me to see him cry, one tear rolls silently down his cheek.

He carefully brushes his hand against my cheek and bites his lip.

"There was an accident, Keeks. You saved the shih tzu, but the van was totaled. It's going to be replaced—with the new model, the one that has a built-in vacuum and a cooler in the center console—so don't you worry about that. You just need to focus on getting better."

Before I can ask about the kids, he says, "The kids are on a plane. My mom took them back to North Dakota to stay with her for a few weeks so you can lay here and focus on getting better."

He's interrupted by a team of nurses. "Kiki?" one asks. "Would you like a special coffee?" She pushes a button, and the bed sits me up . . . just like in the commercials with the elderly people! A second nurse is holding a bottle of Aveda foot cream. "You just relax," she says.

MY FANTASY IS INTERRUPTED BY A HAND GRAZING MY FOOT. It's small and sticky, a disembodied appendage sliding under the bathroom door, searching wildly for me. Gwendolyn recommends that you take five minutes a day to visualize the life you want, but that is very difficult when there are three small children who have a psychotic obsession with you, and another child who may just be psycho. I'd sat the three girls on my bed in front of my iPad to play an educational game, but they'd apparently lost interest already. It has been two minutes, and I didn't even get to the part where the nurse gives me the remote and tells me that there's a twenty-four-hour marathon of *Property Brothers* on.

"MAMA? MAMA. MAMA!!!!" IT'S ONE OF THE TWINS. SHE BIRD-
dogged me, and now there are several small hands reaching underneath the bathroom door. The physics of this barely make sense, but children are kind of like mice. They can squish their bones to get into anyplace you don't want them to be.

In the minuscule amount of time I was allowed alone in the bathroom, the girls have made their displeasure with me apparent. Somehow, even though they each tend to go completely limp when it's time to get dressed, they've all managed to get completely naked. The basket of clean clothes I *just* folded is now upside down, and one of the twins is standing on it proudly, like she has just scaled a mountain. Kent's socks, which I had *just* finished ironing, are unpaired and littered around the bed.

Naptime isn't for another two hours, and I can tell that this will not be the kind of day where the girls fall asleep sweetly after lunch. This won't be the kind of day where I stand outside their door, missing them, wishing I could be in their little unconscious brains.

No, this day is going to be a fight. And even if your opponents' combined weight is half your own, three on one is an impossible fight to win.

DO OTHER MOMS FEEL THIS WAY? BECAUSE IT SURE DOESN'T
look like they do. On Instagram, the other McKinley moms all seem to love their days. *All* their days. They actually post things like that on Instagram: captions that say, literally, "I

love *all* our days," right under beautiful photos of their clean and smiling children. I look at my girls, whose faces are crusted with the remnants of this morning's attempt at yogurt parfaits. I got the idea from Pinterest, from something titled *100 easy breakfasts your kids will love!!!* I spent the morning spooning full-fat, hormone-free unsweetened yogurt into little rame-kins, alternating layers of expensive yogurt with homemade granola. On the top of each little parfait I placed thinly sliced strawberries, fanned out to make a flower. I had them sitting at the table, with real cloth napkins, when the girls came down for breakfast. The twins cried because they wanted toast, and smeared yogurt on their cheeks while I rushed to the toaster. Clara took a single bite and gagged, which I thought was a lit-tle dramatic. I ended up eating what was left, scrolling through Instagram trying to imagine if this would ever happen to the McKinley moms who were always at playdates and special cof-fee dates, who take their well-behaved children to lunch at the diner where they still serve milkshakes in old-fashioned glasses *and* give you the big metal tin they mixed it in.

Kent says that eating out is a waste of time and money, and that if I wanted to spend my days eating fancy lunches, I should have been born the Queen of England. He also says that joining a gym is a waste of time and money, because he spent all that money on the Chuck Norris Total Gym and if I watched the DVD it came with, I would totally get it and I would also trim inches off my buns, waist, and thighs. He also says that I'm starting to sound like a real feminazi, and that if I'm so unhappy we should switch places. "I'd love to spend my day finger painting and taking naps!" he joked the other night. "But, Keeks, *someone* has to keep the lights on. You like electricity, don't you?" I *do* like electricity, so I nodded.

I actually do like electricity. I was considering a major in electrical engineering at the University of North Dakota, but my mom told me I should focus on getting my MRS degree. I got a BA in elementary education, and I got Kent. I thought I'd work for a few years, but when I was pregnant with Bernard, Kent pointed out that my salary wasn't all that much more than we'd be paying to put Bernard in daycare, and that I may as well stay home with him. Not *forever*, just until Bernard was in kindergarten. But then I got pregnant with Clara, and then the twins. And after being out of the workforce for five years, what are the chances I'll earn more than it costs to put the three littlest ones in daycare?

The chances, I've learned, are not great.

I practice the deep breaths Gwendolyn talked about on her blog, and repeat my mantra for the day:

I love my life. I love my life. I love my life.

To: McKinley Mom Squad
From: Megan W.
Subject: Playdate

Hey, Mamas!

Just wanted to let all of you know that Praydon and Aubrianella have openings in their playdate schedules coming up. Please be in touch if you'd like to arrange a time with either of them.

Praydon is GF/DF/NF, prefers dinosaurs to LEGOs, and does not watch television of any kind.

Aubrianella is spirited and independent. She enjoys physical play and is currently working on impulse control and using her hands and words for kindness.

Both are available from 3:00 to 3:25 on the following dates: 1/15, 1/16, 2/8, 5/12, 6/27, and 8/15.

All responses will be considered. I will send a confirmation calendar when the playdate selections have been made.

Best,
Meg

To: Megan W.
From: Jenny M.
Subject: RE: Playdate

Hi Megan,

Thanks for putting this out there. Kermit's avails are below:

1/16
6/27

Would either of your kiddos be able to spare an extra ten minutes? There's a beautiful path at McArthur Park that Kermit and I love to forest-bathe in, but the loop takes a solid five minutes.

With Love,
Jenny

To: Sarah J.
From: Megan W.
Subject: FW: RE: Playdate

Like I'd ever let my kid go forest-bathing with her—remember in our newborn group when she told me I had a "weak aura" because my milk supply was down? Fuck all the way off, Jenny.

To: Megan W.
From: Sarah J.
Subject: RE: FW: RE: Playdate

Oh, she's not that bad. Kidding—I don't even go to McArthur Park anymore because last time I saw her there she tried to get me to eat a raw acorn.

To: Jenny M.
From: Megan W.
Subject: RE: RE: Playdate

Hi Jenny,

Our availability is firm at 25 minutes to ensure the kids stay on schedule. I'm sure you understand.

Best,
Megan

11

AMY

I'm dreading what I'll say to the kids about Mike being gone. I even Googled "how to tell your kids that you think you might get a divorce because their dumb dad was having an affair with someone on the Internet?" I've practiced a very fair speech, where I assure them both that Mike and I will always be on their side, in their corner . . . we just won't be living together anymore. I am ready, when the right moment arrives, but the sad truth is that the three of us hardly notice Mike is gone. Turns out Mike's absence was the same as his presence. *I* took the kids to school. *I* went to work. *I* picked them up. *I* drove Jane to her first soccer practice, and to Mandarin classes.

In the meantime, *I* also solved everyone's problems at work. It was like the Ineptitude Awards, and everyone at the office was vying for first place. Dale *accidentally* forgot to pay last quarter's commission to our sales team, and I am the one who issued the apology and the checks. Tessa *accidentally* forwarded an email complaining *about* a client *to* the client, and I'm the one who made the phone call apologizing for her. Our Ops team realized they hadn't accounted for the cost of storage when calculating the MSRP for our cold brew product, and I'm the one who made the red numbers turn black again.

In other words, nothing has changed. If anything, things are a little smoother, because I'm not tripping over Mike's giant shoes, which he used to take off directly in front of the front door, as though there wasn't a front hall closet with a shoe organizer *right there* next to where he left his giant shoes for the rest of us to trip over. I'm not rinsing his toothpaste crust out of the sink or picking his sopping wet towels off the bathroom floor. I'm not wondering if he'll finally be able to step in to help with pickups or drop-offs. Mike is less of an estranged husband and more like a variable I'd removed from my daily operations.

"WHERE'S DAD AGAIN?" DYLAN ASKS THE THIRD NIGHT MIKE is gone. "Dallas or something?"

This is the moment. The moment for me to jump into my speech, to tell the kids the truth about their parents' marriage and to quell any fears before they can take root and turn them into adults who follow jam bands on tour. I swear I was about to tell them, but Roscoe interrupts us by walking directly into the kitchen cupboards. Like, right smack into them. Now, he's a dumb dog, but not *that* dumb. Our little buddy looks confused, and a little unsteady on his feet. *Bam!* He walks into the cupboards again.

"Is he . . . drunk?" Jane asks, and I instinctively check his water dish for beer, which Mike has been known to share with him on occasion. Nope—just water.

"Roscoe, buddy? You okay?" I ask him, because I am a person who talks to my dog like he might be a person.

Roscoe staggers a bit, and then falls.

ROSCOE IS OUR FIRST BABY. HE WAS MIKE'S FRAT DOG, A weird little mutt who wandered up to the front door of their frat house one day and never left. He was the chapter's unofficial mascot (hence the beer), but there was never a question that when Mike graduated, Roscoe was going with him. But Roscoe's college career was cut short when I got knocked up, and Roscoe moved from the frat house into the tiny apartment that Mike and I shared. He spent my pregnancy curled up protectively beside me, resting his head on my belly.

Roscoe and Dylan were best buddies right from the start. All the grainy digital photos we have of Baby Dylan, taken with our state-of-the-art three-megapixel camera, feature Roscoe's scraggly mug. Roscoe cried if Dylan cried, which was cute until it was annoying. Roscoe became a living vacuum cleaner, sucking up every Cheerio, raisin, or teething cracker Dylan dropped. When Dylan didn't like dinner, he'd tip his entire plate toward the ground, raining smooshed peas and chicken on a very happy Roscoe. Roscoe went from Mike's dog to our dog to Dylan's dog. But not just a dog, because

Roscoe isn't just a pet, he's a pillar of this family. The kids and I would be fine without Mike. But without Roscoe? Hell no.

JANE AND DYLAN STAY SHOCKINGLY CALM WHILE I CARRY Roscoe to the car, wrapped up in his favorite blanket. Dylan even opens the door for me so I can put our little buddy in the front seat. "I love you, Roscoe," he whispers, fastening his old bike helmet under Roscoe's chin. It's weird and sweet and maybe the only thing that keeps me from bursting into hysterical tears.

Roscoe looks so small and scared, even with a helmet on. Jane and Dylan wave from the porch, and I give them a weak thumbs-up and then dash off a quick text to Dale and Tessa.

Family Emergency

Will take the team call from my car

I never text and drive, but I sometimes happen to see the text messages I'm receiving while I'm driving if the phone is already screen up and unlocked and the kids aren't in the car and I'm already running late for everything. Okay? I admit it. I looked at my phone, and I really wish I hadn't.

We're your family, too, Dale replied, and my shoulders shot up to my ears. As if he'd anticipated my physical reaction to his text, he quickly sent an addendum.

Hope all is okay, tho. U know I love family. A photo followed, of his godawful forearm tattoo, an illegible script that he insisted said FAMILY, but looked more like a series of loops created by someone who had never been taught to read or write cursive.

Oh no! Tessa replied. **Xoxoxoxxo**

The thing about team meetings is that they are completely useless. Anything that requires the presence of more than four people and lasts more than thirty minutes is guaranteed to be a waste of everyone's time. Once, I calculated that these weekly meetings cost us about ten thousand dollars in productivity. When I brought this to Dale's attention, he rolled his eyes, "Oh my God, Amy. That's such an old-school way of thinking. You can't put a price on *connection*." Maybe not, but there *is* no connection to these meetings, unless you count everyone on their laptops iMessaging one another about their weekends or commenting on Dale's collection of outdated ironic T-shirts. Still, I dial in to the weekly call, Roscoe whimpering next to me. Nobody notices when I dial in because nobody is ever listening at these meetings. I hear bits and pieces of conversation: someone is still hungover, someone else is still wearing the clothes from yesterday. Someone is *finally* watching *Game of Thrones* and doesn't get what all the hype was about. That's because, someone else pointed out, it was way overhyped. An argument breaks out, and then, apparently, Dale enters.

"Hey, everyone!" I shout. No reply.

"So," Dale starts, "you'll notice that Amy isn't here today. I know, I know, it's disappointing."

"I'm actually HERE. I'm dialed in. I'm on my way to the vet's off—"

"Amy's got her reasons, I'm sure, but I just want to make

sure that everyone *else* here at the CoCo is really *here*, that we're all here to make the world a better place."

I give up, not even trying to fill the awkward silence that has apparently filled the room. There are murmurs of agreement from around the table.

"So, that's my update. Who's next?"

I swear I can hear Dale's stupid smile. This is the first semi-work-related thing he'd contributed to a meeting in ages. The past few weeks, his updates have been about renovations to his pool, or his spot on the waitlist for a solar-powered jet-pack he had backed on Kickstarter.

I mute the phone while I park the car and scoop Roscoe up from the front seat. I keep it on mute while I explain the situation to the vet tech, while the vet tech takes Roscoe into another room, and while I sit in the waiting room, uh, waiting. One by one, I hear more updates that aren't actual updates. There are a lot of words being used, but nothing being said. I hear mumbling about creating alchemy and finding equilibrium, about identifying pain points, but nothing that even remotely corresponds to the meeting agenda, which I write and distribute every week.

I unmute my phone, because I actually *do* have updates. And I *need* updates. And then I get one. My phone buzzes, and like the Pavlovian dog I am, I look down.

To: Amy Mitchell
From: Gwendolyn James
Subject: Everything Okay?

Hi Amy,

Just checking in to make sure that everything is okay on your end. You've been noticeably absent from the Mom Squad this year, and we're all missing your contributions! As a mompreneur, I know the challenges that come with trying to balance the professional obligations with your personal calling as a wife and mother, and I want you to know that I'm here for you.

One of my personal mottos is that when life gives you too much to handle, it's best to open your arms even wider and say, "More, please!" By simply stating that you are capable of handling more, you will be able to handle more. The abundance mind-set will truly transform your ability to manage your time and make you a happier, healthier mother to your children.

With that in mind, I'll see you at tonight's meeting. The start time is promptly at 5, and the program should last no longer than 3.5 hours, accounting for social time and questions and answers. Please arrange for childcare for Dylan and Jane. I know that Mike is staying at the extended stay out by the airport right now—staycation?—but my nanny has plenty of referrals if you need any help in the interim.

All the best,
Gwendolyn James
@GwendolynJamesStyle
Download my eBook, *Rich Mom, Loser Mom,* here!

The sound that emerges from my body is halfway between a growl and a scream.

"Did anyone hear that?" I hear Dale ask.

The adrenaline coursing through my veins is making my hands shake. I can actually feel my heart beating. Is this what dying feels like? Is this what Roscoe feels like? Oh my God, Roscoe. I hang up the phone, suddenly very aware of my surroundings, which include a very concerned-looking vet tech standing in the doorway of the waiting room.

"Ma'am?" she says in the voice she probably uses for dogs before she euthanizes them. "Is everything okay?"

I mean to say yes, but sometimes, when I'm really upset, I can't tell where my thoughts end and my voice starts. Was I really telling the woman who castrates dogs for a living that my husband has left me and my boss hates me and the moms at school all know that I'm a loser and that this dog is the last thing holding me together? Yes, I am. Am I really letting her take me by the hand and lead me back into an examination room so I won't disturb the other patrons, who are starting to look concerned? Yes, absolutely. This angel of a human hands me a tiny paper cup of water and rests her hand on my shoulder.

"Okay." She smiles. "The doctor will be with you in a moment." Before I can panic about what the doctor will tell me, there's a light knock on the door and the vet enters, holding Roscoe like the sweet little baby he is. I brace myself for the diagnosis. I take in Roscoe's big, dumb eyes and his unbelievable eyelashes. I briefly wonder if it would be weird to have him taxidermied (yes).

Roscoe looks at me like he has already been briefed on the situation. His eyes are sadder than usual, which means it's probably cancer. And this is why people buy health insurance for their pets, because when the doctor tells you that your dog needs chemotherapy and radiation you're not going to say no, you're going to hand over your credit card and spend many thousands of dollars to keep that little fur person alive as long as possible.

Dr. Omar takes a deep breath. "It's vertigo," she says, setting Roscoe on the exam table. Roscoe tips over on his side, like he's been blown over by a stiff wind. I scream like I've just found my favorite brand of frozen lunches on supersale at Target. And then I start crying, like they're out of my favorite recipe and I'm on my period.

"Roscoe!" I kiss him on the lips, which I know is disgusting given what I've seen him do with that mouth. "You have vertigo! I'm so happy you're not dying! I'm so happy you don't have cancer!" I pick him up in my arms and sway back and forth.

"I'm prescribing him some sedatives to take the edge off, but it should pass. It's just something that happens in older dogs. Here's a sample to get him through until you can fill his prescription."

Dr. Omar is halfway out the door when she adds, "It's the same sedatives doctors prescribe to people having extreme anxiety . . . if that information is useful to you."

12

CARLA

I've been purposefully avoiding any and all mom-related school activities since Jaxon started kindergarten and the teacher was like, "Make sure you each sign up to be a classroom volunteer at least three times a month!" All the other moms were ready to cut each other to get to the sign-up sheet and I thought, *Isn't that* your *job? How the shit should I know how to get twenty-six kids to pay attention to reading? I can't even get one giant kid to sit still while I get my nails done. My volunteer work is spending every other week just keeping this kid from eating the nickels he finds on the floor of the car. Ask his* Dad *to volunteer his time. He's got almost two months of sobriety and a court order to complete three hundred hours of community service before he can get his license reinstated.*

I'd been so excited for Jaxon to start kindergarten, especially at McKinley. The moms at the spa were always talking about how desperate they were to get in, how competitive the lottery system was for open enrollment, and how impossible it was to find a house in the district these days. These moms were obsessed with McKinley and all the ways it was going to benefit their children. There was a nutritionist on staff supervising the hot lunch program, a music therapist there to help the kids express themselves through song. Several language immersion programs, so that your kid could learn Mandarin or Spanish or for some reason, German? Most of it sounded boring as hell to me, and I know this sounds like the cheesy kind of thing you only hear on TV, but anytime I looked at Jaxon's dirty little face I just wanted him to have every opportunity in the world, even if they were opportunities I didn't understand. But there was no way he'd get them. McKinley was a school for rich kids who had rich parents like the ones whose crotches I was always waxing. Jaxon would go . . . I didn't know where.

One day, when Jaxon was still a toddler, spending his days with our elderly neighbor, Janine, I'd gone to the library to research schools. The first step, the local website told me, was to identify our school district. The computer screen featured a map of our area, cut into what looked like jagged, angular puzzle pieces in different colors. The McKinley district was the smallest, a tiny island of purple smack in the middle of the map. And right there, right on the edge of that purple area? Was our neighbor Janine's house.

Just a measly ten yards south was our house, on the edge of the Colton district. I'd never heard of it, but a quick search showed me that it had the worst school in the state. Their graduates go on to become guys who wear sunglasses on the backs of their heads, telemarketers, and disc golfers. And those are the lucky ones. Jaxon was screwed.

So when I went to pick up Jaxon, I cut a deal with Janine. I would put her address on all my school paperwork, and when school mail would arrive at her house, she would dish it to me. In exchange, I gave her free pedicures. That old lady has some nasty feet. But it was worth it.

Jaxon was in. I was in.

THAT WAS KINDERGARTEN, WHEN ALL THE COMMUNICATION was done in colorful flyers that Jaxon just jammed into the bottom of his backpack. I'd usually find them after they'd congealed into a pulp with spilled water, loose raisins, and other unidentifiable snack residue. Apparently Jaxon wasn't the only kid who made an unreliable mailman, because the teacher eventually wised up and decided that the best course of action was to hand those flyers to parents *personally* at drop-off or pickup. She'd look us dead in the eye and narrate the entire moment, too, just so we couldn't pretend we hadn't known about the Harvest Hootenanny or the Book Bonanza. "Hi, Ms. Dunkler, here's a flyer for next month's volunteer *opportunities*," she'd say, and I'd promise to look it over when I got home and had a better sense of my schedule. Wouldn't you know? I was booked every day of the next month with LITERALLY ANYTHING ELSE.

Thank God for first grade, when Gwendolyn strong-armed the entire teaching staff into communicating only via email. She saved thousands of trees and saved me from dying of boredom at a science museum field trip with a bunch of nerds. Ever since then, my email address has been my shield: taking one for the Dunkler team day after day. "Sorry!" I can say whenever a mom asks if I'm going to whatever fucking carnival they're planning to celebrate something that isn't a holiday. "Musta missed that email!" It's called plausible deniability. You can't prove that I *didn't* not get that email.

KIDS ARE DUMB ENOUGH NOT TO NOTICE THE DIFFERENCES between them right away. Kids don't know that their parents' car costs what I make in a year, or that Jaxon's backpack came from the thrift store. To them, class is a place you learn, not a pecking order that determines your worth and your path in life. So when Jaxon was in at McKinley, he was *in*. He was huge and athletic, and when you're a kid, that's kinda all you need to be popular. He made every team and got invited to every birthday party. But I was not in. I'd walked into that first parent-teacher conference ready to parent the *fuck* out of it. But Mrs. Fagnani—with her boring jewelry and her prim and proper sweater set—had taken one look at me and written me off. She had so many questions: Was I married to Jaxon's dad? Did Jaxon *have* a dad? Where did we live? And were we sure it was in district? I'd gotten the message loud and clear. And I'd ignored it.

I never went to another parent-teacher conference. I never answered another letter or email from the Mom Squad, the administration, or anything else related to this school. Jaxon was in. I didn't need to be.

SEVEN YEARS LATER, I'M TROLLING THE HALLWAYS OF Mc-Kinley *trying* to run into Jaxon's teacher. From everything I've heard about Mr. Nolan, he's single and at least not *not* trying to mingle. *Bam!* I didn't even see her there when I took that corner, poor kid. Except she's not a kid. Though she *is* dressed like a large kindergartner.

"It's okay!" she says, smoothing down her hair. "Oooooh!" Her small, clammy hand clamps itself around my forearm. "Nice tats!" It sounds like she'd practiced saying "tats" before.

"I'm Kiki," she announces, sliding her hand down my forearm until we are shaking hands.

"Okay," I reply, glancing behind me to see if Mr. Nolan had slipped by while I was being accosted.

"Hey, would you like to have a special coffee date with me sometime?"

"Like, an Irish coffee?" I ask. "Because I have some Bailey's in my bag if you want . . ."

"Like, a Starbucks?" she asked, which is confusing because why is she asking me an additional question when she hasn't even answered mine?

This woman has so many questions: What grade is my kid in? Where do I work? What's my *name*? I have one question: What the fuck is *wrong* with this lady?

My dreams of bumping into Mr. Nolan dissolve while this happy little Gollum leads me deep into the caverns of

McKinley. We end up in the auditorium, where dozens of other moms are gathered in what they'd call "small groups" but I would call very small circles of my personal hell. They are *meeting. Gathering.*

My perfect nonparticipation streak is officially over. I've accidentally and tragically attended a fucking Mom Squad meeting.

I'VE WATCHED PROFESSIONAL WRESTLING MY ENTIRE LIFE, and I wish I could take back every penny I ever spent on those tour shows, because going to PTA meetings is free and even a bunch of drugged-up, over-tanned meatheads in spandex can't bring the amount of energy or drama that a roomful of anxious moms provides.

You've never seen so many moms in your life. They're *everywhere*, packed into the McKinley auditorium like they heard there was going to be a pop-up Ann Taylor sale where our kids hold their "talent" shows.

The crowd here is decidedly more sober than at any WWF event I've ever been to, and I'm the only one holding a twenty-ounce bottle of Mountain Dew, but the energy is similar. The most hardcore fans sit right up front in the folding chairs and everyone is in costume: perfect hair, perfect outfits. Even the women who are dressed like they could bust out into a series of walking lunges at any moment are showered and made up.

Bits and pieces of conversation float into my ears:

"That's just one of the pitfalls of having a gifted child, I suppose."

"Me? Oh my GOD, I'm disgusting right now. I swear, I've gained ten pounds since Max started kindergarten, just eating my feelings!"

"And I said that . . . I said it right to her face. I said, Jenn, you're not acting like yourself right now. You're being very hostile."

I need to get out of here, but most of the exits are blocked by tight pods of moms all very intensely discussing whatever it is moms like them discuss: Artisanal diapers? Small-batch peanut-free peanut butter? Grass-fed, organic children?

This is why people have dogs: they're a built-in excuse to have to leave at a moment's notice. Then again, so are kids, and you don't see a single kid in this room. Not one.

The lights flicker. The crowd hushes.

Showtime.

Gwendolyn takes the stage, and I fully expect pyrotechnics to follow. The crowd applauds before Gwendolyn even opens her mouth, and all I can think is, "I really, really wish I were high."

From what I can gather, every woman here is mega into Gwendolyn, the way all the guys I grew up with were mega into Hulk Hogan. Confused, anxious people like a strong leader who promises absolute order. It's a basic tenet of fascism and pro wrestling. And, apparently, the PTA.

Gwendolyn doesn't tan—it "causes premature aging"— but she does pay two hundred and fifty dollars a month to be airbrushed the color of coffee with cream and sugar. It takes a lot of work to make you look like you're effortlessly beautiful. Personally, I don't get it. If I wanted to look like I wasn't wearing makeup, I'd just skip the process altogether. I don't mind people knowing that I've put in some effort. That's kind of the point, actually. But what's really in now is for nobody to know that you've made any effort at all. That everything from your gel manicure to your highlights look *natural*, which seems like a big waste of money and gel polish to me.

I don't get it, but I do appreciate Gwendolyn for bringing this trend to McKinley, because the local beauty community owes her our livelihood. Once she started telling people that the secret to her look was one hundred ounces of water and nine hours of sleep at night, the spa was overrun with women who wanted to look *natural*. The problem with wanting to look natural in a world that still expects women to look fuckable is that you want to look like you naturally looked when you were twenty, when you were maybe drinking a couple ounces of water a day and stumbling in to work hungover, on three hours of sleep, and were still a straight-up hottie.

I don't know how much water Gwendolyn drinks or how much sleep she actually gets, but I can tell you by looking her up in our database that Gwendolyn's "no-makeup" look is the result of bimonthly facials, quarterly Botox injections, and a half-syringe of filler at the apples of her cheeks, refilled twice per year to add some fat to her skinny-ass face.

Look, everyone needs a little help. There's nothing unnatural about that. I like my help to come in the form of a heavy-duty push-up bra, a professional-grade concealer/foundation that could also work to spackle your walls, and the occasional morning margarita. I don't like the idea that anyone should feel bad about the help they get, or the help they need. And I sure as shit don't like when people lie about it.

A face that has trouble matching the tone of your voice is not the "natural and organic" lifestyle that Gwendolyn promotes on her blog and her Instagram, except that botulism *is* naturally occurring, and our tanning solution is labeled as organic because who the fuck is going to check? Only one woman has ever asked what made it organic. She was standing there in her paper panties bent over at the waist like a Barbie doll so I could tan the crease under her butt cheeks. "It's made from the skin of naturally felled acorns," I'd said, and she'd nodded like that made any sense at all. I swear to God you can tell women like this that anything is organic, and they'd pay three times as much for it.

Speaking of organic, Gwendolyn is now discussing the importance of using an organic, nontoxic homeopathic solution whenever treating head lice.

"We're facing a crisis here," she says, nearly whispering. A pause, and then her voice gets louder. "Our *children* are facing a crisis."

Now, look, I had lice for about ten years growing up. Your head is a little itchy because there are bugs on it, but eventually the bugs die. Big deal. It's annoying, sure, but it's not exactly a crisis. A crisis is when your girlfriend has amnesia and doesn't remember who she is and has been pulled into a crime ring that's taking advantage of her lack of memory, which somehow doesn't affect her driving skills. That's from *Fast & Furi-*

ous, by the way, and Dom Toretto got through it and he and Letty got back together and everything.

Maybe I *am* high. Because the crisis Gwendolyn is talking about isn't even lice.

"As you know," she says, smiling, "I'm dedicated to *being* the change I wish to see in the world. I'm dedicated to making our school and our world safer for our kids. I'm not afraid to cause a stir. Or take on big challenges." She pauses here, and the crowd applauds in agreement, like Gwendolyn is some sort of freedom fighter. I gotta admit, the energy here is contagious.

"And that's why I'm so proud to bring the following issue to your attention. An issue that's quite literally poisoning our children . . . right in front of us. Every year. An issue that's been disguised as fun and fund*raising*, an honored tradition that has been tainted by our own laziness and inattentiveness."

Dramatic music rises, and I lean forward in my chair.

It isn't quite pyrotechnics, but a projector suddenly turns on, and two words illuminate the movie-theater-size screen behind Gwendolyn. Her nemesis has been named. The gauntlet has been thrown.

Gwendolyn James is calling out the bake sale. And with that, I am fucking outta here.

13

AMY

Most people know to sneak in when they're late. *I* know to sneak in when I'm late. But sneaking in is for people who are thinking clearly, and there are too many thoughts zipping through my mind, too many things on my ever-growing to-do list. What I'm saying is, I forgot to sneak in. In I walk, like I'm *not* arriving twenty minutes after the scheduled "gathering time." Gwendolyn clocks me right away.

"Oh," she cries out, shielding her eyes from the stage lights, "Amy Mitchell! How nice of you to join us. Right on time, as usual!"

The crowd laughs nervously, but I don't even crack a smile. I just shrug and look around for a seat.

"I was just naming the lead on our Bake Sale Task Force," Gwendolyn continues, "and I think you're just the woman for the job!"

That stops me in my tracks. She can't be serious. I am drowning at work; I am juggling one stressed-out kid, one lazy-ass kid, one sick dog, and a marriage that is hanging by one mangy little thread—and also? I just realized I have to pee. I have not peed today, or if I did, I can't remember it. I absolutely cannot head some stupid, made-up Bake Sale Task Force. I just cannot.

The word is out of my mouth and into the atmosphere before I can even think it through.

"No."

It hangs there for a moment, and then incites a ripple of murmuring through the crowd.

"Pardon me?" Gwendolyn places a hand over her heart as she says this, pretending to truly give a shit.

"I SAID . . . NO."

That came out a little louder than it needed to, I know. It's a bad idea to cross Gwendolyn. The last mom who pissed her off ended up suddenly moving her family to South Dakota. But fuck it.

"No, Gwendolyn. I don't want to be on the Bake Sale Task Force." Once I started, I couldn't stop. "Or the Lice Task Force. Or the Community Recycling Task Force, which I'm pretty sure gave me mercury poisoning last year. I don't want to bring snacks for the class. I don't want to *go* to class. I'm done with school! I finished thirteen goddamn years ago! I don't want to spend my entire life taking care of everything for everyone. I quit!"

Gwendolyn looks like a robot who has just found out she

isn't a real person. "You . . . quit?" She forces a laugh. "You quit . . . what, honey?"

"This! All of this! I quit . . . trying so damn hard. I'm done."

I don't wait for a reaction; I just turn and march toward the exit. I can only imagine Gwendolyn's fake smile and her eyes boring into my spine as I let the door slam behind me.

I hope I don't have to move to South Dakota.

14

KIKI

She *quit*.

She *quit* the Mom Squad.

She walked away from Gwendolyn. From the PTA. From my chance to be friends with her!

I'm trying to horn in on all the whispered conversations happening around me, but my phone keeps vibrating.

KENT: Kiki, where are the diapers??

ME: Top drawer of the changing table. Xo.

KENT: When are you coming back?

ME: Meeting goes until 9. Xo.

KENT: 9pm?? You still have to go to the supermarket.

KENT: I'm out of protein bars.

ME: I know! Xo.

KENT: And milk. Whole, not that 2% stuff.

ME: I know! Xo.

KENT: I'm serious, no almond milk.

ME: Yep!

KENT: And apples. Green ones.

ME: You got it!

KENT: Thick-cut ham.

ME: Alrighty!

Amy is gone. She must have left while I was texting, probably because texting in public is so rude.

My dad always told me that quitting was for quitters. He was talking about smoking, and he later died of emphysema. I never quit anything except my job when I got pregnant, but that's different. As a kid, I still played hockey even after I dislocated my shoulder. "Get back out there!" my coach shouted when I tried to get off the ice, and I did. At the ER later that night, the doctors said they couldn't believe I was able to finish the whole game in such excruciating pain. My dad stood there, beaming with pride while they popped my shoulder back into the socket. Junior year of high school, I was diagnosed with mononucleosis. That's the kissing disease, but you can also get it from borrowing someone's reed in marching band, or drinking from the same cup as Crystal Baumgartner, which are the two places I could have gotten it, seeing as how I for sure wasn't kissing anyone after what they taught us in sex ed. Anyway, mononucleosis didn't stop me from going to the State Finals for Debate even though my doctor said I was in danger of developing hepatitis if I didn't rest. Hadn't Amy had a strict father who taught her better than to just . . .

quit? And why do I so badly want to follow her out that dang door?

All around me are the people I had hoped to connect with: moms who I had hoped would want to get a special coffee sometime, or exchange recipes for dessert bars. What did Gwendolyn have against *dessert bars*? Gwendolyn had a *lot* against dessert bars, it turns out. I happen to know for a fact that they make people happy, but her entire presentation included photos of sad kids clutching their bellies like they had just swallowed a Tide pod, and I saw on *Good Morning America* that some kids are actually doing that and it seems like *that* is a crisis, not my mother's seven-layer bars. Nobody in Minot could *ever* get them as gooey as hers, and here's why: she used *two* sticks of salted butter in every batch. But butter is now outlawed. So is chocolate. And sweetened coconut. And graham crackers. And caramel. And walnuts. And butterscotch. And condensed milk. Any milk, really. The recipe that I was counting on to win over hearts and minds and stomachs at McKinley was now officially outlawed.

My phone buzzes again.

KENT: Mild salsa.
KENT: And chips.

Heart thumping, I grab my purse and stand up.

I'M NOT FOLLOWING AMY; I'M JUST WALKING BEHIND HER FOR a few blocks without saying anything. I *want* to say something, but when I try to think of what I could call out to her on a dark street without alarming her, nothing comes to mind. So I just hang back, hoping that the right opportunity will present itself. I'm just thinking about how much I like the sound of her boots clicking on the pavement when she darts across the street without even looking both ways, and walks into a low, plain building with a big neon sign. The Office.

I've never been to The Office. Kent says that bars are for creeps and lowlifes, but the moment I step inside I realize that he forgot to also list sad-looking people, regular-looking people, and McKinley moms, apparently.

It smells a little bit like the inside of Bernard's mouth after he's had the stomach flu, or maybe the inside of a sippy cup you find on the floor of the van on a hot summer day. It smells bad, but when my eyes adjust to the dark, I see her. My future friend.

Be normal. Be normal. Be normal.

"Hi, I'm Amy! You're Amy. I'm Kiki. My kids go to McKinley." My voice sounds like me, but not like me. I sound like an alien doing a bad impersonation of a human mother.

Good job being normal, Kiki.

Amy Mitchell has the prettiest skin I've ever seen in my life. She has no pores. It's like she's been airbrushed, except you know that she doesn't wear makeup—maybe a swipe of mascara, if she's feeling like it. She's just *that* beautiful. Her hair is so glossy I want to weave it into a pillowcase and sleep with it every night. Even my thoughts are not being normal.

"Oh God." She moans. "You were there? I'm not normally like that. I just have a lot going on right now."

Her voice is so warm and kind that I want to take a nap inside of it. I know that what I say next really matters; I rehearsed this conversation in my head the whole way here. It's my chance to turn the fact that I followed her from a school to a bar several blocks away into the beginning of an actual friendship.

I'm interrupted by Carla, who has been busy ripping through the pile of pull tabs in front of her. Are she and Amy . . . friends? Did I totally blow it by ignoring her to text my husband? Does she totally hate me now?

"Hey!" Carla smiles. "I know you! I tried to get you out the door with me, but you were glued to that fucking phone. It's a tracking device, you know. So. What're you drinking?"

When I was little, my mom would take me with her down to the VFW for the Friday-night fish fry, and I'd get two dollars to spend. I'd get myself one Shirley Temple with extra cherries and six pull tabs, even though it's technically gambling and for sure illegal to sell them to children. I took my time with each tab, double-checking every symbol to make sure I didn't miss a winner.

"Helloooo! Kiki! Drink?" Carla is snapping her long fingers in my face.

"Shirley Temple, extra cherries."

At first I'm afraid that she is gravely injured, but the sound coming from her mouth and throat is apparently a laugh, which turns into a cough that really should be treated by a medical professional.

"You're nuts," she says, stepping behind the bar.

What she hands me is too dark to be a Shirley Temple, so I assume it's a Roy Rogers. I try not to drink Coca-Cola Classic after five PM because it keeps me up, but this is a special friend date and I want to be polite.

It tastes like acid mixed with nail polish remover and whatever is leaking out of the bottom of our van right now, but I keep drinking. The faster I get this over with, the better.

"Easy, mama!" she says. "That's a Manhattan. It's like, pure alcohol. You're gonna be on your ass if you drink it that fast."

Alcohol! And not just alcohol, but a *Manhattan.* Kent and I went to Manhattan once. I thought we'd go to FAO Schwartz and the Statue of Liberty and the Museum of Natural History, but mainly I just stayed in the hotel room while Kent went to his work conference because he said the city was filled with crooks and pickpockets. We *did* go to the Olive Garden in Times Square, though, and when we were walking back to the hotel, Kent stepped in human poop.

This drink of alcohol is warm inside of me. I can feel my self-consciousness unknotting itself. I feel . . . comfortable?

"Amy." I hear my voice before I even know what I'm saying. "I think what you did in there was really . . . cool."

Amy has the kind of smile you know comes straight from her soul. I wonder if she has an Instagram. I should follow her.

"Thanks, Kiki. I think *you're* really cool. How have we not met sooner?"

I'm smiling at her like a doofus, trying to come up with a funny way to say that we should make up for lost friendship time by "grabbing a coffee" soon, when my brain focuses back in on the conversation that Amy and Carla are having.

"I just have too much going on to give a shit about anybody's lice but my own kids'," Amy says, taking a really big sip of her own drink.

"Your kids have *lice*?" I don't mean to, but I jump back. I have four kids, I can't be combing through four heads for tiny bugs and their larvae! We did that last year, and I still find myself keeping my distance if they so much as scratch their heads once.

"No!" says Amy, laughing. "I mean, who knows, don't kids always have lice?" Amy takes another big sip from her drink. "I mean, I don't have time for anything right now. I barely have time to brush my teeth at night."

I run my tongue over my teeth. Did I brush them today? I honestly can't remember.

"My kids haven't been to the dentist in a year and a half, and I don't even have a *job*." This Manhattan is really something. Also, it's gone.

"You have a job," Carla says. "You spend all day with your fucking kids. I would rather wax a thousand nutsacks a day than do that. No offense."

"None taken! At least it's just three of them home now. Although I don't know how long that will last because Bernard's teacher said that the two of them don't seem to be making a connection and it might be time for the two of them to explore other options and I don't know what she means by that but also she doesn't reply to my emails."

"Smart," says Carla.

The silence that follows isn't awkward at all. Which is strange because everything is awkward for me. So, maybe the silence *is* awkward, but I just don't know it?

Amy is the first one to talk.

"This is really nice, guys. I can't remember the last time I just . . . went out?"

"I can't, either," replies Carla. "It's like my life is a revolving door of work, sleep, and other boring shit."

It occurs to me that the warm feeling I have from my shoulders to my waist, this little vest of happiness I'm wearing, might be that I'm drunk? Kent says that drunkenness is a sign of a low intellect.

"I think I'm drunk!" I announce, and the two of them laugh. I think they think I'm joking, but I have been drunk fewer than three times in my life. I took DARE very seriously as a child.

"So, Amy, you said that you have a lot going on right now, Amy?" Kent has a book called *How to Win Friends and Influence People*, and one of the steps is to remember to say people's names a lot, and to ask them questions about themselves.

Amy waves me off. "Oh, forget it. We *all* do. I'm just . . . so tired. It's work. It's my marriage. It's . . . it's so hard to be a good mom. I feel like every day that passes, I'm just closer to the end of a rapidly fraying rope. It's like I'm juggling five bowling balls while riding a pogo stick balanced on top of a ball and if I mess anything up, the entire world is going to end and my kids are going to grow up and write memoirs about me."

Carla is nodding, but I can't even speak. Did I just hear what I thought I heard? That being a good mom is hard for a woman who looks like she could be on the cast of a popular late-nineties sitcom?

"Oh my God, I know," moans Carla. "There are so many rules."

"Yes!" I scream. "The rules! And they always change! Like, children need boundaries . . . but don't say no to them."

"Or," Amy adds, "screen time will make them stupid . . . but no screen time will mean they're behind their peer group and destined to fail at life."

"Yes!" This feeling of validation is *almost* better than being drunk. "And . . . let your child decide how much to eat, but if he doesn't eat fourteen different vegetables a day, he's going to be malnourished and probably die."

"Good moms don't work full-time," Amy points out.

"Good moms volunteer to be the class mom," I reply.

"Good moms have clean cars and clean kids and don't forget to take their kids to the dentist for two years." Amy smiles.

"Good moms remember to pick your kid up from baseball! Good moms don't let their kids have fast food for two meals a day! Good moms don't sleep with the janitor at your kid's school!" Carla shouts.

I hope she doesn't mean Rusty.

"You know what being a good mom got me so far? TMJ, migraines, and carpal tunnel from building my kids' blue-ribbon winning dioramas . . ." Amy leans over the bar to grab a bottle of alcohol and pours some in each of our glasses. "So, fuck it, ladies. Let's be *bad* moms."

Amy raises her glass, and we all clink our glasses together. *My first toast!*

"To being bad moms!" Amy declares, and we all take a drink.

I'm still gagging from the taste of whatever I just ingested when my phone buzzes.

> **KENT:** If you haven't left the grocery store yet, Bernard and I want pork tenderloin for dinner tomorrow.

"Fudge!"

Amy is pouring another round of whatever hellfire she selected, but she pauses to ask what's the matter.

"I have to go to the supermarket." I sigh.

Amy and Carla share a look, then pour their drinks down their throats. Neither of them look like they want to vomit.

"Fuck it," says Carla, slamming her glass on the bar, "let's go get some fucking groceries."

15

AMY

Look, I've worked retail. I know that there's nothing worse than someone waltzing in the front door ten minutes before you close. But sometimes it's 9:50 PM on a weeknight and your new best friend needs to get some essentials for her family and you could use a couple bags of chips for the house anyway, and *yeah, you're kinda buzzed*, so you stroll into the supermarket just before close and avoid eye contact with the manager.

"Oh my GOD, this place is depressing," Carla says in a voice that is the exact opposite of avoiding eye contact with the manager. "Do you come here every month?"

Kiki has dutifully wiped her cart with antibacterial wipes and is navigating through the aisles in the most efficient display of grocery shopping I have ever seen, while Carla and I eat extra-cheesy chips right out of the bag. Kiki and I spent the whole car ride comparing mom notes: how Pinterest should be

labeled as a terrorist organization for convincing every mom
we know that birthday parties need to be themed and decorated as if the party is going to be photographed by *Vogue*,
how crappy it feels when stay-at-home moms tell me that they
can't imagine being away from their kids every day, and how
shitty it feels for Kiki when working moms treat her like she's
an idiot just because she spends her days with her kids. Carla
mostly just told us we both needed to take a chill pill and offered us some weed cookies from her purse (pass).

"Fudge," says Kiki, "I need diapers for the twins. They're
like twice as expensive here."

"That's 'cause they know they've got your balls in a vise,"
Carla explains. "Formula costs more than a case of decent
beer, you know why? Because they *know* you're gonna pay it."

"Just like they know if they put juice boxes with cartoon
character faces on it *right at kid level*, you're going to buy it
because it's easier to spend three extra dollars than it is to
physically wrestle your child in public." I can't imagine Kiki
wrestling her child, but I can see why she wouldn't want to.
She's very petite.

We cruise through the aisles, pointing out all the ways
that the Patriarchal Capitalist Machine attacks us: diet soda in
slim cans, razors for women that cost more than the same ones
for men, scented tampons! I say "pointing out," but to clarify,
we are definitely using outside voices.

We're just rounding the corner from Dairy to Cleaning
Goods when I see her. The face of everything wrong with modern motherhood. No, not Gwendolyn. The "spokesmom" for
a name-brand chemical company whose entire ad campaign

centers on a mom who "does it all." The campaign is called—I kid you not—"Like a Mother," and features a C-list actress showing how much easier her life is with the help of this all-purpose cleaner that smells like lavender. In every video she's breezing through life: working like a mother, cooking like a mother, being very hot in a bathing suit like a mother? This woman haunts me in Facebook videos that blow my cover with loud voiceover when I'm just trying to enjoy a little scroll time during a boring meeting, in commercials when I'm just trying to enjoy a marathon of a show where people suck at baking, and now in the grocery store? Do we really need a life-size cutout of a woman who likely has someone to clean her home *for* her looming over us in this sacred space where we come to page through gossip magazines while we wait to pay for the food our kids will whine about?

The decapitation is Carla's idea. Or maybe Kiki's. Kiki definitely starts it, ramming her cart repeatedly into the display while shouting, "I'll show you how to clean like a mother!" It's Carla who performs the final ritual, ripping off the cardboard head and presenting it to Kiki like an offering.

"For our Queen," she says, bowing down, then hoisting Kiki's little body into the cart. If I have to pinpoint where our night changes, it's this moment. Because once Kiki is named our Queen, once we get her into the cart and start referring to it as a chariot, once we allow ourselves to get sidetracked by the impulse purchases at the endcaps (a lemon-shaped plastic dish to store . . . your lemon?), we are no longer three moms at the grocery store. We are three wild animals with debit cards, spraying diet soda like we're NBA players celebrating a championship, taste-testing the flavored lube (which does *not* taste like cherries), and moving all the full-fat yogurt to the front of the dairy case because *who the fuck decided our yogurt had to be fat free?!*

It's clear during checkout, as Carla slips her number to the manager and Kiki begins to sort her coupons like she's the star of her own reality show about extreme frugality, that I will never be able to return to this Stop-N-Save again.

16

CARLA

Jaxon is supposed to wake me up by seven, but he either didn't try hard enough or I was unresponsive, because by the time I snap out of my near coma, it was time to leave ten minutes ago.

Lucky for me, Jax knows the drill. I slap on some makeup and perfume; he grabs a Pedialyte from the pantry and cracks it open for the drive to school. If I can chug a liter of this shit before drop-off, I'll be okay.

Lucky for Jaxon, his mom only needs six minutes to go from hot mess to just hot. If you can't apply mascara while driving a stick shift, you have no business driving a car.

"Ma," Jaxon shouts from the kitchen, "why is there a cardboard lady head on the kitchen counter?"

17

KIKI

Kent didn't wake up when I came in last night. He didn't wake up when I dropped a gallon of milk on the kitchen floor and tried to clean it up with a broom. He didn't wake up when I tripped over his underpants trying to sneak into our bedroom. But he's awake now, and the smell of his coffee breath makes me want to puke all over him.

"Keeks, babe, you feeling okay?" The back of his hand is on my forehead, checking me for a fever. I *do* feel sweaty. And cold. Should my skin hurt? I remember the time I was drunk in college, when my roommate and I split a Mike's Hard Lemonade and I immediately threw up in our sink and she threatened to report me to our Resident Assistant if I didn't let her borrow my Abercrombie hoodie. This is worse.

I want Kent to leave, and to take his pleated khakis with him. All the things I usually love about him—the smell of his

cheap generic bar soap, the sight of his biceps in a polo shirt—
make me want to drop dead. After what seems like a hundred
years, Kent is done taking my temperature.

"You're burning up. You forgot to use hand sanitizer at
that PTA thing, didn't you?"

Downstairs, I can hear the kids going absolutely bonkers.

"Take a vitamin, you'll feel better," Kent says, heading for
the door. "I'll be home around five thirty. The kids are starving, by the way. And the floor is really sticky."

18

AMY

One of my eyes seems to be glued shut, but with my one good eye, the room begins to come into focus. It appears the sun has already risen. That . . . can't be right. I peel my eyelid up. I slept in my mascara? Jesus. I slept in my *clothes*? What the actual hell happened last night?

Next to me is a life-size cardboard cutout of a popular TV spokesperson used to advertise cleaning products. She's headless. Each of my heartbeats echoes inside of my head, and I realize with horror that I'm . . . hungover. Not "I had two glasses of wine with book club last night and I'm a little fuzzy this morning." No, this is "I disassociated from my body and my life last night and became a college sophomore in a thirty-something-year-old body."

The stairs seem particularly treacherous today, like someone has rearranged them while I was sleeping. Why am I so *sore*? Why are my legs so tired? My brain serves up a small flash of me teaching Carla and Kiki a short barre routine in the cereal aisle. "Tuck! Tuck! Tuck!" Carla scooped her hips back and forth like a natural. Kiki peed a little bit, which is totally normal—she's had four kids.

"MOM."

Dylan and Jane are sitting at the kitchen island, expectantly.

"Where's our breakfast?" My instinct is to panic: to grab two frying pans and four eggs and get my babies fed. It takes two pans because they have different breakfast requirements: Dylan will have two "scrambied" eggs with sausage links. Jane will have two "poachies" with veggie bacon. And I *do* reach for the pans, but there's a dirty baking sheet on the stovetop covered in . . . nachos? Or, at least some tortilla chips covered in what must have been cheese before they were burned to a crisp. I made nachos last night? I pull a few cheese-crusted chips from the baking sheet and turn to assess the situation.

I'm . . . possibly still drunk. I have no business operating anything that involves a flame. And Dylan and Jane are big enough to reach the cupboards. They're smart enough to add milk and cereal together in a vessel of some sort. They're old enough to know that toast is just bread that's been placed in a toaster. You just push *one button*.

Instead of the eggs, I reach for my phone.

"MOM. What are you *doing*?" Dylan is not amused.

"I'm calling the cops," I say calmly. "If your breakfast is missing, I think we should get the authorities involved."

I think this is the best joke I've ever made, but Dylan and Jane look at each other like I should be institutionalized. I've been standing up too long, and my body is starting to break into a cold sweat. *Please*, I pray to any god that is listening, *don't let me puke in front of my kids.*

"You've got twenty minutes till the bus comes. The stop is on the corner. Put your dishes in the dishwasher before you go."

The two of them protest as I shuffle out of the kitchen and prepare to climb the stairs. Dylan and Jane can't believe what they're hearing today. They don't know how to ride a bus, they cry! How will they know when to get off? Does it even have seatbelts? Is it safe? And they're *serious*. My kids are smart, capable children who claim that they don't know how to enter a motor vehicle, sit on their butts, and disembark when they reach their destination? Have I really never made them take the bus? It's a free service provided by the school district. It picks them up less than twenty-five yards from our house. Plus, my car is still in the McKinley parking lot.

By the time I reach the top of the stairs, which might have taken anywhere between two and twenty-seven minutes, I can hear cabinets banging in the kitchen. I smile. They're gonna be okay. They're gonna be better than okay. They're gonna be functioning members of society. Today it's breakfast, but tomorrow it could be doing their own laundry. Changing their own *sheets*. Packing their own lunches. In a few decades, they'll pay their own mortgages and finance their own cars! But first, the bus.

"You'll figure it out," I call weakly from the landing. "I believe in you!"

THE CURE FOR A HANGOVER HASN'T CHANGED SINCE COLlege. It takes thirty-two ounces of red Gatorade, two Advil, and a big, greasy breakfast: three fried eggs, over hard, white toast, and any kind of fried potato product.

When was the last time I ate a meal alone? A real meal, not just shoveling chips and salsa into my mouth while standing at the counter scrolling through work emails at 10:30 PM.

I've read the entire newspaper. The *real* newspaper. The one that's made of *paper*. Usually, I let them collect on the front step until they've become a massive, soggy mess, and then I throw them in the recycling. I could cancel my subscription, but having a newspaper subscription is one of those things that makes me feel like I'm a real grown-up. Actually reading it? I feel like nobody could possibly doubt that I am a woman who has my life together, as long as they don't get close enough to smell the booze seeping out of my pores. I read every inch of that newspaper. I actually chewed my food before swallowing it. And forty-five minutes later, when I had finally read the very last obituary—rest in peace, Beverly Howard—I felt *great*. Relaxed, even.

At this point in the day, I'd typically be in my sixth meeting. It would overlap with two other meetings, so I'd arrive late and leave early, offering apologies to everyone in the room like this wasn't their fault for seeing that my calendar was full and booking a meeting with me anyway. I *almost* feel guilty, except I don't. I'm only a part-time employee. I don't have a 401(k) or healthcare benefits. I don't get paid enough to answer emails before the sun rises, or to spend my Christmas on the phone with Dale, talking through his latest stupid idea. I get paid to do half of one job, three days a week. That's exactly why I took the job.

WHEN DID I GO FROM BEING A PART-TIME MARKETING MAN- ager to being a more-than-full-time CMO/COO/CFO who makes less than our entry-level sales staff?? It happened slowly, the same way anything does. A few more meetings here and there, a few more phone calls taken from the car during school pickup and drop-off. A few more nights where "dinner as a family" turned into me making separate meals for each kid according to their personal preferences. It was raising my hand to volunteer with the teacher who needed help organizing the Fall Ball, the coach who needed extra adults to stand around at practice and make sure we didn't lose track of a kid. Somehow, I went from wanting my kids to be happy and succeed to "helping" with their reports and double-checking their homework for them. I went from having a partner who could help me with bath time and bedtime to becoming the only one who could do it right. The same way I went from helping Dale part-time to becoming the only person at the company who can do anything right.

SPEAKING OF DALE, HE'S CALLING AGAIN.

"AMY. Amy. What is happening, I'm about to issue an Amber Alert for you. You're missing the midweek check-in."

"No, I'm not."

"Yeah, Amy, you are. It's right now. I'm right here, at the meeting, in the conference room, checking in. And you're not here."

"Dale. It's my day off," I say in a voice that's as relaxed as I feel.

"It's THURSDAY, Amy. It's nobody's day off! There are no days off! Not when you have a champion's mentality, and I'm beginning to think you don't have that mentality."

"Dale," I say, activating my Mom Mode. "Dale," I say again, slowing my voice and enunciating clearly, the way I did when Jane used to throw tantrums so violent I was sure she would transform into the Incredible Hulk at any moment. "I am a part-time employee. This means that I am contracted with you to work *part*-time. You've certainly enjoyed my over-working for the past few years, and I understand that this may be confusing for you, but I will now only be working *part*-time. I'll see you on Monday."

Dale is choking on his words when I end the call.

I fold the paper neatly and place my dishes in the dishwasher. The day stretches ahead of me, filled with possibility and wonder.

I can do anything I want with this time. Anything at all.

And even though I've just eaten a full farmer's breakfast, even though I can still feel the effects of last night behind my eyes, I want to go out to lunch.

To: McKinley Mom Squad
From: Gwendolyn James
CC: Principal Burr
Subject: Last Night

Hi Mamas,

Many thanks to those of you who maintained your commitment to excellence in education by fulfilling and exceeding your obligations to the McKinley Mom Squad. We are, of course, only as strong as our weakest link, and some weaknesses presented themselves last night.

As your leader, I feel responsible for the traumatic outburst we experienced last night and want to apologize to everyone who was affected. Amy is a valued member of the Mom Squad and I hope that Amy takes the time to get the mental health support she needs.

Our thoughts and prayers are with her during this stressful time. Marriage and Motherhood are not for the faint of heart, and we hope she and her family come through their troubles stronger than ever. Amy remains a valued member of the Mom Squad, and we are here to support her with open arms. When she's ready, we will accept her apology and move forward, together.

In Love and Light and Style,
G

"The supreme art of war is to subdue the enemy without fighting." —Sun Tzu

Take my eCourse: <u>Mom Enough: Making the Most of Your 18 Years with Your Precious Children</u>

To: Gwendolyn James; McKinley Mom Squad
From: Amy Mitchell
CC: Principal Burr
Subject: RE: Last Night

Thanks, G.

The well wishes are appreciated. A couple points of clarification:

1. I quit, so please unsubscribe me from these emails.
2. Not sorry.

Love and Light,
Amy

To: Amy Mitchell; Gwendolyn James; McKinley Mom Squad
From: Stacy Gordon
CC: Principal Burr
Subject: RE: RE: Last Night

She's my hero.

To: Amy Mitchell; Gwendolyn James; McKinley Mom
Squad
From: Stacy Gordon
CC: Principal Burr
Subject: RECALL NOTICE: RE: RE: Last Night

STACY GORDON WOULD LIKE TO RECALL THE
MESSAGE: RE: RE: Last Night

To: Amy Mitchell; Gwendolyn James; McKinley Mom
Squad
From: Stacy Gordon
CC: Principal Burr
Subject: RE: RE: Last Night

Sorry, everyone! Kid got my phone, not sure what she sent!

To: Amy Mitchell
From: Stacy Gordon
Subject: RE: RE: RE: Last Night

You're my hero.

To: Amy Mitchell
From: Rose A.
Subject: RE: RE: RE: Last Night

Oh my GOD, Amy. Fuck yes.

To: Amy Mitchell
From: Rose A.
Subject: RE: RE: RE: Last Night

Take me with you.

To: Amy Mitchell
From: Jenn P.
Subject: RE: RE: RE: RE: Last Night

If you start a cult, I'm totally joining.

To: Amy Mitchell
From: Jenn P.
Subject: RE: RE: RE: RE: Last Night

PS—I have to ignore you in public and unfriend you on Facebook, though. Gwendolyn scares the shit out of me, and we have three more years at McKinley together.

To: Gwendolyn James; Amy Mitchell
From: Taryn O.
Subject: RE: RE: RE: Last Night

Gwendolyn and Amy,

I want to take a moment to let you know that I see and validate your individual struggles and frustrations. Our roles as moth-

ers and community leaders bring challenges and opportunities. If the two of you are interested in my conflict resolution
services, please let me know. I'm also available for individual
life coaching sessions.

Sincerely,
Taryn (Fern's mom)

19

CARLA

Jesus Christ, are all married moms like hostages with minivans or is it just Amy and Kiki?

Amy texted me at 10:30 AM asking if I'd like to meet for lunch. I haven't even had *breakfast* yet because the Taco Bell near our house doesn't open until 11:00. Kiki replied in under ten seconds.

> **KIKI:** Are we allowed to do that??
> **KIKI:** Let me ask Kent.
> **KIKI:** He's in a meeting until noon.
> **KIKI:** Can I get back to you?
> **CARLA:** I asked Kent. He said it's okay.;)
> **KIKI:** Carla, you asked Kenton?
> **KIKI:** How did you get his number?
> **CARLA:** We go to the same AA meeting.

. . .

CARLA: Kiki, it's LUNCH, not an 8-day sex cruise.

KIKI: :(Sorry. I don't have a sitter.

KIKI IS SHOCKED TO SEE ME ON HER FRONT STEPS. AND EVEN more shocked to see Claudia. Most people are shocked when they see Claudia. She's like nine feet tall and looks like she was created in a lab by scientists who wanted to see what the hottest chick in the world would look like. Claudia's our part-time receptionist and makes the rest of her money posting about diet teas on Instagram, so she's got plenty of free time. I offered her a free facial if she'd watch Kiki's kids for a few hours, and she said yes if I'd throw in a manicure, too. She's savvy like that.

Kiki opens the door, and then just stands there like a mannequin.

"Get your backpack, Punky Brewster!" I yell, pushing Claudia in the front door. "You're going to lunch!"

Kiki's house is . . . cute. It's cozy. It smells like oatmeal and diapers, but you can tell she cares about this place. She has framed photos of her kids on every available surface, and a huge family portrait hanging over the fireplace. They're all wearing coordinating denim outfits and standing in a corn-field for some reason. Kiki's girls are sitting on the couch with a pile of library books, poor kids.

"Kids?" I say, sitting down in the middle of them like the therapists on those shows about having interventions with your family members who won't stop hoarding cats. "This is your Auntie Claudia. She's in charge while Mommy is gone. Listen to her and don't tell her where Mommy keeps the valuables. She's a klepto."

Kiki's children seem confused by the presence of another adult in the house, like they're an endangered species unused to seeing another creature in their habitat. You can sense them wondering what the presence of an Instagram model means for their afternoon, and why their mother is looking for her backpack. I can see in their faces that they're about to lose their shit, but Kiki thinks quickly, reaching into her backpack for some sugar-free, dye-free, organic fruit snacks, shaking the bag like they're dog treats. "Who wants fruit snaaaaacks?" she calls, like a tiny, white Oprah, ripping the bag open with her teeth and pouring the jewel-colored nuggets into her palm. That does the trick: the kids descend on the fruit snacks like a pack of ravenous wolves, and we seem to be in the clear.

Kiki's "quick getaway" takes a solid fifteen minutes, which includes Kiki narrating the entire experience for her children in a tone that implies each sentence ends in a series of exclamation marks.

"Mommy is going to show Claudia the bathroom!!!"

"Mommy is going to talk to Claudia about your snack schedule!!!"

Kiki is in the middle of showing Claudia a three-ring binder filled with step-by-step instructions for each of her children's likes, dislikes, and allergies when I grab her from behind like a kidnapper and carry her toward the door.

"Look, Kiki. Claudia knows enough English, she can figure it out. And if she has questions, she'll call me."

I haul Kiki out the front door and right into my car, which I'd left idling in her driveway so we could make a quick getaway.

"Clara has real attachment issues," Kiki says, worrying, "and the twins are . . . they're just a handful right now. They do NOT do well with sudden change."

"Yeah," I say, throwing my ride into reverse and pulling into the street, "I can see."

On the front porch, Claudia is holding the twins, Clara is hugging Claudia's leg, and all four of them are waving like idiots. I'd stuffed Claudia's purse with all kinds of tasty processed foods: the little snack crackers filled with neon orange cheese, fruit snacks that didn't have even a hint of real fruit juice in them, and full-size candy bars, because YOLO. These kids are about to have the best damn day of their weird little lives.

"THIS IS THE BEST DAY OF MY ENTIRE LIFE!" KIKI GIGGLES, TIPping back her third Shirley Temple. I sniffed each one of them to make sure there was no booze. It turns out that Kiki is absolutely capable of getting drunk on life, the way our gym teacher always said we could be.

In the twenty-minute ride to the restaurant, Kiki told me her entire life story, starting with her birth during a snowstorm in North Dakota when Mom had her on the floor of their bathroom because the snow had piled up so high even an ambulance couldn't get to their house. Because they were snowed in for so many days, her parents had lost track of when she'd been born, so the date on her birth certificate is really just a guesstimate. The only thing more boring to me than a birth story is a dream, but Kiki also had time to tell me about her dream from the night before and the night before that and the night before *that*. Her recurring dream is that she's stuck in a cage, and Kent won't let her out. I'm not a psychologist, but I've watched enough Dr. Phil to know that sometimes dreams are your brain trying to tell you something you already know.

Amy is on her first glass of champagne when Kiki and I arrive. She's picked one of those fancy places where there's a waiter whose job is *just* to pour your water, and it is filled with men in boring suits who have boring jobs and have no idea how boring they actually are. I have this weird thing where whenever I'm in a group of people I don't know, I just imagine what they look like having sex. This dining room is filled with guys who keep their T-shirts on and have to be on the bottom because otherwise they'll get winded.

Kiki's reaction to the bread basket is to cradle the individual buns in her hands like they are kittens. She has tears in her eyes when she sees the tiny little balls of butter they come with.

"Thank you!" she cries to him, like she is a starving orphan. "This is *seriously* the best day of my *life*!" He brings two more baskets to her, and she receives each of them like it is a fucking Oscar.

THE REASON I DON'T HAVE A LOT OF MOM FRIENDS IS BE-cause moms always want to talk about their kids. It's like instead of the default topic of conversation being the day's weather or your last sexual encounter, it's just what your kids are doing on a daily basis. Amy's kids are doing . . . a lot. They're learning Mandarin, which is apparently a kind of Chinese? My kid can barely master English, and the only thing he's interested in is baseball. You know what's interesting about baseball? Absolutely nothing. It's just a bunch of rednecks standing around in pajamas, and the games last at least six hours. I never thought I'd say this, but I am so glad he's into baseball. Because at least it's *just* baseball, and not the dozen random things that Amy's kids are signed up for.

"No wonder you're on the verge of mental breakdown," I tell her. "Carting those kids around to all their shit is basically a full-time job."

Amy nodded. "But I *have* to do it," she says, sighing. "I owe it to them."

That's hilarious to me.

"You *owe* it to them? Like, you made a blood oath to kill yourself making sure they could go to absolutely every activity under the sun? You don't owe them anything but food, safety, and love. I haven't gone to one of Jaxon's baseball games in four years. The last game I went to? The score was one to two. There were seventeen innings and, I swear to you, I would sooner go to Afghanistan than to another baseball game. And I don't even think he's noticed I'm not there. There's like six hundred other moms cheering like they're at a John Mayer concert every time a kid gets up to bat."

"So, how does he get there?" Amy asks, like she'd never

heard of the school activities shuttle . . . or a *dad* doing drop-off.

"You're married, right?"

Amy twists her ring around her finger.

"Well, yeah . . ."

"Then where the shit is your husband and why are *you* doing everything?"

"He works . . ."

"*You* work."

Amy downs the rest of her champagne.

"Is it hard to share Jaxon with your ex-husband?" she asks.

Ah. So *here's* the real issue. I can always tell when married women are thinking about divorce because they start to take an interest in *my* divorce. Otherwise, divorce is something they pretend doesn't exist. They act like it's a communicable disease and they don't want it to pass their lips, or they'll jinx themselves and end up with a 50/50 custody agreement that essentially forces their kid's dad to do the bare minimum of parenting.

Jaxon's dad and I should have never been married, but if you get me drunk and dare me to do something, I'm gonna fucking do it. And it was fun for a while, but eventually you realize that the only thing that feels better than proving a stranger wrong is your freedom. We did a no-muss, no-fuss divorce that cost us a total of $149 because he printed the forms from the library. We didn't use a lawyer, because we didn't have any fucking money, and we didn't argue. I could have been an asshole about it and made him pay me some alimony or child support, but I asked myself WWVDD and I realized that the Diesel thing to do was to remember that this big dummy had given me the most important thing I have: a family. I helped him pack up his shit in a U-Haul, and he got an apartment about a mile from my house. He's married again to a chick who bartends at the bowling alley near our house, and the two of them take Jaxon every other week. Jaxon likes it over there because she's got a parrot that knows swear words, and she always brings home leftover pizza and chicken fingers from the bar. But not everyone can be as blessed as I am.

"HE'S BEEN HAVING AN AFFAIR WITH SOME WOMAN ON THE Internet," Amy admits, and Kiki looks like she's going to throw up.

"But you're so pretty," Kiki stutters, and I have to agree. Amy's hot, so this Mike guy must be a fucking idiot.

"Maybe it's my fault," Amy says, like an actual fucking idiot. "We don't even have sex anymore."

"Kent and I have sex every Friday, after *Blue Bloods*," Kiki says like it's perfectly normal to watch a Tom Selleck cop show before you bang your husband.

This is *not* Amy's fault. It's not even that Internet lady's fault. It's just a shitty thing that shitty guys do, even if you have sex with them all the time.

"Why are you still with a loser who doesn't even help you? Is he like, superhot or something?" I know he can't be *that* hot, or I'd already know who he is. I'm guessing he was real cute when they were younger, but now he wears flip-flops in public, like people want to see hairy man toes when they're at Applebee's.

"I think it's just that . . . I got knocked up, and we got married, and we never got our twenties. We never got to have *fun*."

Wild twenties are a magical time in a girl's life. I swear, in my twenties, it was just raining dicks everywhere I went. I didn't have to swipe left or right, I just stepped out my door and right into someone's bed. Or car. I couldn't even go to the Container Store without locking it down with some hot young shelf stocker. I'm lost in the vague memory of sneaking out of a wedding reception with an uncle of the bride when we're interrupted by one of those I-wear-a-T-shirt-for-sex guys, standing over our table like he's mistaken us for a group of "colleagues" or something.

"Kiki?" he asks, and I watch Kiki's giant eyes pop out of her little tiny skull.

"Kenton! Hi, baby!" she squeaks, her voice rising to octaves I thought only dogs could hear. "How fun to see you!"

So *this* is the Kent who likes his briefs folded before they're put in his drawer. The Kent who requires Kiki to email him the "dinner menu" for the night so he can approve it before she starts cooking. The Kent who needs to get kicked in the throat by a woman who is almost a yellow belt and should have worn jeans with a little stretch today.

"Kiki . . . what are you doing here? Where are the kids?"

"They're with a babysitter, dipshit," I interrupt. "Why are *you* here?"

Kent ignores me. "A babysitter . . . isn't that *your* job, Kiki?"

Even Amy doesn't like the sound of that.

"Really, dude? You think this woman is a babysitter? She's the mother of your *children*. You better get on your hands and knees and THANK her for—"

"You're right, Kent," Kiki interrupts with a smile. "I'll see you at home. We're having pork tenderloin and new potatoes tonight." Kiki puts on her backpack and opens her Velcro wallet, placing four crisp twenty-dollar bills on the table. She has literally no idea what a Shirley Temple costs.

Amy and I sit in silence, watching her walk through the dining room. Across the restaurant, Kent and I lock eyes. He smiles at me, and I raise my glass to the dickbag who just ruined our lunch.

"You're going down, son," I mouth to him, smiling.

20

KIKI

I have six followers on Instagram, and two of them are my mom. She forgot the password to her first account, so she made another. Still, I can always count on her for a like and a comment. When my phone buzzes, I sometimes think, *Oh! Maybe that's a new follower!* Or, *Oh! Maybe that's a text from another mom who found me in the MFM part of Craigslist I've been posting in.*

But usually it's Kent. Kent recently added this app called HNYDO that is supposed to be pronounced "Honey-Do," but I guess they just didn't know how to spell it? It lets him add all the things he's asked me to do, and then it reminds me to do them if I haven't yet. Each time I complete a task, I'm supposed to click a little button, and a little bee pops up and says, "Thanks, Honey!" I told him that I liked my planner just fine, but he said he likes to know what I'm doing all day while he's at work financing our lifestyle.

I took one photo today, the kind that Gwendolyn usually takes, where you hold your camera above your plate so everyone knows what you are about to eat for lunch. I haven't done this before, because usually my lunches are just the crusts from the kids' sandwiches, the milk they leave in their sippy cups, and whatever half-chewed carrots or goldfish crackers they leave behind. Sometimes I'm lucky and they leave half a quesadilla completely untouched.

But today, I ordered a *real lunch*. There were the cutest little rolls, and tiny little butters that went with them. I got a niçoise salad, which I thought was pronounced "knee-coyze" but the cute waiter told me it's "knee-swaaah," and I got a little butterfly in my tummy when he said it like that, the kind of butterfly I used to get in college when Kent would pick me up for dinner in his Toyota Corolla with the windows down.

It's a good picture, even if you can kind of see the shadow of my phone hovering over the salad.

Fun lunch with the girls today! #salad #lunch #instafood

My phone buzzes less than thirty seconds after I post it. Mom.

Glad you're out having fun, Kiki! You deserve it!

Another buzz. Did she accidentally post it twice?

@_jane_and_dylans_mom has tagged you in a post

I have *never* been tagged in a post, and my hands are shaking as I click the notification. Amy's account is mostly photos of the kids: Jane standing in a soccer field, hands on her hips, a medal around her neck. Dylan snuggled up with Roscoe. Mike makes an appearance in some of the photos, but Amy never does. I'm not in any photos with my kids, either. I'm always the one taking them. But this *is* a picture of me. I didn't even see Amy take it today. I'm mid-laugh, probably because when Carla talks about dicks, I get really uncomfortable and have to laugh so I don't freak out. I look pretty. I look *happy*. She's written a caption, too:

So lucky to know this special lady. Here's to new friends. Xo.

I double-tap the center of the photo, and a small red heart appears on the image, right above where my own heart is. I don't like it. I *love* it.

21

AMY

The donut holes were right at the gas station checkout. They were (at least) a day old, so they were practically free. They practically *forced* me to buy them. And I had to pass McKinley on my way home, anyway, and there was an open parking spot right out front, which there never is, so what I'm saying is, it was meant to be.

Ever since Dylan started kindergarten, the bake sale has been my own personal hell. I'd spend months scouring blogs and Instagram for inspiration, weeks hunting down allergen-safe ingredients, and days trying to work out the kinks in the recipe. And then I'd arrive, set up my little shop, and immediately feel my body flood with cortisol while I mentally tallied whose booth had more kids crowded around it, whose cookies were cuter, and which moms did a shittier job than me.

But walking in the door today feels great. I'm just here to *enjoy* myself. I'm going to eat some cookies, and not even think about how many scoops and squeezes the barre instructor would punish me with.

There's an audible gasp when I walk in the door. It's probably only audible because the room is so quiet. There's no hustle and bustle, no laughter, and absolutely no gluten.

There's still one open table on the other side of the cafeteria, so I make my way over. Every other mom has gone full-on Pinterest: they had crafted hand-painted signs that coordinated perfectly with their tablecloths and eco-friendly disposable plates. Beckett's mom had a neon sign made for her booth. Jasmine's mom had branded napkins printed. I knew I was phoning it in with the donut holes, but now I'm actually feeling insecure about phoning it in. Should I have picked up some coffee or something to go with them? No. *No.* That's the old Amy talking. This is New Amy. And New Amy is just here to enjoy herself and raise money for . . . what exactly are we raising money for?

I settle into my spot, wedged between Anna's Avocado "Cheese" Cake and Vicki's Veggie Bites.

"Those look amazing," whispers Vicki, not making eye contact.

"Oh my GOD, Amy. You're killing me," whispers Anna. "I can *smell* the sugar."

My insecurity vanishes. I'm just giving the people what they want. I'm *fine*. I pop open the BPA-filled plastic clamshells and sit back, putting my feet up. The combination of lard and sugar is sniffed out immediately by a kid from Jane's class holding a bar that appears to be made of condensed bird food.

"Ten dollars," I say, and the kid reaches for his money agreeably.

"*How* much?" I hear a man ask, and look up to see the Hot Widow. I mean, he has a name. It's Jesse. But he's hot and he's a widow. Beside him, his daughter grins.

I throw a donut hole to the birdseed kid. "Enjoy! Tell your friends!" I turn back to Jesse. "They're . . . ten cents?"

He hands me a crumpled dollar.

"I don't have change," I realize, embarrassed.

"That's fine," he replies, smiling. "I know where you live." What?

"Okay, I meant that as a *joke*, but I'm a man and I shouldn't say those things to a woman, because it sounds threatening and inappropriate. I just meant that we live close to each other."

We live near each other? I do *not* remember seeing him around the neighborhood.

"Your daughter is my daughter's Big Kid Buddy. She talks a lot about Jane . . . SO! I've made this weird enough. Have a good night, Amy."

He turns away, his ears turning red. It's been a while since I've felt anything other than cramps in my lady area, but *something* is happening down there. Jesse's thumb had grazed mine when I took the dollar bill, and that small, accidental touch flipped a switch inside of me.

I'm sitting, feet up, licking powdered sugar off my fingers and fantasizing about what Jesse looks like without a shirt on when Gwendolyn strikes.

"Amy. Mitchell." She is trying to whisper, but her rage makes it seem more like a shout. "What exactly do you think you're doing here?"

"It's the bake sale, right? I mean, I know I resigned and all, but I'd signed up, and I didn't want to leave you hanging. Donut hole?" I hold the plastic container up like a peace offering, as if Gwendolyn has let an artificial flavor pass her lips since the millennium.

"Is this funny to you?" she whispers, her pack of Moms gathering behind her, creating a wall that shields the rest of the room from Gwendolyn's true nature.

"Look," I say, "I was going to make them at home, but honestly I kinda lost track of things lately—"

Gwendolyn's arms—lean and long—strike quickly, the left knocking the donuts from my outstretched hands, and the right sending the second package tumbling to the floor. Her kickboxing classes are really paying off.

"Listen here, Amy Mitchell." She says my name like it's in quotation marks. "I know that everyone thinks you're sooooo sweet. And soooo relatable. And sooooo smart. But you know what I think you are? I think you're a liability. This might be a joke to you, but it isn't to me. Because this school has high standards. And *we* have high standards. And that's why our school's test scores are the highest in the state, has the best college acceptance rate in the state, and, yeah, the best *bake sale* in the state, six years running. Maybe that doesn't mean anything to you, Amy. But I happen to believe that excellent schools make excellent children. And that's what we want—excellent children."

"Don't we want happy children?" I counter, tentatively.

"Excellent children *are* happy children, Amy! Because losers are never happy, and nobody *wants* to be a loser! Did you forget that when Mike left you?"

That hits me in the gut. How does she know all this Mike stuff? Did I make some announcement that I forgot about? Is Mike out there parading his new Internet girlfriend around town? Normally I'd burst into tears, but for some reason I've broken into a reflexive smile. And my reflexive smile is making Gwendolyn even angrier.

"Now, I know that you are hurting, and I wish you peace and love, and I pray for the healing of your marriage."

I know how angry I have to be to pray for someone, and I'm a little afraid at this point. But Gwendolyn isn't done.

"I want to remind you of something: which is that I am not just the head of the Mom Squad. I'm the chair of the board. The largest donor to McKinley *in the history* of our school. I sit on forty-seven councils and committees and task forces across the school and the school district. Nobody takes a class, kicks a ball, or plays a clarinet at this school without my say-so, and I can and will make life a living hell for you and your dirty little children, do you understand?"

Yesterday, Gwendolyn had posted a guided meditation to her blog. The entire basis of it was to "cultivate a mindfulness practice based in loving kindness." Today, she is foaming at the mouth, threatening my children over a few boxes of donut holes and *one* public outburst of mine. I am speechless.

Gwendolyn closes her eyes and takes a deep breath, sighing openmouthed in my direction. Her breath smells like hay. When she opens her eyes, she smiles at me, as if she has just rebooted, and turns to her pack of acolytes, who turn and follow her like a row of baby ducks chasing their mother. Just one hangs back. Stacy and I have never had a conversation deeper than the typical pleasantries you exchange when you pass another mom in the hall, so I don't know what I'm expecting when she lingers at my now-empty table.

"You're . . . so fucked," she whispers. It doesn't sound like a threat. It sounds like a fact.

To: Amy Mitchell
From: Ingrid Dawson
Subject: Referral for Mental Health Specialist

Dear Mrs. Mitchell,

I'm Ingrid, one of the fifth-grade counselors here at McKinley. Today I had the pleasure of meeting with Jane, who was sent to the nurse's office with stomach cramps and a racing heart. I'm so glad that she and I had a chance to connect. She is certainly a very driven girl, and you and your husband must be very proud of her.

As you know, high-achieving girls tend to have high stress and high anxiety, as well. Per the voicemails I left you today, I am including several referrals to mental health counselors who specialize in childhood anxiety.

Please contact me with any questions.

Best,
Ingrid

The email should read, "Congratulations! You've failed
your child! She's a walking ball of anxiety, and even an adult
who barely knows her can tell she's wound a little too tightly!
Don't worry, it'll definitely get worse when you tell her that
her parents are getting a divorce!"

I add "call counselors" to my to-do list, tap out a reply that
I *hope* reads as grateful and not guilt-riddled, and then call the
McKinley Absentee line.

"Hello, this is Amy Mitchell, calling to let you know that
Jane and Dylan Mitchell will be absent tomorrow due to a . . .
family emergency. Thank you."

"MOM!"

Jane clatters down the stairs like a newborn foal just trying to get her legs under her.

"MOTHER. AMY!" Jane bursts into the kitchen, still
trying to pull her leggings over her scrawny little bod. There
is rage in her eyes. Behind her, Dylan stumbles in, more confused than upset.

"School started ONE HOUR AGO," Jane shouts, grabbing the keys to the van. "Why didn't you wake us up? Stop
smiling! We need to go. NOW."

I sip my coffee while she taps her foot impatiently.

"No school today," I say, turning the page of my newspaper.

Jane rushes to the McKinley calendar that we keep on the
fridge.

"Yes, there is!" she shouts, jabbing her finger at the page.

"Well, there *is*. Just . . . not for you two. I called you in sick."

Dylan gives a fist pump and runs over to hug me. "You're the best mom in the whole world," he whispers into my hair with his sleepy breath. "Can I go play Xbox?"

Jane looks at me as if I'd just told her that what was in my coffee cup wasn't coffee, but the blood of orphaned puppies.

"You can't . . . *do* that," she says, but her face has softened.

"I can do anything I want!" I say. "I'm a mom! Now, we have a full day to do anything we want. Except play Xbox. What do you all want to do? Go for a hike? Go to Fun City and ride some roller coasters? Go see a movie and order all the junk food we can handle? Jane, I'll even let you eat popcorn and I *won't* tell your orthodontist."

Jane's agitation is obvious. Her shoulders remain tucked up by her ears as she kicks off her shoes and shoves me over on the banquette, reaching for my toast.

"So we're just going to do *nothing*?"

WE LAST APPROXIMATELY THREE HOURS BEFORE JANE GETS antsy.

"What if I just checked in online to see what assignments I'm missing, so I don't fall behind?" she whines, as if watching Harry Potter on a weekday morning is an unjust punishment and not the dream day of basically any other kid.

"JANE," Dylan reprimands her, turning up the volume to cover her whining, "CHILL."

She points out that it's easy for him to chill, because he's never tried at anything. She is right. And today was supposed to be for Jane, anyway; I just felt bad making Dylan go to school if I was going to force Jane to play hooky. Dylan needs no help relaxing or going with the flow. If anything, he needs to learn how to swim. Jane, however, is already mentally calculating the potential hit her GPA would take from her missing one reading assignment. There is no amount of *Judge Judy* or *Price Is Right* that can cure this. I need to do something more extreme. To take her to a place where she'll have no access to screens or clocks or to-do lists. A sensory deprivation chamber would be ideal, or even a solitary confinement cell, but I don't think that prisons allow you to just pop in for the afternoon.

"That's it," I say, standing up and brushing the crumbs off my jammies. "Jane, get dressed. Dylan, you're on your own for the rest of the afternoon."

CARLA IS ALREADY SMOKING BY THE SIDE DOOR WHEN WE arrive. "Welcome!" she coughs, tossing her cigarette in the dumpster and waving the air around her. "Get inside, and don't make eye contact with anyone."

Inside the spa, the air smells like eucalyptus and lavender, and, if you get too close to Carla, a faint hint of Marlboro.

"You're a lucky girl," Carla says to Jane, guiding us both to the lounge. "I never got to do this with my mom."

Jane doesn't say anything, and neither do I, because I'm

too busy getting high on the essential oils flowing through the air.

"It's a special blend that's scientifically proven to relax your brain and also get you to spend a fuck-ton of money," Carla says, "and I tell ya what, it works. I'm Zen as fuck after a day of work."

"Now," she says, handing us each a plush white bathrobe and a pair of slippers, "the place is yours. Tea and coffee and snacks are in the lounge. Steam, sauna, and Turkish baths are down the hall; mud baths are just off the atrium. If anyone asks . . . say she's a Make A Wish kid. She looks sad enough."

Carla's right. Jane does look sad. She looks more than sad. She looks . . . depleted. She looks like me, and she doesn't even have a boss or college debt to worry about!

"What?" Jane snaps, and I realize I've been staring at her like a mom in a life insurance commercial watching her baby sleep.

"Nothing!" I lie. I step out of my jeans and pull my sweatshirt over my head, and Jane squeals in disgust. I forgot how embarrassing it is when you realize that your mom has a *body*. I pull on my bathrobe and realize what Jane is screeching about. It isn't her mother's body that shocked her, it's her mother's body hair. Not just a little bit of stubble under the arms, but a full-on mane. And a coat of leg hair that makes it look like I'm wearing leggings. Okay, I'm exaggerating a little.

"This is perfectly natural, Jane," I say, "so hush. And grab me some of those free razors by the sinks. Three at least."

IT'S AMAZING HOW TIRED YOU CAN GET FROM DOING ABSO-
lutely nothing. Or, nothing that involves your body moving
at all. Jane and I soak, steam, and bathe all day. We don't
even need to use Carla's excuse. Jane blends in perfectly,
probably because she's the only twelve-year-old I know who
worries about having a solid retirement plan. We sit in the
sauna so long Jane's glasses nearly melt off her face. We leap
into the plunge pool, not realizing it's freezing cold, then
head directly into the steam room, feeling our bodies thaw
in the heat.

"MOM." JANE SIGHS AS SHE LIES ON A LOUNGE CHAIR IN THE
sunroom after a relaxing lunch of sliced fruit and water with
slices of cucumber floating in it. "Thanks for today. I don't
think I've ever been this relaxed in my entire life."

I look at her, in her fancy bathrobe and her hair wrapped
up in a towel, and I smile. My girl does look relaxed, really
and truly.

"As someone who has known you for your entire life, I
can guarantee that you have never been this relaxed. Ever. You
were born tense. The only time you aren't running at a hundred and ten percent is when you're sleeping, and even then,
I'm sure your dreams aren't any fun."

Jane considers this for a moment, nodding. "They're
mainly just going over the next day's to-do lists. It's a habit
I developed from researching the world's most efficient mil-
lionaires." So much for Jane becoming a more relaxed person.

"The point is, Jane, you needed a break. It's just a lot going on right now, with soccer, and school, and Mandarin, and Dad—"

Shit.

"Dad? What about Dad?" Jane's voice is back to its rapid-fire, high-octave panic mode. "Oh GOD," she shouts, melting into her chair, "is he sick? Does he have what Emily's dad has? Is he going to get all skinny and then die??"

The few women on the other side of the sunroom sit up, alarmed or maybe just annoyed at the volume and pitch of Jane's voice.

"No, honey! He's not sick," I reassure her while my brain tries to piece together a plan for how exactly to tell her the truth. But my brain isn't fast enough, and Jane gets there first.

"You're getting a divorce! You're getting a divorce, and I'm going to have to stand up in court and choose between you!"

"JANE." I grab her bony shoulders. "Your dad and I are not getting a divorce . . . I don't think. Not yet at least."

That didn't help.

"Yet?! That means you're getting a divorce! And I'm going to have to live in an apartment! And Dad's going to get a trashy younger girlfriend, and everyone is going to ask if we're sisters!"

Wow. Nothing gets past this one.

"Jane. I am going to be honest with you: your dad and I are probably going to get a divorce. I don't know when. But the important thing is that you know that we both love you, and that this isn't your fault."

Jane's eyes widen.

"My *fault*! Why would it be my fault? Now of course I think it's my fault! Why would you even say that?!"

If there were a rewind button for this conversation, I would be smashing it at this moment, desperately trying to get back to the blissful moment when our biggest problem of the day was whether to order another pressed juice. But there is no rewind button. There is only the present moment, and my scared, insecure daughter, and a few women actively eaves-dropping nearby.

"I don't know why I said that!" I try to whisper. "Jane, I've never done this before. I think I saw a grown-up say that in a TV show once?"

Jane's eyes soften.

"Where am I going to spend Christmas?!"

Christmas? I hadn't thought about Christmas. Oh God, I'm going to have to split holidays with a man who has never picked out a Christmas present on his own?

"Christmas is months from now, Jane."

Jane wipes tears from her red cheeks with the palms of her hands.

"This just isn't how I thought my life would turn out. I just want a normal life where everything goes perfectly."

Join the club, I think.

"Honey. A normal life is where *nothing* goes perfectly. And I should have probably done a better job of showing you that. Life is messy. I'm messy! I just hide it really well. But life can be messy *and* wonderful." I sound like an inspirational Instagram meme, but it might be working.

"Like Dylan." She smirks.

"Exactly like Dylan. You know, I do his laundry, and I'm pretty sure he doesn't know how to wipe his butt. But he's still a pretty good kid. He doesn't need to be perfect. You don't need to be perfect. Our life is never going to be perfect. But we're all going to be just fine."

"How do you know?"

"Because I'm your mom. And I know what you're made of. Did you know that when you were born you spent three extra days in the hospital?"

I know she knows this, and I also know that she loves hearing her birth story.

"They give every baby a few tests, to make sure they're okay. And you know what? You failed them! You failed them over and over and over and the doctors said, well, we have to keep her."

Jane laughed a little.

"Your dad called it Baby Jail, because you were in this incubator, and you had so many tubes connected to you, all because you just would NOT pass the test! Jane, the first grade you ever got was a big, fat F. And look at you now. You're amazing. And that has nothing to do with being perfect. It has everything to do with *you*. You're tenacious and amazing and so intense you sometimes scare me. And it doesn't matter where you live or if your parents are married, you're always going to be Jane. Your mom will always love you. Your dad will always love you. Your brother will always love you. You will always have us cheering you on and helping you up when you fall. We love you so much, Janer."

"And I'll probably get two Christmases."

Ah. There it is. The balm that heals all children of divorce: consumerism.

To: Principal Burr
From: Amy Mitchell
CC: Gwendolyn James; Coach Craig; McKinley Mom Squad; McKinley Staff
Subject: Jane Mitchell

Hello All,

Just a quick note to let you know that my daughter, Jane Mitchell, will be respectfully withdrawing from the following activities:

- Mandarin Club
- Recycling Committee
- Feelings Club
- Math League
- Debate
- Model UN

She will remain on the McKinley Soccer Club (go, Mustangs!).

Thanks so much for your understanding.

Best,
Amy Mitchell

To: Amy Mitchell
From: Gwendolyn James
CC: Principal Burr; Coach Craig; McKinley Mom Squad;
McKinley Staff
Subject: RE: Jane Mitchell

Hi, Amy.

Thanks so much for keeping us updated on Jane's condition. I hope that you reached this decision with the help of a mental health professional, as I'd hate for Jane to grow up and resent you for projecting your own unhealthy behaviors on to her. Said with love: our children look to us to be examples, and structure and activity is paramount to raising healthy, happy children.

Please let us know if you and Jane change your minds, and if there is anything we can do to support your family through this difficult time.

Best,
Gwendolyn
Download my eBook: Happy Kids, Happy Mom: A Selfless Journey Through Motherhood

22

CARLA

I've been leaving my phone on silent lately due to an unfortunate case of mistaken identity. I know better than to answer an unknown number, but the local radio station gives away a trip to Cancun every fall and I filled out, like, a hundred giveaway forms and I thought maybe my time had come? Instead it was Mr. Nolan asking if he had Carla Dunkler on the line. Mr. Nolan, the only hot teacher at our dumb school. Mr. Nolan, who I was hoping to bang. After I said in my sexiest voice that yes, it was Carla, he said he wanted to "talk about Jaxon." Shit.

I'm not a great mom, but I know what those three words mean. For a boy like Jaxon, it means that I'm about to get an earful from some dumbass with a college degree who is going to tell me that my kid is too "spirited" or too "disruptive." I know that after "it's about Jaxon" comes a bunch of bullshit about how he may benefit from medication, or how his energy levels have become a problem in the classroom. And look, I don't think my kid is perfect by any means. I'm not the kind of parent who goes to parent-teacher conferences to give the teacher a bunch of shit about how *special* their kid is, and whether the teacher is doing enough to challenge my precious little flower of a human being. I mean, I'm not the kind of parent who goes to parent-teacher conferences, period, but that's only because the kindergarten one ended with Mrs. Fagnani trying to give me a bunch of books about raising "a kid like Jaxon."

I'd told Mr. Nolan I'd get back to him with a time that worked for me and made a mental note to avoid the shit out of him for the rest of the school year. I haven't been answering my phone since.

But this incoming call? This was the call I've been waiting for ever since Amy told me about her frat-boy husband having an Internet affair with some hosebeast in Wisconsin. Or maybe Missouri? Somewhere with cows.

"I need to get laid," Amy whispered.

I didn't need any more details than that. Amy was still talking when I snapped my phone shut and shouted down the hall to Jaxon that I'd be home late and there were pizza rolls in the freezer.

It ticks me off to think about Mike out there sampling from some Internet sex buffet while Amy's at home with two kids, a demented dog, and a vagina that's only met one penis. Women don't even reach their sexual peak until at *least* thirty-five. I look around at the moms at McKinley and see a bunch of wild vaginas just waiting to be set free.

When I was a little girl, my grandmother had to have her vagina removed. I can't remember the medical term for it, but it was a full-on vagectomy. Like when you accidentally rip off your doll's leg, and there's just an empty cavern? That was Grandma. I mean, I never saw her lady cave, but that's how I imagine it. Grandma didn't sit around feeling sorry for herself, either. My mom always said, "Your Grandma's the happiest woman I've ever met. And she doesn't even have a vagina!" You know why? Because when Grandma *had* a vagina, she used it. When the time came for her to part with her lady parts, she did it with a clear conscience, knowing she'd done all she could while she could do it. And she passed that same joie de vagina on to me. She told me from a young age, "You don't use it, you lose it. And sometimes you lose it anyway!" Then she'd laugh and ask me to relight her cigarette for her. It was Grandma who told me that premarital sex was the only responsible way to make sure you didn't "bag a dud." It was Grandma who told me that, sometimes, it's a *benefit* to bang a dude who is significantly shorter than you because then you don't have to kiss him so much. Grandma told me that the only way to get over a guy was to get on top of, under, or in front of another one.

Grandma's advice makes me a certified sex Sherpa for all my friends, *especially* the divorced ones. I don't have a résumé, but if I did, I would put "getting my friends laid" right at the top. It's a special skill of mine, and my talent comes down to two things: dedication and good old-fashioned market research. I've seen every Dad Bod and Dad D there is, and I don't say that insultingly, either. There is nothing wrong with a Dad Bod. Or a Mom Bod, either. Most people get better with age. And thank God, because if we peaked in high school, we'd die thinking the best life could be was having a guy with two first names dry hump you in the backseat of his grandma's Caprice Classic. That may have been the peak of ninth grade, but there is no way the best days of my life were going to involve me sucking in my stomach for an offensive lineman whose thighs were bigger than my waist. Moms are conditioned to hate our bodies. From the minute your kid comes out of you, the clock to get back to your "prebaby body" starts ticking. You're expected to take about two months to lose the weight that took you the better part of a year to gain. From the moment we have a kid, our goal is to look as though we never had one at all. Three days after having twins, my neighbor Jenny was sprinting down the street behind a double-wide stroller while wearing a weighted vest. I could see her diaper through her lululemons, and she looked at me like I was the crazy one for enjoying a breakfast margarita on my porch at seven AM. We live in the Midwest; we gotta get our citrus in any way we can.

Point is, there's a lot of pressure put on a body that expelled another human from one of its most tender orifices. And *that's* why I tell all my single friends to focus on bagging themselves a divorced dad. Or a single dad. Any unattached dad will do. Because a dad didn't carry a kid, but his body sure looks like it did. *And they don't care.* They're almost proud of it, or at least not ashamed of it. A dad doesn't pretend to be anything he's not. He knows he has shoulder hair, and that his naked body looks like an orange balancing on a set of toothpicks. He knows that the population of the world depends on women like you, women who have sacrificed their bodies for the love of the species. He won't say this specifically, but there's a quiet . . . deference, maybe? A sense of having given up. And that giving up is critical. It means that he's *grateful*. He knows just how lucky he is for any opportunity to paw at your rack. He's beside himself with the prospect of a visit to your secret garden. That gratitude makes him blind to your c-section scar, your bikini line, or the fact that your white bra is now . . . more of a gray? Here's the thing about dads: they respect a map, and an instruction manual. You can tell a dad where to put his hands, where to put his dick, and the exact tempo and pressure you expect, and he'll *do* it. He'll do it accurately and he'll do it proficiently, and if you're like, "Dennis, too much hip!," he'll adjust. Dads have had time to learn from their mistakes, time to perfect either their penetrative or oral skills (rarely both, but you can't have it all). They have something better than confidence: they have competence. A dad is just happy to be there. As he damn well should be.

I've got the plan laid out before I barge into Amy's front door: doll her up, get her out, and let her loose. The dads of the greater Chicagoland Area will have no idea what hit them. I hope. Amy's been with Mike since college, so we're going to need to reawaken her slut instinct and suppress her intimacy instinct. We need her to not be the girlfriend of the first guy she bangs, okay? It's fine for Amy to sleep her way through the dad directory. It's too soon for her to be jumping right into another relationship. We need to get her on some training wheels first.

IF KIKI THINKS YOUR CLOTHES AREN'T SEXY ENOUGH, YOU have a problem. And Kiki, whose "going out" outfit is a thick black turtleneck sweater, is not impressed with Amy's outfit choices for the night. Amy has more than a problem. She has a goddamn *situation*. It's a situation that includes blazers and beige and for some reason, corduroy? It's a situation I was not prepared for. How does the hottest woman I know have a closet built to prevent boners in human males? When I asked her to pull out her best "fuck me" heels, she pulled out some Clarks like I'd asked her to show me the best shoes for trying to pick up an orthopedist.

"I just have work clothes and mom clothes!" Amy tries to explain while I pull out piece after piece of shapeless, bland, sad, depressing, awful clothing from her closet. I'd call them mom clothes, but I would find it personally offensive to myself and generally offensive to all moms. It's more like every cliché about motherhood got shoved into one closet. I'm talking the wardrobe equivalent of abstinence education. We could donate the entire thing to the Catholic high school and, actually, maybe I'll go back and do that later. I can tell them it has been proven effective: Amy has only seen one penis in her entire goddamn life, and it belongs to her husband.

"What if I get a weird one?" Amy asks, swiping mascara

on her ridiculously long eyelashes. I am the #1 waxer in the tri-county area, and 20 percent of my clients are men. Trust me, I've seen a lot of weird dicks in both my personal and professional lives. I'm ready to jump in with a pep talk, but Kiki beats me to it.

"Oh, they're all weird!" Kiki reassures her, and Amy and I eye her suspiciously. How the hell would Little House on the Prairie know anything about peni in the plural?

"They are," she insists. "I had kind of a wild time freshman year of college. Whenever my mom wasn't staying in my dorm room with me, it was like *Game of Thrones* in there. Without the murder or the incest. I saw a lot of penises and they're all gross. Truly, it makes no sense that we like them. Kent has a really weird penis and I still married him! And we have sex every Friday night—"

"WE KNOW," Amy and I shout together. I've never met someone with a regularly scheduled sex life that's coordinated with their TV schedule, and frankly, it's starting to ruin TV *and* sex for me. I just imagine Kent lying in bed, holding the remote control . . . okay, that's enough.

"Really, I was on Reddit, and there are so MANY strange penises out there," Amy agrees. "Like, what if he has priapism?"

"Has what?"

"Priapism," Amy reads from her phone, "is a prolonged erection lasting hours or even *days*."

"Sounds like a bonus. Good for him."

"What if he has penile psoriasis?"

"That's purely aesthetic. Just wrap it up and pretend you never saw it."

"Peyronies disease: a condition that causes erections to be curved."

"Just curve with it!" I shout. "Use your imagination!"

"One in five million men are born with diphallia: two penises!"

"Again, Amy, that's a bonus." I hand her the beer she forgot about while she scoured the depths of the Internet for nightmare material.

"Kent's a never-hard," Kiki says, and Amy puts down her phone. Kiki meets my eyes in the bathroom mirror, where I begin applying lipstick to prevent myself from interrupting her. "He never gets *fully* hard," she explains, "so I just kind of"—for this part, she uses hand gestures I hope to never see her use again—"fold it up, and jam it in, and that gets the job done. But at least he's circumcised!"

Amy slams the rest of her beer, eyes bulging.

SOMEWHERE UNDER A PILE OF SWEATER DRESSES THAT I SIN-cerely hope will not be donated anywhere and will instead just rot in a landfill like they should, Kiki has spotted something black and tight. She holds it up like a trophy. A *tiny* trophy. It looks like it might fit Jane. It's perfect.

"*That?*" Amy scrambles across her bed, trying to wrestle it away from Kiki. "That's an old Halloween costume from college. I think I was a slutty Harry Potter?"

I don't know where Amy learned the definition of "slutty," but I'd like to buy her a dictionary the next time I'm at a thrift store because she looks about as slutty as a nun once we convince her to try on that dress. It *would* be pretty hot, but bunched up under the slick black fabric is . . . a bra? No. A bra is supposed to just hoist up your boobs, to display them in their best possible form. This flesh-toned monstrosity covers too much surface area to *possibly* be a bra. I can only assume it's something she needs to wear for religious purposes?

"Do you have, like, a sexy bra? I have a sexy bra that I wear on Fridays only. I put it on right before *Blue Bloods*, and it comes off when the credits roll."

Amy looks . . . confused, and not by Kiki's *Blue Bloods* kink. "This *is* my sexy bra," she says. "Look, it unhooks right at the top, for easy access." Amy is doing some sort of shimmy that she believes to be sexy, and Kiki looks like she's about to cry.

"Amy Louise Mitchell—I don't know your middle name, but this is a middle name situation—that is *not* a sexy bra, that is a nursing bra!" Kiki lowers her voice. "Are you . . . still nursing? Because sometimes Bernard still wants to, and I don't know if I should just let him?"

I take it back: I'm not a good friend. I'm a fucking incredible friend. Because Carla Dunkler doesn't leave the house without a spare bra and panties. I don't know where the night is going to take me, and I like to be prepared. But tonight, it isn't about me. It's about Amy dusting off the cobwebs, using that vag before she loses it. And she needs this deep-plunge, maximum-push-up bra more than I will. I wear all my bras two cup sizes too small because I like a pillowy cleavage, something dense and inviting, something that says to men, "Wouldn't you like to put your face right here?" On Amy, my

bra looks like it does on the models at the store: it lifts, it sepa-
rates, it turns her mom boobs into two perfect globes.

"Amy Fucking Mitchell," I gasp, "you're gonna catch a D
tonight."

I PICKED THE FANCIEST BAR IN OUR AREA CODE. IT'S DARK IN
a fancy way, not a trashy way, and it's filled with guys who get
biweekly paychecks and paid vacation.

I almost feel bad for these men. Amy isn't sexy, she's unde-
niably hot. I feel like I'm unleashing a man-killing robo-hottie
on all these boring suburban guys in their flat-front khakis. I
briefly consider packing her back up and taking her home and
sparing them the pain, but then she opens her mouth.

"How funny! Their menu says drinks are twenty-five dollars. Typo much?" Amy laughs.

Kiki joins in. "That's, like, two hours' worth of baby-
sitting! Yeah, right!"

"Actually, it's right. That's what drinks cost now when
you're not at a bar with health code violations."

I probably should have started Amy off somewhere a little
less intense, but if you're trying to meet a man you want to
use solely for sexual pleasure? Your best bet is always the darkest bar with the most expensive drinks. It takes somewhere
between forty-five seconds and a full minute before Amy is
swarmed by boring, standard-issue white men. Kiki and I are
gently shoved farther and farther away from her until we're on
the other side of the bar, observing her from a distance. I feel
like parents must feel when they drop off their kid at college:

like Amy is all grown up now, and I can only hope that in our time together, I have given her the tools she needs to succeed.

Watching Amy talk to these guys, I know that any of them would be a good practice ride for her. They've got sensible side parts and think that Under Armour polo shirts are "going out" clothes. I'm willing to bet that 50 percent of them use their mom's birthday as an ATM PIN. They are all sensible, the male equivalents of a Honda Accord.

Kiki can barely contain her excitement. About Amy. About being out in public. About life in general. Every ten seconds, she's pointing out a new guy that Amy could bang. Everyone she picks out looks like Kent: boring, blond, and like he has a basement filled with bodies and/or model trains. Possibly both. "I'm so excited for Amy!" she shrieks. "Kent just might get a special treat tonight. If he plays his cards right, I'll let him keep the TV on *and* I'll get on top."

I'm trying to unimagine the idea of Kiki jamming Kent's soft penis inside of her when she gasps and points toward Amy. Our little lady had reeled in someone new. And not a boring Kent lookalike. No, Amy was always too big-time for that shit. I should have known. She's going right for the white whale of McKinley.

I feel like my panties could burst with pride. Like my vagina is ready to live vicariously through her.

Amy Mitchell, who has only seen one penis in her entire life? She's about to bang *Jesse*.

23

AMY

Being at this bar makes me feel lonelier than I've ever felt in my life. Who do I think I am, sifting through a group of guys like they're objects? Why am I dressed like a college sophomore who just got her first fake ID, and why am I pretending to laugh at everything these guys say? They are in no way deterred by how often I look at my phone, either. And I've been constantly looking at my phone because my mother is bombarding me with text messages about Mike, including photos from our wedding. Or, photos she took of our wedding photos, which are framed and hanging in her living room. I can see her reflection in the glass.

These guys don't even notice that they're talking to the top of my head while I try to fend off my mother's text messages.

I realize that if I want to disengage from future conversation, I have to be forthright and honest.

"I should go call my kids," I shout over the music whenever a new guy approaches me. It works. "Yeah!" I say for good measure, as they look around for another option, "I gave birth to two kids. *Vaginally.* No medication, either! I felt every tear!"

Finally alone, I find an open couch. An *entire* couch, all to myself. I wish I'd brought my Kindle; it would have been nice to catch up on some reading.

"IS THIS SEAT TAKEN?"

Jesus H. Christ, *really*? I've been alone for approximately ten seconds.

I'm ready to tell this guy that I have a highly communicable skin disease when I realize . . . I know him. Or, I've met him. I *want* to know him. Or I at least want to know what it feels like to have his naked body pressed against mine.

"Hi . . . Jesse, right?"

Every single part of me lights up at once when he sits next to me. His thigh is *touching mine*, and I swear to God I could orgasm just from that contact alone.

"I'm glad to see you!" he shouts over the music. "What are you doing here?"

"What are *you* doing here?" I scream back.

He shrugs, and gestures to a group of men I assume are his friends, who are clustered around a group of women who are definitely pretending that these guys are funnier than they are.

I nod and gesture toward where I imagine Carla and Kiki are. It's so *dark* in here, I wish I'd brought my glasses.

I don't think the bar got quieter, but there's something about Jesse that makes it easier for all the noise to just fade into the background. I've never had someone be so *interested* in me. I've never been so *interested* in anyone. I want to know everything about him. I want to know about his dead wife, and how he raises a little girl on his own. I want to know what his most vivid childhood memory is and how he takes his coffee.

And he wants to know about me. *Me.* He wants to know what I studied in college, and how I ended up working at a coffee startup. He doesn't ask me about how I "do it all" or "work-life balance" or any other question that implies it's strange for a woman to both hold a job *and* parent.

And I'm sure I'm violating every single flirting rule ever written, but I *tell* him. I don't feel a need to be mysterious or coy. When he asks what book I could read for the rest of my life, I tell him it's the one about a mama bunny who tells her baby bunny why he's the most special baby bunny in the whole world. I'm embarrassed, but Jesse doesn't laugh. His deep brown eyes get wider and he says, "Oh! I love that one! I cry every time the mama bunny says, *You may be a big boy soon, but you'll always be my baby bunny.* I shed actual tears."

I cry at that part, too. I cried the first time I read it out loud, when Dylan was two days old and slept through the entire thing. And I've cried through it every time since, even though it's been sitting on the shelf in Jane's room for at least five years now.

"This is a weird thing to say, but you know my wife died, right? I never know who knows and who doesn't, and I never know how to bring it up without ruining the moment."

"I know," I say. "I mean, I don't know anything other than that she died. I'm sorry."

This is where an awkward silence should go, but our silence is already comfortable.

"So," he says, "do *you* have a dead spouse you'd like to tell me about on your night out?"

That's my cue to tell this perfect young widow about the demise of my marriage. Which I'm pretty sure is over, given that Mike hasn't even texted me since I kicked him out. Jesse either isn't judgmental or has a very good poker face, because even after I give him a play by play of discovering Mike's digital affair, he's still listening. Not just hearing my words, but *listening,* with his whole body.

"God, Amy," he says, not breaking eye contact, "that sounds like a nightmare."

"Anyway!" I say sarcastically. "Cheers to fucking up our kids!"

"Amy," he says, smiling, "we're all fucking up our kids. But you're a really, really good mom."

Never in my life have I heard a sexier sentence come out of a man's mouth. My head turns off, and my body takes over. I *want* this guy more than I want the appetizer platter that was just delivered to the table next to us. I want his pretty mouth all over me. Or at least on my mouth. Sure, it's been over a decade since I had a first kiss, but how hard can it be? Nothing is hotter than two parents making out in public, right? I'm going for it. I bite my lip, I tilt my head. I let my hand reach for the collar of his shirt and—*thunk*—that is the sound of my face smashing against Jesse's. I wasn't sure if I should go left or right, and I changed direction halfway through, and I *think* I grazed Jesse's cheek with my incisor. Yeah, I'm pretty sure I bit his face.

"I am so sorry!" I blurt out.

Jesse laughs and rubs his cheek. "It's obviously been a while since either of us has kissed anyone. Maybe we should try that again?"

I nod, smiling so hard I feel like my cheeks might break right off my face. We get it right the second time.

And the third time . . .

To: McKinley Mom Squad
From: Gwendolyn James
Subject: Mom Squad Update

Hello, Ladies:

The following weeks are a crucial time for our children, and therefore ourselves.

Fall is a time when the rhythms of life naturally slow down, preparing us for rest and renewal. Let us take our cues from the world around us and continue to embrace the season of change we find ourselves in.

To that end, I have attached the updated parameters for our classroom Fall Festivities. The document includes updated guidelines on games (per Carly T.'s suggestions), nutrition (including new custom recipes for children on keto-vegan diets), and décor (with Pantone swatches to help create a cohesive brand story across the school).

Thank you so much for your compliance and your dedication to making this school an incredible place for children to learn and grow.

In Love and Style,
Gwendolyn James

PS—get 20% off my eCourse <u>Fall into Happiness</u> *with code GWENDOLYN.*

To: McKinley Mom Squad; Gwendolyn James
From: Carly T.
Subject: RE: Mom Squad Update

Thanks so much, Gwendolyn, for acknowledging the seriousness of BINGO and Scavenger Hunts as gateways to gambling, and a slippery slope when it comes to our children.

To: Carly T.
From: Hannah R.
Subject: RE: RE: Mom Squad Update

Have we fully considered the implications of eliminating BINGO from school celebrations? Generations of people have enjoyed this game, and it helps our younger children with number and letter recognition, hand-eye coordination, and time management.

Just my thoughts!

To: Hannah R.
From: Carly T.
Subject: RE: RE: RE: Mom Squad Update

Thank you for your email, Hannah. While I like you as a friend, I do think we fundamentally disagree about childhood development. I'd like to put a pin in this conversation until it can be moderated in a face-to-face discussion with a member of the McKinley faculty.

24

PRINCIPAL BURR

867.

I always thought I'd retire someplace like Arizona or Florida. Twenty-some years in Illinois means that I've earned the right to bake my bones wherever I please, in either a godforsaken desert or a godforsaken swamp. But I've been looking at places in Arkansas lately, and I have to say the price is *right*. For just a fraction of what it costs to live in Scottsdale, I could have a turnkey townhouse on the edge of the Ozark Mountains, where it's possible to golf at least six months of the year. One of the communities has a hospital *right on the premise*, so you can just die on site without wasting money on an expensive ambulance ride.

Jan says no way, she did not spend twenty-something years on her feet as a nurse to retire in hillbilly country. But

Jan *also* spent the last twenty years spending her little heart out buying diamond-*like* necklaces on TV, so I don't think *Jan* understands the financial reality of retirement.

"SIR?" MY SECRE— ADMINISTRATIVE ASSISTANT ALWAYS AN- nounces himself *before* he knocks, which makes absolutely no sense. Rick was hired by the school board after Gwendolyn noted there was a gender disparity in our workforce here at McKinley. "Our children need more positive male role models," she insisted. I agree, but Rick? Rick can't be a role model, he isn't old enough. The kids do seem to love him, though. Maybe because he looks like a second-term eighth grader?

To hide all my web surfing, I found a desktop image that looks like my email inbox. If anyone ever catches me off-guard, I just press "command H" and all the windows disappear, leaving only a photo of a full email inbox. You learn all kinds of tricks when you've been doing the same job for over two decades. Rusty the janitor used to hide his whiskey in an emptied bottle of bleach on his cleaning cart. It worked for years, apparently, but all it takes is one mix-up and the school needs to find a new janitor.

"*Sir.*" Rick's eyes seem to be rolling wildly. Is he having a seizure? "*Gwendolyn James* is here to see you."

I have just enough time to hit command H before Gwendolyn pushes Rick aside and strides into my office in a blur of blond hair and heavy perfume.

"Principal Burr," she says, coolly, "we need to talk."

THE SECRET TO TALKING WITH GWENDOLYN IS APPEARING TO
write down whatever she is saying. The other secret is to
make sure she doesn't see what you're writing, because after
twenty-eight minutes of her monologue, your mind is going
to wander and you're just going to start making your to-do
list. I straighten some papers on my desk, including the credit
card statement I meticulously review every month, because at
this stage in the game, every penny spent is a penny we don't
have to spend in retirement.

Usually when Gwendolyn wants to meet with me it's because she's discovered a new potential allergen in our school
or because she wants to make sure the kids have access to aura
cleansing at least once a week.

This time, the problem seems to be something else. Some
lady named Amy Mitchell?

I've never even heard of Amy Mitchell, which means I
like her. Gwendolyn, I gather, does not like Amy Mitchell.
Mitchell's list of offenses includes:

Insolence
Disrespect
Something about the bake sale
Look into Alabama coastline—more bang for your
    buck than Arkansas?
Call Jan—$348 in charges to the Discover card this
    month.

The problem with Amy, Gwendolyn explains, is that she
is mediocre and fine with it. Further, Amy has two children

at McKinley, who will likely absorb all her shortcomings and then spread those shortcomings to other children, and then McKinley won't be a school that is known for excellence but for mediocrity.

I make what I hope is meaningful eye contact with Gwendolyn at the appropriate times but otherwise let her continue uninterrupted. Gwendolyn is not unlike our kindergartners. Sometimes they just need to scream at the top of their lungs to get it out of their systems. Sometimes Gwendolyn needs to just sit in my office and present a PowerPoint indictment to get it out of her system.

But even after she snaps her laptop shut, Gwendolyn doesn't look satiated.

"This woman," she says, "is a *problem*."

"I see," I reply, though I truly didn't see at all what she was talking about.

"I knew you would," she says, winking at me conspiratorially as she breezes out the door. Or maybe one of her eyelash extensions is caught.

Either way, this Amy Mitchell is totally screwed.

And I need to call Jan about these charges.

25

AMY

On the list of things I expected for today, none of the following would be included:

- A Good Morning text from the hottest man I've ever kissed in my entire life, telling me that he can't stop thinking about last night.
- My cheating husband begging my forgiveness moments after that text arrives.

It's almost normal that he's sitting in his usual spot at the breakfast nook, slurping from a bowl of Lucky Charms—our *weekend* cereal, that I always knew he was sneaking during the week, that liar—and reading an *Us Weekly* like we were still a normal couple and he hadn't been carrying on an Internet-based affair with a dairy farmer for the better part of a year.

It's almost normal, but it isn't because in the weeks since he's been gone, he hasn't even bothered to be in touch with me. No calls. No texts.

"Mike, what the fuck are you doing here?" I'm not yelling, but I'm also not in the mood for whatever this is. How long has he been here? Did he see Jesse sneak out the front door at three AM? Can Mike tell I'd made out with someone else? Am I now excreting a pheromone that indicates I recently let another man grab my boobs?

"I thought you'd be at work," Mike says between slurps of his cereal, "and I'm out of underwear." Ah. Of course. In the time we've been apart, Mike still hasn't figured out how to operate a washing machine. I don't know if it's the fact that I spent the night pawing at the hottest dad in school or if it's just that dishonesty makes people uglier, but Mike looks *rough*. His tousled hair doesn't look boyish; it looks messy and sad. Maybe because he doesn't have me to schedule his haircuts for him. There's more gray at his temples, which is actually kinda hot, but his bright eyes are weighted down by dark bags, probably because when he left for the hotel he took an Xbox with him. I would almost comment on the fact that he's wearing sweatpants, but I'm wearing my basketball shorts from high school.

"Aim," he says in his sweetest voice, spilling the milk from his cereal bowl as he tries to get up from the table, "I want to get back together. I never should have left you, that was a real dick move."

I have some other ways to describe it, but "dick move" will

have to do. I notice that he doesn't even attempt to wipe up the milk he spilled. *That* is a dick move.

"Mike," I say in the same voice I use when Dylan asks me for a bowl of ice cream after he said he wasn't hungry for dinner, "you *just* told me that you have feelings for another woman that you've been seeing online for nearly a *year*."

Mike sighs like a child who has been told he's up past his bedtime.

"Yeah, but then I met her and she's super weird! And she's not even that *hot*. I think she just had those fancy lights that YouTubers use."

"So. Because your other option isn't as great as you thought it'd be . . . you'd like to come back."

That seems to stump him, at least for a moment.

"Amy, haven't you ever just needed a *break*?"

Time stands still. Did this man just ask *me*, the mother of his children, the maker of dinners and school projects, the manager of the social calendar, the woman who remembers *his* mother's birthday and sends the perfect gift every year even though she still calls me "Michael's wife," ask *me* if I ever just needed a break?

"I've been talking with your mom, and she agrees you should give me another chance. She said that Mitch Feinstein got a hand job from a stripper and his wife still took him back."

Of *course* he's been talking to my mom. That explains all her text messages.

"I don't give a shit what my mom or Mitch Feinstein's wife thinks, Mike!" I need something to do with my hands

so I don't wrap them around Mike's neck and squeeze until
he loses consciousness, so I start to wipe down the counters.
Every mom I know has ripped shoulders from years of wiping
counters and butts.

"Babe," he says in his fake-sorry voice, "I miss you. I miss
the kids."

The kids.

"Mostly Dylan—he hasn't even been on Xbox—but Jane,
too. And Roscoe. I miss my family. I'll do anything to make
things right again, Aim. Anything."

"Like . . . therapy?"

Mike's head snaps back like a Pez dispenser. "Therapy?!
No! Therapy is so dumb. Come on, Aim. I was thinking, like,
a weekend in Wisconsin Dells. You know, your mom said
you're totally overreacting."

Of *course* she would say that. Once I broke my nose during a basketball game and she put a Snoopy Band-Aid on it
and told me it was fine. I turn Mike toward the door by his
shoulders. He needs more than new underwear, he needs to
grow up.

"Thanks for stopping by, Mike. Since you like my mom so
much, maybe you can date her!"

"No, no, no!" he whines, digging in his heels. "I'll go! I'll
go to therapy!"

THE FIRST TIME MIKE AND I WENT TO THERAPY, HE READ A
magazine the entire time and told the therapist that he was a
visual learner.

"There's a difference between *going* and participating, Mike."

"Oh God! You just want me to cry, don't you?"

"Would it be so hard? You just ruined your entire family! Doesn't that kinda make you sad?"

"Sure, but I don't cry about it! I haven't cried since Jordan retired!"

"Which time?"

"Every time! He's the greatest athlete of all time! Every time he retired was an emotional experience!"

I give up. On all of it. On this conversation, on him. But not on my counters. I go back to wiping crumbs that aren't even there, but Mike just stands there.

"Okay, Mike. Goodbye."

"Amy? I'll go to therapy. I'll cry and everything. I'll cry the whole fucking time. Just please, please? Give me a chance."

I SPEND THE DAY "WORKING FROM HOME," WHICH I LEARNED from Dale and the other kids at work is code for "responding to the occasional email but otherwise just sitting around doing whatever you want."

From my inbox, which is now too full to receive any new messages, I glean the following: that Dale is desperate to expand our direct-to-consumer business, that Tessa has pierced her right eyebrow, that the Ping-Pong Cup has been passed to a new champion, and that nobody has implemented the solution for the logistics issue that I proposed weeks ago. Seventy-four of the emails in my inbox are part of a chain about a one-legged foster dog looking for a home, and the merits of having an office pet that the entire staff could look after, like the rat we had in our fifth-grade classroom. That rat, by the way, grew a giant tumor and died a painful death over Spring Break 1992.

Thirty-nine of the emails are from Dale and seem to just be forwards from sales, logistics, and clients.

I resend my previous email about our logistics issue and delete the rest of my inbox.

Inbox Zero: achieved.

I TRY TO GET TO SOCCER PICKUP JUST A FEW MINUTES EARLY. Parents aren't allowed to attend practices since the incident with Julia's dad a few seasons ago, and even though he swears he only acted in self-defense when he clobbered the coach from behind with a full water jug after learning his daughter wouldn't be starting in the home opener, the end result is that the closest any of us are allowed to get to the field is the sidewalk that divides the parking lot from what Gwendolyn had renamed the James Athletic Complex for Childhood Excellence in Sports.

There are fifteen minutes left of practice when I pull the van into the lot. Hopping out, I see the girls across the field, blending into a mass of burgundy practice jerseys and bouncy ponytails. Two years ago, these same practice jerseys looked like dresses on them, and Coach struggled to keep them on task for more than a few minutes at a time. Even hyper-focused Jane would spend a good portion of the practice lying on her belly in the grass, looking for four-leaf clovers. The girls look so *big* this year, all spindly legs and coat-hanger shoulders. I squint into the sun, trying to pick out which one is Jane.

She isn't playing two on two.

She isn't blasting practice penalty kicks at the goalie.

She isn't running laps around the complex.

Where *is* she?

I'm startled by a tap on my shoulder, which I assume is another parent who wants to talk to me about how I still haven't sent in my twenty-five dollars for the coaches' gifts.

It's not a parent. It's Jane. Blotchy-skinned and red-eyed, struggling to breathe through her sobs. Oh God, has Mike called her? Kids are geniuses now; did she hack into his phone and find out about his smarmy affair? Did Kyle Jensen find out she has a crush on him? I don't know, but I pull my snotty, sweaty little girl into my arms, where she cries harder than she did when she found out that Justin Bieber married someone who isn't her.

"It's over," she sobs, "it's over."

"Janey Bear," I whisper into her hair, "what's going on?"

Jane wipes her nose on the front of my shirt, and I watch her angst turn into anger. "I'm a loser, Mom. I'm on B squad."

"Bee squad? Like, bumblebees?"

"Like, the kids who *just* practice. Who don't actually play in the games. A benchwarmer, Mom."

Look, I'm not a Sports Mom. I hardly know what the hell is going on during a soccer game, and I'm pretty sure that anyone who claims to actually know what offsides is has to be European or just a liar. But I know that Jane was named MVP of her traveling team this summer, and that her summer traveling coach said Jane had the fastest and most accurate first touch the league had seen in a kid her age. I know that she's quick and aggressive and that since she put on a Mustangs jersey, she's hardly even *seen* a bench, let alone warmed it.

A flash from the bake sale repeats in my head. I'd laughed when Gwendolyn tried to flex her McKinley muscles at me. What had she said, exactly? That nobody kicks a ball or plays an oboe without her say-so? That if I didn't back down, she'd come for me and my kids?

"Go to the car, Janey Bear," I whisper, and double-click my key fob to open the automatic door for her. "There's a red Gatorade in the center console for you. It should be nice and cold."

Jane shuffles toward the car, struggling to walk across the concrete in her cleats. "Mom," she calls from her seat in the back, "are you coming?"

"One second, babe!" I call over my shoulder, clicking the button to shut the door. Across the field, Coach is wrapping up practice while the girls pull off their cleats and chug from the giant insulated jugs their moms had filled with ice and filtered water.

At my feet, a painted yellow line shouts "PARENT ZONE: DO NOT CROSS." On the other side is a carpet of plush grass, a mixture that Gwendolyn bragged needed hardly any water and could be eaten or juiced by anyone in the community who needs additional antioxidants.

From the car, I hear Jane's muffled shouts, but the time to hesitate has long passed. The consequence for breaking this rule, if I remember correctly, is a two-game ban for the offending parent. *Fine,* I thought, *make it five.* Let the whole Mom Squad come for me. This is not the first time a line has been crossed.

COACH MAKES A BREAK FOR HIS OFFICE WHEN HE SEES ME striding across the field. He's trying to look casual, but he's basically run-walking away from me as fast as you can run-walk while carrying a mesh bag full of soccer balls.

"Mrs. Mitchell," he calls over his shoulder as we near the doors of the Athletic Center, "you know I can't discuss team business directly with parents. Any complaints need to be handled through the proper channels."

I dash around him and open the door for him, following him into the dark basement where McKinley keeps athletic equipment and coaches' offices and apparently doesn't ventilate properly. I feel like I'm breathing in decades of body odor, which I probably am.

"What's the proper channel, Coach? Is it . . . Gwendolyn?"

He turns around nervously. I've struck a nerve.

"I cannot comment on that matter at this time," he says slowly. "I would like to have my lawyer present."

I feel bad. I do! He isn't even old enough to rent a car and whatever he gets paid is not going to cover the cost of the therapy needed to deal with parents like me, but this isn't an interrogation. At least not formally.

"It was Gwendolyn, wasn't it?" I challenge him, and he gives a nearly imperceptible nod. My fists instinctually tighten.

"Our rosters are set for the year, Mrs. Mitchell," he says, reaching for the door of his tiny office. "I-I look forward to having Jane as a valued member of our team. Please address any further questions to Gwendolyn James and the rest of the Athletics Committee."

"Thanks, Coach!" I slam the door harder than I mean to, but I'm satisfied by the sound the door handle makes rattling in place. "I'll do that!" I shout toward the closed door. "I'll follow up with Gwendolyn!"

26

CARLA

I've seen a lot of crazy bitches in my life. I mean, I once saw a girl rip out another girl's eyebrow ring in my high school cafeteria. There was so much blood that two guys from the football team threw up. The mid-nineties were *insane*, but so are angry moms nowadays.

I would give my right boob (it's smaller, anyway) to have been there to see Amy go apeshit on Gwendolyn at the bake sale in front of her little posse of prim and proper moms. Amy claims she was "calm and respectful," but I was waxing Glenda Whitaker's hoo-ha today and she was on the phone the whole time talking about how Amy dropped the c-word, and how Amy threatened to stab Gwendolyn with a blunt scissor she grabbed from the kindergarten room. It's an inspiring amount of exaggeration, and I'm proud of Amy even for the shit these moms made up.

I can't blame Amy one bit. I always knew that Gwendolyn was a stone-cold bitch. You can tell everything about a person by how they tip, and Gwendolyn tips as if she's one day away from foreclosure. She tips 5 percent on salon services for the love of God. And I mean, exactly 5 percent. She's a human calculator, and she rounds down to the nearest penny, not up. Maybe that's how rich people stay rich? By giving exactly 5 percent to the women who shave off their calluses and laser off the top layer of their faces and wax their *incredibly* bushy lady parts?

If Amy was "calm and respectful" at the bake sale, she's currently "buzzed and angry," pacing around her living room like a rabid dog. I'm probably not helping the situation, but sometimes when I see a fire, I just want to throw some lighter fluid on it and see what happens.

"Look," I suggest, "why don't we just go settle this the old-fashioned way and slash her tires?"

Amy shakes her head. "Not good enough."

"We could burn her house down! It happens all the time and it's hard to catch a first-time arsonist." Kiki makes a good point, but Amy isn't having it.

"No," she barks, and I swear her eyes turn jet-black like the girl from *The Ring*. "She fucked with my *kid*. I'm going to get her where it hurts."

"That's a good idea, actually," Kiki agrees. "Bernard kicked me in the vagina a few months ago and he actually broke my vagina bone. Did you know that's possible? But you have to hit the right angle."

"*Kiki*." Amy grins like the Joker. "What does Gwendolyn love more than anything?"

"Coconut oil. You can use it as a makeup remover, a supplement, a cooking oil, a vaginal lubricant, a hair conditioner . . ."

Amy shakes her head.

"The Mom Squad."

Kiki and I are silent. This is better than arson. Better than a good old-fashioned street fight. This is diabolical. It's genius.

"So, you're going to kick *them* in the vagina?" Kiki, apparently, is having a hard time connecting the dots. She's had half a glass of boxed wine, which is almost enough to get her blackout drunk.

"She's going to run for PTA president, you dumbass!"

Kiki gasps like she's just been told Amy has six months to live.

"Amy!" she cries. "You can't do that! Gwendolyn owns this school and every mom in it! She'll kill you! Even worse . . . you'll lose!"

DO LESS!

VOTE FOR AMY

Are you tired?

Are you sick of trying to be perfect?

Then cast your vote for

AMY MITCHELL FOR PTA PRESIDENT

Fewer meetings

Less BS

More free time

Maybe I'm old-fashioned, but I figure the best way to get the word out about Amy's presidential bid is to print up some flyers. Well, I figured wrong. Because I spent a good thirty minutes this morning letting some old man named Craig stare at my boobs at Kinko's and none of these bitches will even *look* at a flyer. I blame Kiki. Or, her twins, at least. I didn't even know it was possible to fit two kids into those backpack thingies, but Kiki has her two mongrels strapped to her torso like a bomb vest. "Bote! Bote!" they parrot back and forth to each other, pawing at the flyers with their sticky little hands. Kiki has had at least one cup of coffee this morning, and it shows.

"A vote for Amy is a vote for FREEDOM!" she shouts to nobody in particular as we stand at the drop-off line, waiting for our moment.

"Vote for Amy Mitchell for PTA president! She'll do a really good job!" she pleads to a group of moms who pretend not to hear her.

"Please just take this flyer! Just consider your options!" She's losing it now.

If I'd known Kiki needed to bring her entire collector's set of kids to do this, I would have just told her to stay home.

I wish I hadn't printed so many of these. I also wish I hadn't given Craig a nip slip. It was a total waste of paper and of sexual favors.

"Do you think this is what those poor Mormon kids feel like when they go door to door?" Kiki asks, looking like someone peed in her Cheerios.

"No. Because they at least get a sweet bike out of the deal. This is what it feels like to dress up as the Statue of Liberty and stand on the street corner spinning a sign that says TAX TIME IS HERE!"

Kiki pauses for a moment to think, which I can't believe she can do with two human beings tugging at her hair. One of the twins keeps squeezing Kiki's boobs and shouting, "Eaaaaaaat!"

"I think I'd rather be dressed as the Statue of Liberty right now," she says, desperately trying to make eye contact with a mom who is just as desperately trying to avoid it.

"Come on," I say to Kiki and the girls, "I've got an idea."

McKinley may have gone purely digital with their student communications, but moms are still stuck doing a nightly backpack check for their kids. You have to, or you end up with mice in your kitchen and a permanent funk in your house because your kid thinks his backpack is a traveling trash bin for his old Arby's bags and sweaty baseball socks. There are hundreds of moms checking hundreds of backpacks every night. Which means that each of these sweaty little kids is a little Trojan Horse.

We trail the last kindergartner into the building as if we're class moms ready to help out with today's organic spelt-spaghetti craft project. We spend the next hour shoving our flyers into every available backpack, cubby, and locker we can find. And while I'm at it, I tear down every Gwendolyn James sign from the wall. That bitch is going *down*.

27

GWENDOLYN JAMES

To: McKinley Mom Squad
From: Gwendolyn James
Subject: Election

A gentle reminder that while we are certainly dismayed at the recent developments concerning the PTA election, McKinley *is* a democracy run by the adults.

As such, I would like to remind everyone that we are beholden to a sacred code of election ethics that run in line with our McKinley Mission Statement, bylaws, and Best Practices. While I will not stoop to name-calling, I do know that several mothers expressed concern about the amount of propaganda being distributed on school grounds. I apologize for my own use of paper to create my campaign posters and am happy to report that I am planting 1,000 trees to atone for my misuse of resources.

I hope that my opponents learn from this situation, as I have, and that we can all agree that politics aside, our biggest responsibility is not to our own ambition but to the well-being of our children.

Xoxo,
Gwendolyn

PS—you can save 25% on my eCourse "First Class Kids: A Guide to Raising Exceptional Children" using code VOTEGWENDOLYN. Click here.

28

KIKI

My parents had their talks in the kitchen after I went to bed. It was always less of a talk and more of an argument that they attempted to make as quiet as possible. I would try to piece together the gist of the conversation based on the few words that would waft up the stairs and into my bedroom. Kent's parents have never had an argument. Not once. His mother told me that on my wedding day. She said, "Kiki, if you're wondering what the secret is to a long marriage, it's this: pick your battles. And most of them aren't worth picking." She told me that whenever she *thought* about picking an argument with Kent's dad, she smiled instead. Soon, her brain would believe her mouth, and she would feel happy.

Kent and I have our Big Talks on the loveseat in the living room. It was a gift from Kent's mother last year. It's very floral. She said that another secret to long-lasting love is always being close together, and that big sofas mean big problems. Tonight, I was in the kitchen after dinner texting with Amy about the campaign when Kent used his Serious Voice. *Sometimes* that means we're going to have sex, but it's not Friday, and we're on a pretty strict sex schedule.

"Kiki," he says to me as I settle into the space he left for me on the loveseat, "I'm worried."

"Kent, I don't know how many times I have to tell you, I'm fine with your erectile disFUNction. We make it work!"

Kent gives me a tight smile and shakes his head as he unlocks the iPad. "No, Keeks, I'm worried about *you*."

Me? I rack my brain for what would worry him. I check my blood pressure every time I go to Walgreens and it's great. I eat oatmeal three times a week to keep my heart healthy. I definitely get ten thousand steps a day. Our sex life has been like clockwork: three positions, six minutes from first kiss to cleanup. What could he be talking about?

Kent taps away, and then pulls up a series of charts in the telltale yellow and black of the HNYDO app.

"It seems like you're really disengaged. Your performance has been slipping. Is everything . . . okay? Do you have something on your mind?"

You know how sometimes you don't even know you *have* something on your mind until someone says something like "Do you have something on your mind?" and then all of a sudden, the entire contents of your brain are pouring out of your mouth and into the air and you can't stop it? I hardly ever do this when I'm with Kent. Usually, the cashier at the grocery store will ask how I am, and then four minutes later I'll realize that I just shared a very intimate story about my life with a teenager who was just trying to make small talk and definitely did not need to know that rhubarb holds a lot of emotional significance for me as it reminds me of my dead grandmother, and *that's* why I had been crying in the produce section.

Tonight, though, *Kent* is the cashier looking for a way out of this one-way conversation. I can tell he just wanted to talk about the app, about how I haven't been approaching my homemaking with the zeal of my youth, but I can't stop myself. I tell him all about what's been happening with the McKinley Mom Squad. All about my new friends and all about my former idol, Gwendolyn. Surely he'd recognize the ridiculousness of Gwendolyn's cult of personality. He would *love* Amy. Maybe he would even help us with the campaign? He had run for student government all four years in college; certainly he'd learned *something* from all those losses. Carla would frighten him, so I soften her rough edges just a little bit. I tell him that she works in gynecology, which isn't exactly true but isn't false, either, because I'm pretty sure she's seen more vaginas than my own lady doctor has.

When I'm finished, Kent takes a moment before responding.

"So . . . that's what's wrong? Those two moms I saw you with the other week? *They're* more important than our kids? Than our family?"

Kent's hands grasp mine, and our eyes lock. In his lap, the HNYDO app buzzes away, undoubtedly creating more data about what a bad job I'm doing at keeping our household running as smoothly as Kent's slacks, which I steam for him every morning because he doesn't like to put on cold pants.

"They're not more important than our family, but they're important. They're fun. They make me happy. They like me."

"Keeks, everyone likes you!" Kent kisses the top of my nose, which is one of my favorite kinds of foreplay. But not tonight, Buster.

"Kent, I just want to have a *life*. I don't want everything I do to be about the kids and this house and HNYDO. I haven't seen my college friends since Emily's wedding."

Kent blinks.

"That was five years ago, Kent!"

Kent smiles, and then . . . yawns? Wow, I guess 8:30 really snuck up on us tonight.

"I'm glad we had this chat," he says, tucking his iPad under his arm. "It's good for us to be on the same page." In the distance, I hear the song that haunts my dreams: three notes played over and over. The dryer is letting me know it's time to fold laundry.

"THE SAME PAGE! HE SAID IT'S GOOD TO BE ON THE SAME page! Well, I'd like to know what book he's reading because he participates in three fantasy football leagues. He spends the third weekend of October on a Guys Trip with his friends from college, who are really our friends from college, who also leave their wives at home with the kids. He lives for those weekends. And you know what he says? You know what he tells me? He tells me, 'Kiki, it's important for me to be able to get away and cut loose sometimes so I can come home and be a better husband and dad.'" My Kent impression is getting really, really good. I can tell because Amy and Carla have a look on their faces like they want to puke their guts out.

Tonight is draft night. Or, the first of three draft nights, so Kent won't be home until after nine PM. I'd planned to relabel the shelves in our pantry and get my HNYDO app rating up, but then Carla called and said she had a major case of the fuck-its and didn't feel like cooking and was I interested in all-you-can-eat breadsticks and salad and stuffing the kids full of carbs?

I TAKE ANOTHER SIP OF MY SHIRLEY TEMPLE AND LEAN IN. "Cut loose? Cut loose! Well, doesn't *that* sound amazing! You'd think my hours as a full-time, twenty-four-seven mother would earn me just a little time off but apparently, nope!"

Kent's mother told me never to discuss my private issues outside the confines of my marital home or with anyone other than my husband, but it feels so good to vent.

"Kiki," Amy says, "you're right. That sounds really hard, and really lonely, and I'm sorry."

Never in my *life* have tears sprouted from my eyes this quickly, but Amy's words have touched the little button of truth inside me I was scared to push. I *am* lonely. How can I be lonely when I have four kids and a husband? The math doesn't make sense! I'm wiping the corners of my eyes with my napkin when Carla interrupts.

"How'd you even get out of the house tonight?" Carla asks. "Does he have a monitoring bracelet on you like a parolee?"

My phone buzzes on the table. *Does he have a monitoring device on me?* A photo from Kent fills my screen. He is wearing a Minnesota Vikings jersey he's had since college and giving a thumbs-up.

KENT: Guess who has two thumbs and just got first pick?

I self-consciously open the camera app, temporarily stunned by what I see when my face appears onscreen, mostly chins and nostrils. I make my own awkward thumbs-up and snap a photo quickly, hoping that nobody notices.

ME: Guess who has two thumbs and is so proud of you!

Carla is staring at me when I put my phone down. "Is that him?" she asks. "Do you *ever* get a break? Like, from all of this?" She gestures at the table next to us, where our collection of kids are enjoying a dinner of cheese bread and cheese pizza and breadsticks. The waitress had gotten tired of bringing refills, so she'd left a big plastic pitcher of milk in the middle of the table. Carla's son, Jaxon, is chanting "Chug! Chug! Chug!" while Dylan drains a glass of 2 percent. Bernard and Clara are watching him with rapt attention, holding their own glasses of milk and waiting for their turn to join the tiny frat party. Jane is studying, her face about two inches from a textbook about plant biology that I'm fairly certain is two grades ahead of where she should be. The twins are quietly dipping their breadsticks in vats of ranch dressing, their chubby little arms covered in grease and sauce.

"Repeat after me." Carla pauses, then coughs violently into her hands. You're supposed to do the Dracula cough— even the twins know that!—but at least she wipes her hands on her jeans before she reaches for another breadstick.

"Kent," she continues.

"Kent," I repeat.

"Stop being such a whiny little bitch and let me have my own fucking life!" The dining room of Frankie's Pizza momentarily pauses, unused to the shouting of expletives in a fast casual family restaurant.

"Stop being such a whiny little b and let me have my own fudging life," I whisper.

"Atta girl," says Amy, encouragingly.

DYLAN FINISHES HIS GLASS OF MILK, SLAMMING IT UPSIDE down on the table. Jaxon celebrates by lifting Dylan in the air like the two of them have just won the Super Bowl. "Dy-lan! Dy-lan! Dy-lan!" The little kids all join in the chant—does Jaxon know how to speak, or just cheer?—and Amy and I gesture at them to shut their beautiful little mouths before we're asked to leave. Carla, of course, could not care less that our children are the center of attention.

"Jesus," Carla says, "I can't believe that giant came out of me. You know, I'm still not the same down there? It doesn't matter how many Kegels I do, either. My vagina is like a hospital hallway. It's like a double-wide trailer. It's like—"

"Do you think anyone is going to come to the meet the candidate night?" Amy's giant dark eyes looked . . . scared. Is that insecurity showing? It's actually criminal for someone who looks like Amy to be insecure. I'm sure if I could find one of her old yearbooks in her house, I'd be able to prove that she was voted Most Popular her senior year. And not popular in the Gwendolyn way, where you're really just scared she might slit your throat if you don't follow her on Instagram, but popular in the genuine way, where you just want to be around her because it's probably how lizards feel when they lie on a sunbaked rock.

"They fucking better," Carla shoots back, leaning across the table, "or I'm not gonna be so gentle with the wax next time."

I might have laughed a little too hard, because Jane looks up, startled, and shoots a look our way that clearly indicates she would like to have some quiet study time at this casual family eatery. Amy mimes locking her lips and sighs heavily toward us.

"I'm trying to get Jane to chill the fuck out. Sometimes I think she *almost* gets it, like she's *almost* going to enjoy her life, and then she cries because she wasn't invited to the gifted and talented camp at some school I've never even heard of and I think, *What the fuck have I done?* Like, do you see any other kids reading *next year's* biology textbook at the dinner table? No. No you do not, because it's bonkers."

"That's a good problem," Carla says, dunking her pizza crust in my milk. "I'm pretty sure that if you gave Jaxon a book, he'd just try to karate-kick through it. Or rip it in half, maybe? Good news is, I'm off the hook for a college savings account. *Clearly.*"

I think about my own mom, and if she ever wondered about her own mothering capabilities. I doubt it. She delighted in people asking if we were sisters, sometimes calling me "sissy" in public just to try to encourage the question so she could gleefully exclaim, "Kiki, did you hear that? They thought we were *sisters!*" I *hated* that, just like I hated my mom asking me to prom. Just like I hated *going* to prom with her—in matching dresses, of course—just like I hated how she'd "pop in" to the dorms at the University of North Dakota as if she *had* just been in the neighborhood, and not that she'd driven over four hours with an overnight bag. I hadn't realized how weird it all was until my roommate and Kent pointed it out to me, but I'd never brought it up to her. How *were* moms supposed to know if they were doing a good job? Should we be giving our kids comment cards? Having the kinds of check-ins Kent and I have? Or just waiting until they're grown-ups and it's too late to do anything about it, and hope that we haven't raised serial killers or multilevel marketers who are badgering their high school friends to come get rich quick with them while working from their phones?

"The worst part is that she's just like me," Amy says as Jane adjusts her glasses and leans even closer to her book. "She wants everything to be perfect all the time, and it makes her insane, and it makes me kind of hate her sometimes? Lucky for Dylan, he turned out just like Mike, and he's lazy as shit. I found a bottle of pee in his room yesterday, because he's too lazy to walk to the bathroom in the middle of the night."

My brain crackles with excitement. *Amy's* kids are weirdos, too.

"Yesterday," I confess, "I gave Bernard the wrong kind of juice and he called me an idiot."

"Jaxon still watches *Sesame Street*, and I'm not even sure that he *gets* it, you know what I mean?"

"Dylan failed study hall. Principal Burr said nobody had done it before. Nobody. Ever."

"Clara took money out of a homeless woman's cup."

"I'm only seventy-five percent sure that Jaxon's dad is his dad."

"Dylan tried to make a grilled cheese sandwich on a lamp."

"Clara killed our neighbor's ferret with her bare hands, and we all said it was an accident but sometimes I think . . . was it?"

"Yesterday, in the shower, I spent ten minutes fantasizing that Mike would take Dylan in the divorce and Jane and I could just spend our days in a house where nobody celebrates their own farts."

"I left Bernard at the mall on purpose."

GEEZ LOUISE THIS FEELS GOOD. ALL THOSE THOUGHTS THAT I was certain made me a terrible, awful, no-good mother? They were normal. Or at least normal to these other two psychos. The three of us are laughing. Not the nervous kind of laugh I usually throw in when the silence feels awkward, but a real laugh. My eyes are watering, and my stomach hurts, and every breath I manage to sneak in just turns into a bigger giggle. It's so consuming, we hardly notice that our kids have stopped destroying the restaurant and are staring at us with a mix of fear and embarrassment. I wipe tears from my eyes and give Bernard a thumbs-up, which he returns with his middle finger. As the high of our giggles subsides, something quieter creeps in.

"Ugh," moans Amy, looking at her kids, "I love them so much it doesn't even make sense."

"The other day, Jaxon fell asleep on the couch, and I could see what he'd look like as a grown-up, and then I imagined him moving out and getting someone knocked up and me being a grandma before I was fifty, and I just cried like a baby."

"I think I'd die for them," I agree. "Like, any of them. Right now. A bullet, a train, a gradual poisoning? Whatever. I'd do it."

It's all true: the good parts and the bad parts. It's all true, all at once. We may not always like them or want to share a home with them. But gosh dang it, we love them.

29

AMY

MOM: Amy. Mikey told me that you're having problems.
MOM: I hope you're not being too hard on him.
MOM: Amy. Just talked with Mikey. He's heartbroken.
Give him a chance.
MOM: I'm calling you.
MOM: Answer.

My mom has always loved Mike. He's hard not to love, especially if you're an older woman. He makes intense eye contact with those sparkling eyes of his, he laughs at all the right points in a story, and he is quick with compliments. I'd warned Mike right before our Meet the Family and Tell Them We're Pregnant dinner that my mom could be tough and would probably hate him seeing as how he'd knocked up her high-achieving daughter. But no, no such thing. My mom was full-on obsessed with Mike, right away.

She'd known Mike for about two hours before she found out she was going to be a grandmother, and she'd already started calling him *Mikey,* even though she'd told me as a child that nicknames were "low class." When I finally choked out the words "I'm pregnant," she had a moment of shock before she broke out into a wide smile.

"Well," she said, "what a blessing!" She'd said this to *Mike,* by the way, even though I was the one crying and carrying her first grandchild underneath an oversize college sweatshirt. From then on, Mike was her favorite kid. He started calling her Ruthie, and she allowed it. The two of them *always* ended up picking each other for my family's Secret Santa gift exchange. They *had* to be partners whenever we played card games. In a lot of ways, they were more compatible than Mike and I ever were. Gross, no, I'm not suggesting that my mom should hook up with Mike. Just that she'd ended up with a guy so meek and deferential that my dad was commonly referred to as Ruth's Husband.

ME: Mom, it's a divorce. Not a death.
ME: Mikey will still be in your life, don't worry.
MOM: Call me! Your father is very upset!

My dad, I knew, was not upset. My dad was never upset. Not when my mom traded in his car for a minivan without asking him. Not when my mom had his home office turned into a crafting studio while he was on a work trip. Not even when my mom paid three thousand dollars for some fancy cat even though my dad is allergic. In response to his protests about Jenny (yes, she named her cat Jenny), she bought him an EpiPen.

My phone rings again—Jesus, Mom!—and I put it on airplane mode. Not now, Ruthie.

YOU KNOW WHY COCO HAS A GREAT RATING ON EVERY WORK-place ratings website you can find? Because it's fun to work here! Or, it has been fun for everyone else. Also, because at one point Dale was paying our interns twenty-five dollars an hour to create fake profiles and write good reviews for the company.

Per my actual work contract, I decided to show up at the office today for some facetime of the non-Apple variety.

"Hey, bitch!" Tessa screams when I walk into my office. She is at my desk, with a paper face mask on, listening to a guided meditation that is urging her to offer loving kindness to a difficult person in her life. She peels off her face mask and throws it toward the garbage can, missing by at least two feet. "Swish!" she cries, holding her hands up in the touchdown formation. I pick up the soggy, face-shaped piece of paper.

"Do you want one?" Tessa asks, handing me a foil packet covered in Korean writing. "They're . . . brightening? Or tightening? I don't know, I don't read Chinese."

I do want to do a brightening or tightening face mask, actually. Tessa restarts her meditation, and the two of us practice noticing our breath and ignoring everyone who walks into my office.

After my facial, I join the frat pack downstairs for a game of ping-pong. It turns out, the fast-twitch muscles I thought

I'd lost are still here and still ready to dominate. "Damn, Mom!" Brett (or Brendan? Maybe Brian?) shouts, ducking as I send yet another ping-pong ball straight for his face. "Where did these skills come from?"

"Game," I declare, slamming my paddle down in victory. "And quit calling me Mom."

Tessa had warned me that Dale was "really peeved" about the hotel project. I could tell he had something up his ass, because he spent the entire day in his office, pretending he didn't know I was there. The problem is, all our offices are made of glass, and I could see him up there all day, struggling to look as if he wasn't looking at me. He was pretending to be looking at his computer all day, which is hilarious because he can't look at anything for more than thirty seconds.

"Deep concentration is over," he'd told me one day, when I'd sent him a one-page memo updating him on our sales projections for the coming year. "I need everything in bite-size pieces of information." I'd pointed out that the memo had fewer than three hundred words in it and was truly just a series of bullets, but he'd balked. "It's over!" he'd shouted. "It's all about skimming now." In the end, Tessa had ended up texting him all the information, bullet by bullet. "Brilliant!" he'd shouted each time he received a message. "This is *perfect*, Tessa!"

I'd thought about that moment this morning, when Dylan was preparing his breakfast. He'd poured the milk in *before* the cereal and was frustrated that the results of his breakfast attempt were all over the kitchen floor.

"I can't believe this shit," he'd said, whining. "I have to cook my own breakfast *every* morning?" He stepped over his mess, leaving it for me to clean up, and dumped the rest of his perfectly edible if not perfectly executed breakfast in the sink, leaving it for me to put away.

In the past, I would have grabbed a paper towel, run the garbage disposal, and put the bowl in the dishwasher. But today, *no*. Because boys like Dylan grow up to be men like Dale and Mike: men who believe that the world owes them something, because they've been coddled by their well-meaning but dumbass parents too long. Parents like me and Mike, who let a perfectly capable kid skate by on the excuse that he was a "slow learner" even though the kid can build an entire Minecraft world that I don't even understand. Parents who tried to protect their kid from the sting of imperfection and ended up the kind of people who do their kids' science projects? Last year—and I'll deny it if I'm ever asked directly about this by any member of the McKinley administration—I got a blue ribbon for Dylan's science project. It ended up going to the State Fair, sitting in a glass display case next to science projects by *actual children*. And I wasn't embarrassed, I was proud!

THIS IS HOW IT STARTS: WE LOVE OUR KIDS SO MUCH THAT WE keep helping but forget that they need to be *learning*. We pick up their clothes and pack their lunches and tie their shoes and erase the wrong answers on their math worksheets . . . and we keep doing that, because we love them and honestly because it's faster to do it ourselves and do it right than to teach them and watch them fold a T-shirt incorrectly. And then, without looking, we've created a kid who is given everything, and believes he's earned it and owed it. The next thing you know, you've created another entitled white dude who thinks he's awesome for no reason. And he becomes some vaguely financial guy like Mike, whose biggest point of pride is some dumb muscle car he didn't even restore himself, but lets people believe he rebuilt. Or some dumbass like Dale with an illegible tattoo on his forearm and a startup that gets more funding than nonprofits dedicated to feeding starving kids. Worst-case scenario, they start a friggin' rap career on SoundCloud and drag all their girlfriends to every awful show.

No. Not this white boy, at least.

"Dylan," I'd said in my fair-but-firm voice, and watched him freeze in the doorway, "get back here."

I pointed toward the mess on the floor, and the mess in the sink.

"Take care of this. Use a wet paper towel so the floor isn't sticky and rinse all the cereal down the drain. Thanks so much."

I'M NOT DALE'S MOM. BUT I'M JUST AS GUILTY OF CODDLING him as she is. I considered calling her—as part of his "we're all a family" credo, Dale had included his own parents in the company directory—but I doubt that a woman who cashed in her own retirement to be her son's first "investor" would see where I was coming from.

THE HOTEL PROPOSAL I'D SENT TO DALE WEEKS AGO IS THREE pages long. It includes a timeline for implementation with two of the largest extended-stay chains in the continental US, both trying to shed their image as sterile, impersonal places to stay in lieu of corporate housing or while trying to ride out a divorce settlement. Both desperate to compete with the fact that today's younger business travelers preferred to stay in small, independent hotels furnished and stocked with local wares, or to rent an Airbnb. Their desperation was palpable on my initial calls, and I'd gotten both to agree to a five-year exclusive contract that included the purchase of a small bag of our dark roast as a welcome gift for their patrons and a kiosk with our full product range in the lobby. I could see, checking the history of the document on our shared drive, that Dale hadn't even bothered to read it, instead sending email after email insisting that I was shirking my responsibilities.

I resend the hotel proposal I'd sent him weeks before, cc'ing Tessa. And then I go back downstairs to the rec room for karaoke hour, which runs from one to five PM every day.

If Dylan can learn how to clean up after himself, Dale can learn how to do his job.

THE SELF-ESTEEM BUBBLE I'D BEEN FILLING STEADILY AT THE office is slowly and steadily deflating. I'd spent the late afternoon at Costco, still riding high on my ping-pong wins and the standing ovation I'd received after my karaoke performance. Tonight is my campaign party, if that's the right way to put it? It's a party at my house to get to know the moms I've passed by for years in the pickup line or at class parties. Moms I know by their affiliation to their child, and not by first name.

It's dedicated time to convince them to cast their vote for me. I'd filled two carts—two—with mid-range bottles of champagne and wine and light beer and diet soda and sparkling water and every kind of bite-size snack I could find. I got frozen mini egg rolls and frozen mini quiches and frozen spanakopita and frozen mini tacos. I got two trays of crudités and a gallon of hummus. While I was at it, I loaded up on protein bars and printer paper and batteries and lightbulbs and tampons.

It was more food and drink than I'd had at my own wedding, and ten minutes after the official party start time has passed, I'm convinced I'll end up eating all of it myself. Or, most of it myself. Carla is doing a good job on the wine, and Kiki has had at least four LaCroix since she arrived here. I'm not sure if she knows there's no alcohol in it, because she tends to get a little silly after one.

Kiki checks her watch nervously, then her phone. "You know, most people like to be fashionably late," she announces. "They'll be here any minute, I'm sure." Kiki does not like to be fashionably late. She likes to be fashionably early. She got to my house before I did today. When I got back from Costco, she was just sitting on the front porch like a latchkey kid, with a case of Pamplemousse and a two-liter of Diet Coke.

On cue, the doorbell rings, and I'm not sure why, since there are at least thirty balloons outside and a sign on the door that Kiki made with poster board and Magic Markers that says in joyful bubble letters, COME ON IN! THE PARTY IS HERE! On the other side of the door stands a very concerned and slightly confused woman.

"Is . . . this the party?" she asks, and suddenly I see myself through her eyes: my disheveled living room, when had I last cleaned? My two friends, one drunk, and one high on life. My dog, stumbling around with his vertigo. Streamers and balloons like we're celebrating a baby shower and not a political campaign. Political campaign sounds a little extreme, but this is very political! This is about ending the reign of terror that Gwendolyn has imposed on moms in our community. It's about standing up to the bad guys, even when the bad guys look like really hot moms with a lot of Instagram followers.

"The crew is gonna be here any minute," says Carla, opening her flip phone like it had the capability to do something other than place phone calls and send very, very incomprehensible text messages.

"Really?" Our guest seems surprised. "I thought everyone was over at Gwendolyn's house."

If we'd been playing a record, this is the moment it would have scratched.

"Gwendolyn's house?" I ask, trying desperately to sound casual. Our guest—what the hell is her name?—spoons hummus onto a plate nervously.

"Yeah. She's . . . having a meet-the-candidate party, too. Martha Stewart and Chrissy Teigen are doing cooking demos."

Carla slaps the plate out of this poor woman's hand, sending a dollop of hummus smack onto the dining room rug, where Roscoe is resting.

"Are you fucking with us?" Carla asks, going into her Dom Toretto/Vin Diesel mode. "You better not be fucking with us."

Our guest puts her hands up in surrender. "Check Insta-gram!" she shrieks. "You'll see!"

"Instagram is a way for Big Brother to watch you through your camera phone." Carla growls, but Kiki and I are already scrolling frantically. Gwendolyn *is* having a party. With Martha and Chrissy.

And every fucking mom at McKinley.

HERE'S THE THING: THERE IS A BIG DIFFERENCE BETWEEN THE photos that Gwendolyn posted and the rest of the photos hashtagged #GwendolynForPrez. Gwendolyn's are perfect, of course: perfectly framed and filtered images of the kind of party you wish you could throw. The first photo is Gwendolyn's perfectly manicured hand, delicately holding a flute of cham-pagne. In the background, you can see Martha and Chrissy laughing in Gwendolyn's professional-grade kitchen. More photos by Gwendolyn: her driveway, filled with minivans; her living room, packed with moms; her hand holding the eve-ning's *agenda*, which it appears she calligraphed by hand. She's scheduled out every moment of the evening, including a forty-five-minute keynote presentation by . . . herself?

I want to snark on it, but it looks fucking amazing. The election isn't even here yet and I've already lost. I slump onto the couch, defeated.

"Don't you dare believe that Instacrap." Our guest/hostage laughs, pulling out her phone. "Jenn F., Archie and Trinket's mom? She texted me and said she's so fucking bored she's making her husband call her in five minutes and say the kids are going into anaphylactic shock and she needs to meet them at the hospital."

Carla emerges from the kitchen with two bottles of tequila, which Mike always kept on hand for "special occasions," like a Tuesday night when he felt like getting blackout drunk.

Carla grabs this lady's phone and takes a photo of the tequila. "Well, tell Jenn F. to get the fuck over here. We're doing shots."

THAT TEXT WORKS ITS WAY FROM ARCHIE AND TRINKET'S mom to Declan's mom and Plum's mom and Willow's mom and Gertrude's mom and the mom of every kid at McKinley named for an obscure flora, fauna, or historical figure and the mom of every kid named a regular name, but with an inexplicable *K* or *X* dropped in to make it unique (sorry, Jaxon), and every kid named for a character in a fantasy novel (we have three Aryas, and all their parents are trying to claim they never watched or read *Game of Thrones*). They trickle in, one or two moms at a time, greeted at the door by Carla, who offers everyone a shot of tequila. For all the time I've spent with and around these women, I've never seen them actually have *fun*. I've seen them do pickup and drop-off, and wipe vomit and/or blood from their kid's shirts. I've seen them chaperone a field trip to the Science Museum with thirty-two first graders. I've seen them give standing ovations to school concerts that absolutely didn't deserve it. I've seen them display happiness and joy directed at their children, but not just happiness and joy for themselves.

What really gets the party started is my playlist of late-nineties hits. Because nothing bonds a group of women on the cusp of middle age like harmonizing to "This Is How We Do It" by Montell Jordan. Hearing the first three seconds of "Pony" by Ginuwine makes it physically impossible for us not to grind on each other like we're the cast of *Coyote Ugly*. Kyler's mom—sorry, Lindsi—knows the *entire* choreography to Britney's "Toxic" and we listen to the song eight times in a row just so we can watch her do it. It's amazing.

"Amy!" a mom screams over the sounds of "Genie in a Bottle," "I puked in your dishwasher!" I give her a thumbs-up as I survey my Most Successful Party of All Time.

I think it was Kiki who started it. The girl loves to chant. At first, it's just a few drunk voices, not quite in unison. "Speech! Speech! Speech!"

Eventually, it's the entire party, and I realize when I see Carla and Kiki standing on my sofa that the speech they're waiting for is supposed to come from me.

"Welcome to meet the fucking candidate night!" shouts Carla, like she's announcing a professional wrestling event. Someone stops the music, and Carla has the undivided attention of every mom in the house. Kiki tries to pipe up, "My best friend Carla and I are so honored to be working on the campaign for our third best friend, Amy Mitchell. A lot of people think you can't have two best friends, but—"

Carla places her hand over Kiki's mouth. "Are you ready for Amy FUCKING Mitchell?" she shouts, and the chanting resumes.

"A-my! A-my! A-my!"

I've spent twelve years yelling at the kids not to stand on

the furniture, but here I am, standing on my sofa trying to figure out what to say to a group of drunk moms who really just want to get back to playing flip cup.

"Hey! Hi." I know, I know. Real dynamic start to my first stump speech.

"I'm Amy. You know, I wasn't ready to give a speech or anything. Just like I'm not really ready for anything, ever. I don't know about you, but I feel like I spend a lot of time pretending. Not the fun kind, not make-believe. I spend a lot of time pretending I'm perfect, that I have it all together, and the truth is, I have no idea what I'm fucking doing. All I know is that I'm really tired. I'm really tired of having to work so hard on shit that doesn't matter to my kids, or to me. I'm tired of marathon PTA meetings and insane bake sales. I'm tired of all the bullshit." I had to pause here. Not for dramatic effect, but because people were cheering. Like, cheering the way we usually cheer for our kids. I heard a few "fuck yeahs" in there, too. Maybe I'm not so bad at this.

"I know we all want to have happy kids. Of course we do. And I don't think you can have happy kids without a happy mom. And that means we need to give ourselves a break. It's not selfish to need some time to yourself. It's not selfish to be here tonight. Holy *shit* I needed this! So. If you're tired of feeling like you're not good enough. If you're tired of feeling like you're not doing enough. If you're just *tired*? Vote for me."

By the time I step down from the couch, I'm mobbed with moms. Someone had flipped the music back on, but all around me is a crush of earnest, slightly (okay, extremely) inebriated faces.

"I want to be your best friend! Can we be best friends?"

"Amy Mitchell, you're the hero we've been waiting for!"

"I will do whatever you tell me to do! You're my sister. I love you sooooo much!"

I nod and smile and hug every single mom who comes my way.

THE PARTY WENT ALL NIGHT LONG LIKE LIONEL RITCHIE. OR, until 11:30 PM, which is basically an all-nighter when you're a mom or when you're Lionel Ritchie's current age. In college, we used to judge the success of a party on how trashed our house was. The best party we ever threw ended with all our living room furniture being burned in the front yard. Tonight was the grown-up version of that party. Someone had beaten the Little Tikes playset to smithereens with what I can only assume used to be a baseball bat, before that too was smashed. Every surface in my house is covered in beer bottles, LaCroix cans, and Dylan's and Jane's old sippy cups with a few swallows of wine left in them. Kiki and I are sorting the debris into garbage and recycling while Carla finishes doing whippets out of a can of store-brand whipped cream when a tall, dark figure appears in the doorway.

"Don't fucking kill us!" Kiki screams, ducking into a fetal position.

"I won't!" the figure screams back, stepping into the kitchen. "Did I . . . miss the party? Carla made it sound like it was raging."

Jesse.

"Jesse!" Carla shouts suspiciously. "So good to see you!

Fun party, Amy, see you another time!" Carla grabs a very confused Kiki by the arm and starts for the front door.

"Bye, Jesse. I like your face and your clothes and your body," Kiki whispers before Carla spirits her away.

It was all very natural and not at all uncomfortable for me or Jesse, whose beautiful caramel skin is starting to blush.

"Should I . . . go?" he asks, in a voice that said he had no intention of going anywhere.

I shake my head, and feel Jesse's hands on my hips, pulling me closer to him.

Our first kiss may have almost given us each a concussion, but it turns out, kissing is like riding a bike. You *can* forget how to do it, but you'll get the hang of it after a few tries.

I feel like someone just offered me a glass of water after wandering through the desert. I feel like a deaf person hearing music for the first time. I feel like a mom finally being treated like a sexual being. Everything is sexy to me in this moment. The feeling of my countertops under my thighs, the way Jesse's hands move across my hips and up my shirt. I know that Beyoncé and Jay-Z can do it all night long in a kitchen, but I do find the location where I serve dinner to my family to be a little distracting. And I don't want to be distracted right now, not when Jesse's mouth is on my neck and I'm pulling off his shirt. I pull away from kissing him and grab him by the hand, pulling him up the stairs behind me.

Jesse's body is not what I expected. It's *better*. It doesn't even make sense that someone can be this good-looking. Even his shoulders are hot. Can you be attracted to a shoulder? I would make out with just his shoulder if that were socially acceptable.

It's not like Mike's got a *super* hairy back, but it's not like Jesse's: smooth and lean, and tapered into an actual waist, not just a barrel bod.

The last time I did this, I was . . . nineteen? Twenty? Twenty. I spent the entire time sucking in my stomach, like having internal organs was a crime and Mike or any other man-child I was with deserved a nymph with a concave stomach. This time, I don't have time to think about what my body looks like. I'm not embarrassed when Jesse tries to pull down my skinny jeans and they get stuck on my ankles like they always do. I just laugh, and he laughs, and that makes it hotter. All my nerve endings are alive at once, lighting up in every place that Jesse touches, and kisses. We've fallen perfectly into sync: my back arches to make room for his hands under my lower back, and he slides off my Target underwear in one pull. My legs make room for him as he kisses down my stomach, running his hands along the stretch marks Jane left on my inner thighs. This is what I want, so badly that I can't imagine ever wanting anything else. I push my hips up to meet his mouth, and Jesse gets to work.

And then: *kaboom!* The kind of eye-rolling, earth-shattering orgasm you don't think is actually possible until it happens. I'm out of body and inside my body at the same time. I see nothing but stars and the entire meaning of the universe. Over and over and over.

And just when I think it couldn't get any better? He speaks the seven most beautiful words in the English language:

"Can I go down on you again?"

30

CARLA

The worst part of being in your mid-to-late thirties (okay mid-forties but *looking* like your mid-thirties) has to be that a hang-over isn't just an inconvenience, it's completely debilitating. I know enough not to try to call in sick, since my manager was at the party last night. I considered it, though. I saw *her* start a wet T-shirt contest with a bunch of the other Fit Moms, so if she started throwing stones, I could toss a few at her glass house.

Instead, I chug a Diet Mountain Dew, eat two pieces of slightly burned toast, and head out to do my part to beautify America, right after I drop the kid off at school.

"Oh hey, Mr. Nolan said he emailed you," Jaxon says as he gets out of the car. "Did you get his email?"

I freeze. What the shit is going on now? Mr. Nolan must

really want to talk to me, and that can't be good. "Uh, musta gone to my spam? I don't remember seeing it, bud."

Jaxon rolls his eyes.

"Dude, go! Tell Mr. Nolan if he needs to talk to me, he can come find me." And I decide not to step foot on campus again.

When I walk into my treatment room, my first client is already there, tits up, legs spread, a cold sleep mask covering her eyes.

"Hello," I coo in my special spa voice. "And what are we doing today?"

"A bikini wax," she snaps back. *Oh. So this is how it's going to go.*

"All right. It looks like you've been getting French waxes. You don't have a lot of regrowth, so I'm just going to do some maintenance today, sound good?"

She sighs. "Fine." Where have I heard that bitchy voice before?

When you've been in the vagina business as long as I have, you can do a wax with your eyes closed. I don't go to sleep, but I definitely go into autopilot and before I know it, the job is done.

"All set," I say, rubbing a soothing balm over her inflamed vaginal area.

"Wow," she says, "thank you so much. I think I fell asleep there for a moment. You're incredible."

"My pleasure," I say. "Now, I'm sure you know the after-care instructions, but I just want to remind you that witch hazel is your friend for the next few days: don't be afraid to soak a pad, pop it in the freezer, and then wear it between two pairs of underwear. It's weird, but it works."

She nodded. "Witch hazel. Got it."

I pull the blankets down over her legs and stand up to leave, disappointed to see a giant rock on that left hand. All that pubic hair for a shitty tip.

THE "MOTHER'S LOUNGE" AT THE SPA IS NEVER OCCUPIED BY the actual McKinley Moms, just by the women who are employed by the McKinley Moms. The nannies who have babies to watch hang out on the couches in the mother's lounge, because they've gotta be ready to run the baby in to breastfeed at regular intervals. Nannies with school-age kids just sit and read or scroll on their iPhones or Skype their families, waiting for their boss to finish her treatments. If you're wondering, *Why would a nanny have to tag along to the spa if there aren't even any kids for her to watch?*, then please excuse me for ruining your innocence when I tell you that the nanny's job is no longer to look after the children. Instead, it's a nanny's job to take care of the rich mom. It's basically like getting paid to be someone's friend/servant, I guess?

I fucking love nannies. They've got all the best dirt. Did you know that Roman's parents don't even live in the school district for McKinley? They use their grandparents' address, and the nanny drives over there every single day so they can walk out the front door and down to the bus stop, just in case there are any snitches around. Sydney and Kit's nanny told me that their mom isn't away on business, she's away at rehab. For the fourth time. Porn addiction is real. Mostly, I've learned that behind every successful white woman is a bunch of underpaid women of various racial backgrounds making her life run smoothly and getting no credit for it.

I was hoping to use the mother's lounge for a quick nap before my next wax, but when I walk in, the best couch is already occupied by some chick all snuggled up under one of our weighted anxiety blankets. I try to catch her eye as I pass by so we can talk some shit, but she's fully locked into whatever she's got going on her laptop, which has her typing away like a crazed cartoon character.

I grab one of my sudoku books from behind the fiddle-leaf fig tree and settle into one of the massaging chairs on the opposite wall. If I can't sleep, I can at least loosen up my muscles and work my brain.

I'm stuck on page four when a well-manicured hand with one helluva ring on it pushes the door open, followed by a thin, tan body.

"Oska?! I've been looking all over for you. What the fuck are you doing in here?"

That bitchy voice belongs to Gwendolyn, who also owns the vulva I'd recently been touching. I thought for sure she'd recognize me, if not as one of Amy's friends then as the woman who was just up close and personal with her labia, but her eyes scanned over me like I was nothing, and landed directly on the nanny, who must be Oska.

I put my nose in my sudoku and try to turn on my listening ears, but it's hard. Gwendolyn is so good at whispering, and she's got her lips practically glued to this poor lady's ear.

Oska is what the Hippie Moms would call *a natural beauty*. Duh, it's easy to be naturally beautiful when you're twenty-five and your skin is still rich with collagen and your metabolism can still burn through a bagel like it's nothing.

I can make out a few of Gwendolyn's words. Something about hurting? About pain? If she's talking shit about my waxing . . . No, she's talking about someone else.

"There's no way for her to charm her way out of *that*," Gwendolyn snips, standing up and brushing invisible lint off her expensive-ass workout clothes. "Now bring the Tesla around."

I know enough about Gwendolyn to know that whatever she's plotting, it's probably as bad as the tip she left me today.

GWENDOLYN JAMES STYLE

Winners never quit.
Quitters never win.
—UNKNOWN

It took 37 hours of labor before Gandhi was born. Now, my birth plan called for no more than 20 hours, max, so I was not pleased. I had expected her to arrive the way we had discussed: the morning of her due date. But my stubborn little lady took her time. For over a day, I bounced on a balance ball, soaked in the tub we'd installed just for this purpose, and chomped on ice. My husband and doula *begged* me to go to the hospital. But I said no. And at 9 at night, our family was complete. You know why? Because I didn't quit.

I will never forget the way she looked at me, with total admiration and awe. She may have been just a few minutes old, but she already knew that I was her North Star.

Our children are watching us. Even before they're here, they're absorbing our thoughts, our attitudes, our approach to life. They know when we've given up, or when we're not living up to our potential. When we sell ourselves short, we sell our kids short. Selling our kids short is like selling every kid short. So here's my promise to you: I'll never quit. Because your kids depend on me, too.

In Love and Style,
Gwendolyn James

PS—Witch, Please! Do you know the natural soothing properties of witch hazel? My Spooky Season guide to natural beauty is here! Click here *for the free PDF download!*

31

PRINCIPAL BURR

854.

The school board is asking for my five-year plan for Mc-Kinley. A five-year plan? What am I, a recent college graduate? My *plan* is to walk out the door in five years and never look back. What happens in the interim is nobody's business but my own. I *plan* to spend five years doing the bare minimum: the kids will be taught; the teachers will be paid. We will, eventually, find a new custodian.

Recently, Gwendolyn James proposed that we become the First School in Space, and she wasn't even joking. She told the school board that a school known for innovation (are we?) owes it to the community (do we?) to think out of the box, out of the school, out of the stratosphere (can we?). I know I've been wrong about a few things. I'll admit that in 1999, I did tell the school board that we didn't need to teach the kids about the Internet because it was just a place for geeks and pedophiles. I stand by that assessment, because the Internet of the moment was little more than AOL chatrooms. But, as has been pointed out ad nauseam on the Facebook page "OK, BOOMER," I failed to see the merits of the Internet, and the potential it held for developing the education of the future.

So no, I don't always have my finger on the pulse of what's next, but is that really what you want from a principal? Do you really want someone who is obsessed with what the future holds, or someone who is just happy to be here, in the now? A principal who knows every kid's first name, and dresses up as his "long-lost sister, Brenda" on the last day of school every year? Apparently Brenda is no longer welcome here. One of the parents sent a strongly worded letter to my office telling me that my heteronormativity and homophobia were showing. I was flabbergasted, even more so after Rick explained what those words meant. The bottom line is, as Rick explained to me, that Brenda is problematic, and I will no longer be dressing as a woman to entertain the children.

"PRINCIPAL BURR?"

There's no telling how long Rick stood in my doorway, waiting for me to notice him. I've told him a million times, "Just knock," but he refuses, and instead just stands there, motionless, until I'm startled into noticing him.

"Mail's here," he says, smiling and dropping a modest pile of envelopes onto my desk. Per my preferences, they've all been neatly opened with a letter opener, which Rick mistook on his first day for a knife and asked me to remove in the interest of fostering a safe work environment.

I TAKE MY TIME WITH THE MAIL, AS IT'S A GREAT WAY TO EAT up some of that long afternoon stretch between the lunch hour and the final bell. I read through each credit card offer, noting to once again talk with Jan about her spending habits. I page through the entire Costco magazine and fold down a corner promising a great twist on the classic chicken Waldorf salad.

And then the phone rings.

I have a habit of letting calls go to voicemail, but when it's an unknown number, you *have* to answer. It could be anyone—what's more exciting than that?

"Hello, Principal Burr speaking. How can I be of service to you on this fine day?"

There's a pause on the other line, and for a moment I'm disappointed. Is this a butt dial? And then, she speaks.

"Good afternoon, Principal Burr. I'm a concerned member of the McKinley community."

It's not a voice I recognize, but then again most parents at this school are from the generation that decided phone calls are "intrusive" and routinely ask if they can text me, which they may not.

"How may I help you, ma'am?" There's a pause, and I instantly regret using gendered language.

"Principal Burr, you're a busy man so I'll make this quick. We've heard rumors that a student at McKinley has been abusing illegal drugs . . . and selling them to other children."

I hold the phone away from myself as I groan. Really?! Drugs at McKinley? When I *just* paid for that Drug-Free Is the Way to Be mural?

"Does this student druggie have a name?" I ask. There's a pause on the line.

"I heard . . . it's Jane Mitchell."

Jane Mitchell? The Jane Mitchell who recently asked for a meeting with the school board so she could review our district's conservation and recycling program? Then again, she does seem to be pretty high energy. Maybe she's snorting Adderall in the bathroom like I heard about kids doing on *60 Minutes*?

I'm about to tell my mystery caller that I'll look into it when I hear a click. Seriously, did telephone etiquette die with Gen X?

It takes me approximately ten minutes of clicking around on our intranet (which is different from the Internet) before I find our locker directory and another four minutes of scrolling until I reach the center of the alphabet.

Mitchell, Jane

Locker 126

There's no need to go pulling an A student out of class just yet. I fish around in my junk drawer for the master key ring that holds the keys to every locker, office, and classroom in this building. I slip my shoes back on, grab my coffee cup, and check the clock. I've got thirteen minutes. That's plenty of time for a quick investigation.

32

AMY

The last time we went to therapy—three years ago, maybe—Mike left halfway through the session. Not because that was a planned part of the therapy, but because he'd decided he'd had enough, and that it was a waste of his time. Dr. Karl had said nothing as Mike stood up, and nothing when he shut the door.

"Is that . . . normal?" I'd asked, knowing that I didn't want to know the obvious answer. A good rule of thumb is this: If you have to *ask* if something is normal, it isn't normal.

Dr. Karl had made unwavering eye contact with me, playing with the ends of her afro contemplatively.

"That's normal," she said, "when your marriage is fucked up."

MIKE AND I HAD SETTLED INTO THE SMALL SOFA, SITTING AS far apart as you can on a couch that was built to force couples into close physical proximity. Dr. Karl started with all the usual therapy stuff: how being here was a good sign for us, that all marriages can be saved, that the work *starts* in this room, but the most important work will be done outside of these walls. I didn't even have to look at Mike to know he was rolling his eyes.

"Let's start with some affirmations," Dr. Karl suggests. "I want you each to tell your spouse three things that you *like* about them." She over-pronounced *like*, just to clear up any confusion.

"Can I go second?" Mike asks, because of course he did.

My mind goes blank. Blanker than blank. What did I *like* about him?

"Well. I like that you gave me my children. That was nice of you." I say the words slowly, hoping my brain will come up with two more reasons while my mouth was talking.

"You're welcome," he shoots back, in that self-satisfied way that I used to find appealing.

"I like that you sometimes pick up the kids from school; that's really helpful. And . . . I like that you came to therapy."

Dr. Karl nods in Mike's direction.

"Okay. Um, I like your spaghetti. And your calzones."

Dr. Karl and I wait patiently for him to mention something that isn't Italian food.

"Is that three?" he says after several moments of silence.

"Oh!" He continues, "I like that you've never crashed the car."

So. That's it. That was what we like about each other?

Dr. Karl pages through the file folder in her lap, probably reviewing her notes from our last session.

She breathes deep, and exhales loudly. Without thinking, Mike and I do, too. Dr. Karl asks us to close our eyes, and to imagine ourselves as our partner. We aren't to say anything aloud, just imagine life in their shoes. What do they see when they wake up? What do they think about? What does their day look like? She will ring a small bell when our exercise is finished.

I close my eyes and disappear into Mike's life for three hundred seconds. It's . . . nice. I wake up, and the coffee is already made. My wife has already hit the gym and fed the kids, and all I have to do is stumble to the shower and get downstairs for breakfast. During the workday, I take a few phone calls and spend the morning picking a restaurant where I can spend two hours chatting with a client. After lunch, I set my phone to silent and take a nap. I come home to a clean house where my wife has made a balanced dinner, where my laundry is folded neatly and arranged by color.

The bell rings before I can even finish the day, which surprises me because Imaginary Mike hadn't even done anything yet. I blink open my eyes. Mike is playing on his phone. I try my best not to let the rage blooming inside of my chest take over.

Dr. Karl clears her throat. "Mike? Why don't you go first? Tell me what it's like to be Amy."

Mike puts his phone down and sits up straight. Is he making fun of me?

"Hiiiiii," he says in a patronizing voice that is supposed to be me, "I'm Amyyyyy. I'm sooooo perfect. My life is sooo perfect! I spend all day just rubbing lotions on my face and talking and talking and talking and making sure everyone around me lives up to my ridiculous standards!"

"We—we don't need the voice," Dr. Karl tries to interject. "Focus on how it *feels* to be Amy."

"Oh, it feels great to be me! Why wouldn't it? I have a fully tricked-out minivan and my husband still has all his hair and I have a ton of expensive clothes, but I still wear these boner-killing sweatpants every night and I don't know what I sit around complaining about all day because my life is great!"

I pride myself on my ability to navigate conflict with maturity. Which is why I'm *not* proud of what I say next.

"OH, HEY!" I shout in my best bro voice. "I'm Mike! I have no idea how good I have it! My wife actually buys all her clothes on sale, takes care of literally everything for me, and all I had to do was not jerk off all day online with a stranger but whoops! I'm still the same fuckup I was in college!"

"Oooooh!" Mike squeals. "I'm Amy! And I've never jerked off on the Internet because I'm sooooo perfect!"

"Hey, Doctor," I bellow, "mind if I splooge all over your computer?!"

"Please don't joke about that," Dr. Karl whispers, eyeing her MacBook Air, which sits on the coffee table between us.

"The bottom line is that she is a perfectionist, and I'm never going to be good enough for her. And she doesn't even bother with sex anymore. I haven't gotten a blowie since my birthday, which was like, months ago."

"You know what, Mike? You're right. You haven't gotten a blowie since your birthday. Maybe because you still say things

like 'blowie'? Or because you think I owe you sex in exchange
for you meeting the minimum requirements as a parent and a
spouse. And by 'minimum,' I mean just being alive. You know
what would be so hot to me? If you took care of the kids, or
me, in any way. If you ever walked the dog. If you took care of
anyone outside of yourself, I would give you so many blowies
your dick would explode."

Mike scoffed. "That would never happen. My dick is in-
destructible."

Sometimes, you don't know what the truth is until it slips
out of you on its own. I sigh, and it comes out: "I am so tired
of pretending to love you, Mike."

Mike nods. "That's *exactly* how I feel."

Dr. Karl snaps shut the folder in her hands.

"Okay, you two. I know earlier I said a lot of stuff about
how all marriages can be saved? But that was hyperbole. This
marriage? It's not going to happen for you. I'm not going to
refund you for our time today, but I won't be booking another
session with you. I can refer you each to an individual therapist, which I highly recommend."

"Wait, don't you think we should stay together for the
kids?" Mike asks, and Dr. Karl shakes her head, citing statistics that kids whose parents stay in a loveless marriage are two
times unhappier than kids whose parents got divorced. I think
about my parents, and how even as a child I could tell that my
parents loved each other and belonged together, even though
my mom is an absolute tyrant. Was *that* why I believed that
marriage was like a staring contest? Because my parents hadn't
blinked? Did I want Jane and Dylan growing up thinking that

marriage was more important than love, or happiness? That misery was noble?

"So," I wonder aloud, "what now?"

"As a therapist, I'm not allowed to tell you what to do. But as a human being with two fucking eyes in my head, I will tell you to get a divorce as soon as humanly possible."

DIVORCE.

Why have I been so afraid of saying the word before? Now that it was out there, the fear had been drained from it.

"Hi," I said to my rearview mirror, "I'm Amy. I'm divorced. Oh, it's okay. It's a good thing. The divorce was really amicable. Really!"

It would be amicable, I knew. Eventually, at least. I'd walked into therapy hating Mike and hoping to work it out, and walked out of therapy planning for a divorce and hating him at least 200 percent less than I had for the past month. By the time I got to work, he'd already texted me five times:

MIKE: Everything 50/50 sound good?

MIKE: We don't have to get lawyers, do we? Lawyers suck.

MIKE: And I'll pay for all the kids' shit because I know they're expensive.

MIKE: Can we split custody of Roscoe?

MIKE: Can we please not hate each other?

It will be amicable eventually. It will be okay eventually. But right now? It's just really, really fucking sad.

JESSICA IS OUR "HUMAN RESOURCES" TEAM. BY THAT I mean, her business card reads "People Person," and her qualifications for running an HR department are that she is a human and that Dale assumed she would be a very resourceful person. Most of her job description is having "one-on-ones" with the younger staff members and promising them ever-loftier job titles. At one point, all the VPs here at CoCo were under twenty-five years old. The other part of her job is exactly what's happening here. Jessica fires people. Always in the conference room closest to the entrance. Always when the person has just arrived at work. Always—always—with a witness present.

I'm seething. It's one thing to say you're divorced; now I have to practice telling my mirror I am divorced and unemployed?

"What the fuck, Dale? You're firing me?"

Dale looks as if he's been fed a lemon. "What? Yuck, no! I hate that word! You're being positively transitioned, Amy."

"What do those words even mean, Dale?" I'm going to make this smarmy little dink say it.

"It means that you used to have a job here, and we're so grateful for the many ways you've contributed to our company, and now . . . we are so grateful, we are . . . positively transitioning you somewhere else. Home. So you can just, do your thing."

"You're firing me."

"Amy, you haven't even been coming to work!"

"I'm *part*-time!" I remind him.

"Okay, but you only came in once this week. That's less than part-time."

I'd only come in once this week, yes, but that's because it's only Tuesday. Isn't it? Oh. Shit. It's not Tuesday. It's Friday. I *had* only come in once this week. And I don't remember checking my email, either.

"Look," I reason, "I have been slacking off. Sure. But Tessa took two weeks off when Jon Snow died on *Game of Thrones* and he's a fictional person, so . . . can't you let this slide?"

Dale winced. "You know I'm not caught up on *Game of Thrones*, Amy. And besides, I already sent out an email telling everyone you were being positively transitioned so I can't take it back or I'd look stupid. Jessica has your severance info."

Jessica, who has been sitting here silently with a pasted-on smile, just nods. A small gift bag has materialized on the table, next to the folder.

"Just, sign these?" She wasn't asking a question, she just always sounded like she was. "And . . . the team wanted you to have this special gift?"

I scrawl my name at the places Jessica had flagged with tiny sticky notes and dig my hands into the gift bag. Was this? No. A *four*-ounce bag of CoCo coffee. Four ounces. The size we sell to hotels. All this time here and they couldn't even spring for a pound?

I consider throwing it at them. I glare at Jessica. At Dale. And then at the two mountainous security guards.

"Well!" I say, shoving the coffee into my purse. "Fuck off, then!"

33

CARLA

The smell coming from Jaxon's backpack is from a few bites of what might have been deli ham at some point. It's hard to tell, but it's clear the whole thing needs to be thrown into the washing machine or possibly burned. I dump the backpack onto the kitchen table and sort through all the junk. We've got chewed-up pencils, a baseball schedule, some spiral-bound notebooks, a math textbook, a calculator, some kind of melted candy, and one sealed envelope that looks too clean to have been in this bag for long. I separate the usable school supplies from the pencil shavings and food remnants and pick up the letter.

"CARLA DUNKLER" is written in neat block letters on the front, and I pray it's not another library fine like Jaxon got last year for trying to get into *The Guinness Book of World*

Records by *eating* a *Guinness Book of World Records* to entertain his classmates.

I unfold the paper and wince. It's worse than a fine.

Hello Ms. Dunkler,

I'm just checking in again to see if you're available to join us for conferences. Midterm conferences are a great time for educators and parents to connect about a child's development and performance this year, before the crunch of the holiday season.

Let me know if you're available. Spots are filling up, but I'm more than willing to accommodate your schedule.

Sincerely,
Peter Nolan

Shit, this guy is relentless. What has Jaxon done that would necessitate a conference? Every time I ask him about school, Jaxon grunts and says his day was good, or that everything's fine. Sometimes he'll even smile about it and tell me something they learned that day. Mr. Nolan needs to step the fuck off and let Jaxon and me just live. I use the paper to sweep the backpack trash into the palm of my hand, then crumple it up and dump it all in the trash.

34

AMY

My life is teetering dangerously close to the lyrics of a country music song. My husband has left me. I just lost my job. My dog hasn't died, but he is on anxiety meds. I'm driving home, playing through all the scenarios that could arise when my mom finds out that I'm also unemployed. It's chilly, but the windows are down, and Alanis Morissette is up, because when everything has gone to absolute hell, I find that angsty music from middle school is really the only thing that helps.

And, the only thing that can interrupt my word-for-word rendition of a song about the heartbreak of losing Dave Coulier to another woman is the sound of my phone ringing, which blasts through every speaker in the van. I have to admit that Mike was right, and I do have a very nice minivan.

Any sense of fine-ness I'd achieved with Alanis disappears when I see the number calling me. It's the generic number from McKinley, which means it's the school nurse calling to let me know that one of the kids puked or has chicken pox or lice or whatever else could possibly go wrong this week.

"Hello!" I shout, trying to roll up the windows and keep an eye on the road. "Amy Mitchell here."

"Hello, Mrs. Mitchell." It's a deep, kind voice. Not like our nurses aren't kind, but they are also not men my father's age.

"Hello?" I reply. "Can I . . . help you?"

There's a cough on the line. "Yes, it's Principal Burr. Could you come pick up Jane from school? She's in my office."

Jane? He must mean Dylan. "Jane? Jane Mitchell? My daughter? Is she sick? Is she getting bullied?!"

My body has already rerouted the van toward McKinley, and I know from memory that I'll be there in approximately eight to eleven minutes, depending on how many parking spots are available.

"No," Principal Burr says, sighing, "she's not sick. And she's not being bullied. We can discuss it in person."

The line goes dead, and I push the gas pedal. What the fuck is going on?

AFTER I'VE DOUBLE-PARKED IN ONE OF THE VISITOR SPOTS and gotten buzzed in the front door and rushed down the hallways papered with sponge-painted sunsets and posters about the scientific process, I've worked up a sweat to go with my anxiety.

"Hello, Mrs. Mitchell," Principal Burr's secretary greets

me, gesturing to the small pleather loveseat where sick kids wait for their parents to show up.

"Hey," I say, blatantly ignoring his unspoken request that I wait my turn and instead pushing my shoulder into Principal Burr's office door. Jane looks so small and so scared as she turns toward the door. She's sitting in one of the two chairs facing Principal Burr's desk, wiping tears from her red, blotchy cheeks. Principal Burr looks bewildered and more than a little bit uncomfortable. Did Jane get her period?

"Janey Bear," I coo at her, and she looks at me with wide-eyed bewilderment.

"Janey? What's going on, bear?"

No response.

Principal Burr sighs, and I take my seat.

"Are you aware of the code of conduct by which all McKinley athletes are expected to abide?" he asks, and I shrug.

"Sure," I say, "is Jane getting an award or something?"

Principal Burr slides a small baggie toward me. It's made of eco-friendly craft paper, and I open it. Inside are three *perfectly* rolled joints. And I mean *perfectly*. I'm . . . confused. Is he offering these to me? Am I supposed to know what this means?

"He found those in my *locker*," Jane chokes out, and I can't help but laugh.

"*Your* locker? *Honey*."

"Mom! They're not mine, you have to believe me."

"*Believe* you? Of course I believe you!" I turn to Principal Burr. "You know Jane. You know there is no way these are hers. Kids don't even roll joints, they vape marijuana juice out of those little flutey things. It's an epidemic! I saw several tweets about it."

Principal Burr pulls the bag back toward himself.

"It doesn't matter who rolled them," he says. "They were found in Jane's locker."

"Then someone must have—" My face suddenly falls as I recall Gwendolyn's meltdown at the bake sale. "*Oh my God . . .*"

Jane snaps to attention, grabbing my arm.

"Wait, Mom, do you know something about this?!"

"It's possible I pissed someone off . . . and it's possible they came after you."

"WHAT?! This is so unfair! Principal Burr! Are you hearing this?"

If Principal Burr is hearing this, I'm sure it sounds absolutely bonkers. Am I really going to accuse Gwendolyn of planting drugs in my daughter's locker? And how exactly would I prove that? "J-Jane, it's . . . it's . . ." I stammer, not sure what to say.

Jane starts crying. When I turn to Principal Burr, he just shrugs.

"The code of conduct is clear," he says, opening the student handbook to read me a passage. "The possession of any drugs or drug paraphernalia is grounds for immediate ban from all extracurricular activities."

I wince. "*All* activities?" I ask.

"*All* activities. Jane is off the soccer team. I'm sorry, Amy, but I answer to the PTA and the school board on this one and my hands are tied."

I bite my lip to keep it together and do my best to smile.

"Thank you so much for your time, Principal Burr," I say, standing up and reaching out to shake his hand. He looks relieved, like he'd expected this meeting to go differently. His hand is warm and clammy, and once he lets go, I swipe the bag of joints from his desk.

"I'll just take these for safekeeping."

THE CAR RIDE IS ICY COLD. JANE HAS STOPPED CRYING, BUT she's also stopped talking to me. Instead, she stares out the window like a captive plotting her escape.

When we pull into the driveway, she's out of the car and into the house before I can even put it in park. I grab my bag, and her bag, and a few empty cans of sparkling water that have been rolling around in the back and walk in after her. I know enough to let her cool down, but it's *hard*. I halfheartedly tidy up the living room, which is an absolute garbage dump. I haul out the trash and recycling. I let Roscoe out, and give him a treat when he comes back in. I glance through the freezer to see what I can thaw and reheat for dinner. I do my absolute best to pretend that I am not the worst thing that has happened to my children, but the moment I *hear* her crying I'm up those stairs two at a time and *thunk*—running directly into her locked bedroom door. I knock. I knock again. There's silence, and then the sound of Jane turning the lock.

The door whips open, and Sad Jane has been replaced by Angry Jane. Angry Jane scares me, and always has.

"What do you *want*?" she snarls.

"I'm just, I'm just checking on you, baby."

"Well, don't bother. You haven't bothered for the last month or so, so why start now?"

"Janey, that's not fair—"

"No, it's not *fair* when your mom decides that partying with her new friends and sleeping in and kicking your dad out is cool. It's not *fair* when you get kicked off the soccer team because your mom pissed somebody off. It's *not fair* when *my* life falls apart because I have a terrible mom."

"Jane, I'm sorry—"

She's already turned her back on me, rifling through her desk. "Here," she says, stepping back into the doorway and shoving an old notebook into my hands. "Take it. I'm nothing like you, and I hope I never am."

The door slams. My heart breaks. She gave my journal back.

GWENDOLYN JAMES STYLE

I believe the children are our future.

—W. HOUSTON

Nobody thinks it will happen to their child. But the sad fact of the matter is that today's kids are turning more to drugs at a younger age than ever, and for all kinds of reasons: divorce, parental neglect, genetic predisposition to self-destruction . . . the list goes on.

Now, as moms, we know we *all* make mistakes. One of my most popular posts is all about the 78 most common mistakes made by new moms—and how to avoid them (click here to read). But the biggest mistake we make is thinking that it won't happen to our kids.

As part of a community that has recently been affected by drug use and trafficking, I feel a responsibility to my fellow moms to help educate one another on how we can *all* do better, to make sure our kids do the absolute best.

1. Talk to your kids about drugs! A Google Image search of "people who use drugs" will help illustrate the life consequences for their poor decisions.
2. Know who their friends are! And more importantly, who their friends' *moms* are. Apples never fall far from the tree, do they?
3. Pay attention. Is your child irritable? Too calm? Sleepy? Not sleeping enough? Hungrier than normal or without an appetite? It could very easily be drugs. Urine tests are cheap to procure online (click here to use my affiliate link!) and will give you peace of mind.

In Love and Style,
Gwendolyn James

35

KIKI

This is the worst week of Amy's life. Which makes it the worst week of *my* life, because the thing about having a best friend is that you really feel for them. You feel their highs and their lows. It was more fun to feel like I'd had sex with Jesse Harkness than it is to feel like I'm getting divorced and my kids hate me and I'm also unemployed, but this is what friendship is.

Amy's front door is unlocked, which is strange. Usually, Roscoe barks his head off before my feet even touch the front porch, and Jane is shushing him from the armchair where she's snuggled with a book. When I peek my head inside, there's no Roscoe, and no Jane.

"Hello?" I call, stepping into the living room, where Dylan is usually talking into a headset and playing some sort of violent video game. No Dylan.

"Amy?"

I tiptoe up the stairs, ducking my head into her bedroom, her bathroom. No Amy. I find her snuggled in Jane's bed, curled up under the covers. She pokes her head out to look at me, and my heart breaks. I've never seen Amy like this before. She's so . . . sad.

"I'm such a fucking fuckup," she whispers, and I do what I do best: I curl up next to her and listen.

WHEN I WAS A LITTLE GIRL, MY MOTHER USED TO MAKE ME Bad Day Banana Bread. We called it that because it was filled with chocolate chips, and nothing makes a bad day better than fresh banana bread with more chocolate than any bread should have. I played with Amy's hair while she cried and talked. Dylan and Jane and Roscoe had left to stay with Mike for a while. Mike had been nice about it—and I personally wouldn't mind if Kent took our kids for an indeterminate amount of time—but Amy is really, really sad, and saying that I was envious of her would not have helped.

Once she's at least able to sit up and drink a glass of water, I leave Amy in Jane's bed and go downstairs to her kitchen. Jane, I hate to admit, had a point. The sink is piled with dirty dishes, which is my pet peeve because the dishwasher is *right there*, right next to the sink! How much time do you save by dropping your dish in the sink? None! The floor is sticky, like someone hadn't bothered to wipe up a spill properly. And the counters are cluttered, absolutely covered, with junk mail.

It's clear that Bad Day Banana Bread is not my only task for the day.

I'VE KNOWN A LOT OF KIDS WHO DID DRUGS. OR, I KNEW OF them and they weren't anything like Jane. They were always a little too old and a little too street smart for their age. Jane can't even say the word "bra" without being embarrassed. Once, after school, I'd tucked her fallen strap back into her T-shirt, and she'd turned maroon with embarrassment. When I was her age, the bad girl in my grade was named Devon. Devon *definitely* smoked drugs because she talked about it all the time. Seriously, she would say stuff like "I smoke drugs." Her parents were always out at the casinos and she spent a lot of time alone. I looked her up on Facebook the other day and she looks older than my mom. I know things have changed since I was growing up in North Dakota. On *Oprah*, I once saw a bunch of teenage girls who said they put vodka-soaked tampons into their vaginas to get drunk. They got drunk through their vaginas! And I'm sure their parents just thought, *Hm, she sure goes through a lot of tampons, I hope her period isn't too overwhelming.*

By the time the banana bread is ready—perfectly crisp on top, spongey in the middle—the kitchen is not quite sparkling, but certainly better than I'd found it.

"Hey." It's Amy, bleary-eyed and bed-headed, standing in the kitchen doorway. "You did this for me? Kiki, I'm so sorry, you didn't have to come over and clean up my dumpster house."

"Of course I didn't have to. But I wanted to. That's what friends do." I cut her a generous, butter-covered slice, trying not to stare at her while she takes her first bite.

"This is really fucking good." She smiles, chocolate smeared across her perfect white teeth. It worked. It *always* works.

BOOM. BOOM. BOOM. We're startled by the sound of pounding on the front door. A muffled voice floats through the front door.

"Open the door, bitches!"

36

CARLA

What Would Vin Diesel Do?

Well, I'll tell you right now, he wouldn't let some bitch get away with framing their friend's kid for possession. No way.

I knew the moment Amy texted me who was behind this shit.

First off, Jane wouldn't know how to smoke drugs if her life depended on it. I *was* the bad girl in middle school, and in middle school, bad girls don't know how to hide it. They don't *want* to hide it. I walked around my middle school telling everyone that my mom was at her boyfriend Randy's house for the weekend and I had four wine coolers and half a joint to share.

Now, bad *women* know how to hide it. And nobody, I mean *nobody*, does more drugs than the white women of McKinley. Pot is the new . . . pot? Stressed-out white ladies everywhere, the kind who love calling the cops when they smell even a hint of weed at a public park, are all secretly toking up because it helps their "stress" and "anxiety." They'll call it something cute, like microdosing, but vaping in your minivan isn't microdosing, it's just . . . dosing. The moms who used to casually ask my colleagues and me where in the world someone would even *buy* drugs? Now, they grow it themselves, tucked into their gardens among tomatoes and wildflowers, or in basement grow spaces just off the laundry room. It's like they thought *Weeds* was an instructional documentary.

Normally, what other people do is none of my business. I firmly believe that not getting into other people's bullshit is what keeps me young. But like Vin says, I don't have friends, I have family. And when someone fucks with my family? I will literally drive a car through a building to save them, if that's what it takes.

I WAS ABOUT TO TAKE A LITTLE CATNAP IN THE MOTHER'S lounge when I saw her. Gwendolyn's little nanny pal, sitting on the same couch, tapping away on her laptop.

"Hey," I said, getting up and taking the seat across from her, "you're Oska, right? Whatcha working on over there?"

Oska crumbled like a cake. All I had to do was show the tiniest bit of interest in her as a person and she sang like a little bird.

Look, I pride myself on not knowing jack shit about the Internet, but this lady was basically the inventor of that shit. She isn't just Gwendolyn's nanny, she's *Gwendolyn*. Or, the Internet version of her at least? She takes Gwendolyn's photos. She writes her blog—whatever the shit that means—she writes her eBooks. Gwendolyn James is a big fucking phony.

37

OSKA

It wasn't always like this. In the beginning, Gwendolyn was a totally nice, normalish rich lady. I was nervous just walking up to her giant house for the interview, but then Gwendolyn and I played on the floor with Blair and she asked me about my childhood and my family. Gwendolyn offered me the job after twenty minutes, and then I stayed for two hours just to hang out and drink coffee with her while the baby napped. I knew she was my boss, but she felt like more of a friend. A really, really rich friend who bought me the skincare products I could never afford and took me along to all her fancy parties because her husband was always traveling for work or standing in his home office barking into a Bluetooth headset at someone in a different time zone. I was supposed to be watching Blair so Gwendolyn could have some free time, but instead, the three of us just hung out together. It was nice.

Here's where things changed: Blair's first birthday party. Gwendolyn had invited all of Blair's friends from her New Mom Group. We'd made a sheet cake and bought some juice and some party hats, and Gwendolyn had strung up one of those HAPPY BIRTHDAY signs made from the interlocking letters. We only had one *A*, so "birthday" was spelled "BIRTHD4Y." Close enough, right? Wrong! It was so not close enough. Because then Paisleigh's mom showed up and started asking things like "Does the juice have added sugar?" And "Is this cake made from a mix?" Which felt more like an accusation than a question. She wanted to know when the photographer would show up, and where the smash cake was.

Gwendolyn and I had no idea what a smash cake was, but we figured out later that it was apparently a small version of a birthday cake that you had made just so your baby could smash it into a pulp while your photographer took pictures. Gwendolyn didn't have a smash cake. She didn't have a hand-lettered birthday banner or a photo backdrop for the parents to pose their children for professional photos. She'd assumed that a first birthday party—which the baby would never remember—was, you know, just for fun.

"And what's the entertainment today?" one of the other mothers asked, and before Gwendolyn could totally lose it, I ran to the basement to rifle through Gwendolyn's storage closet. Five minutes later, I was back in the living room in one of Gwendolyn's old ball gowns, in full character as a Disney princess. The babies had, of course, not noticed, but the mothers were impressed, and cell phone photos were taken and uploaded to Facebook. Gwendolyn spent the entire next day scrolling and counting the likes and comments, which she read out loud to me. The moms called it a "throwback party" and apparently thought Gwendolyn now the coolest mom ever.

That Facebook attention was good for her self-esteem, but Pinterest was even better. I'd never heard of it, but Gwendolyn's husband had mentioned that there was this website that had just been blocked by IT at his work because his younger female employees were spending up to three hours a day on a website that was just . . . pictures? It pissed him off, but it also smelled like an opportunity, and he'd been an early investor. He never talked to Gwendolyn about business, but he did talk *around* her about business, and while he slurped down his dinner one night, standing at the kitchen counter, she overheard him shouting into his Bluetooth headset.

"It's crazy!" he said. "The referral traffic from this site is *absolutely insane*. It's where women go to create their dream lives. And once an image is on Pinterest, it's *everywhere*. This is the democratization of taste-making." He'd smacked his lips. "Anyone can be important now."

That night, Gwendolyn had signed up for an account. She'd stayed up until three AM, scrolling and pinning images to digital boards. Her husband was *right*, this was exactly like creating your dream life. Gwendolyn created boards for everything from the garden to the living room and filled them with beautiful images. It was addictive. And she wasn't alone. Sitting alone in the glow of her laptop, she watched her list of followers climb. A few dozen at first, and then a few hundred. By morning, she had ten thousand people following GwendolynJamesStyle.

At first it was a hobby. Then it was a habit. And then it was like a sickness that took over our life, and their house. Gwendolyn spent hours "curating" perfect boards of the ideal home, the ideal dinner menu. But the ideal Gwendolyn didn't just want to be sitting on her MacBook compiling inspirational photos posted by other women. She wanted to *be* the inspirational woman. She wanted to be making the perfect photos, the perfect homemade bread. She wanted dads to want her, and other moms to want to *be* her.

The problem, of course, was that she had no talent. Like, none. I mean, anyone can throw a pack of pizza rolls in the oven and call it dinner, but not everyone knows how to make kale look like more than just a pile of leaves. But I do. I learned it from my mother, who learned it from her mother. When you grow up poor, you learn how to make something out of nothing. That's why I could spend an hour every morning making dinosaurs out of fruit for Blair and Gandhi, or look into the fridge that Gwendolyn thought was "so empty" and pull together a decent meal for our dinner.

I'm not stupid. I knew that everything I did and wrote and made ended up on Gwendolyn's blog. I didn't care that Gwendolyn got all the attention, either. It was actually cute how nervous Gwendolyn was the first time a stranger had pointed her out in public. We'd been pushing Blair and Gandhi on the swings at the park when a mom who'd been staring at us from over by the slides walked over.

"I follow you!" she announced. "I'm, like, obsessed with you! Those fruit dinosaurs are incredible . . . so creative!" My ears had burned, but Gwendolyn had pretended as if nothing had happened. The moment passed, and a sort of understanding formed. G was the face, and I was the brains. That Friday, G handed me an envelope of cash. It was three times my weekly salary. And every week, the same envelope would appear. It was a good arrangement, until Gwendolyn turned into an asshole.

"Whatcha working on over there?"

I recognize the woman sitting on the couch next to me in the mother's lounge. She works at the spa, and I sometimes see her napping in here. Now, though, she's peering over at my laptop, which I've been staring at for the past three hours while Gwendolyn got acupuncture and a massage and then left without me so I could "buckle down" on writing *her* next eCourse. I don't even care about meditation, or motherhood!

"Oh, just . . . you know . . ." I trail off, shutting the laptop and rolling out my neck.

It's not like I've been waiting for the opportunity to rat G out, but when this spa lady asks me about my work, I can't stop talking. It's been a while since anyone asked about me. Since anyone has been interested in me. Even Gwendolyn, who used to tell me I was like the little sister she never had (she does, by the way, have a little sister), only talks to me when she needs me to make content or run her errands or get her a glass of lukewarm water with a pinch of Himalayan sea salt and a squeeze of lemon. I've been pretending to be Gwendolyn for so long that I forgot I even exist. But this Carla lady is nice, and she gave me a cold washcloth soaked in cucumber water to put over my eyes while I take a break from the screen. I lay down on the couch and breathe in the essential oils Carla is spritzing around me.

"Let me get this straight," she says after I've finally stopped talking. "Gwendolyn had been a regular mom, and other moms made her feel bad, so then she took your skills and used them to make other moms feel bad?"

I nod. That's pretty much it.

"One last question, and don't fucking lie to me, either. Did she put that pot in Jane Mitchell's locker?"

"Of course not!" I sit up, and the washcloth falls from my face. "Gwendolyn would *never* do something like that. She made me do it."

38

CARLA

Kiki's Bad Day Banana Bread is good, I'll give her that. But banana bread isn't going to put a bitch like Gwendolyn in her place. Actually, I take that back: a gluten-filled, dairy-filled slice of banana bread would probably destroy Gwendolyn.

I was hoping to kick in the front door at Amy's house for dramatic effect, but Kiki opened it before I had the chance. The house was a goddamn mess, but Amy and Kiki had been sitting in a clean kitchen having a Lifetime Movie moment together. I kid you not, they were each drinking a mug of herbal tea. I have never seen someone do that in real life. It was disturbing. Didn't these bitches know we had somewhere to be?

"Did you hear?" Amy asks, looking like a dog just waiting to be kicked again.

"Yeah, Amy. I heard. Everyone heard. Your life sucks. But

I know for a fact that it was Gwendolyn who had those drugs planted in Jane's locker."

Amy hesitates. She's clearly not as shocked by this as I am.

"What difference does it make?" she asks, and I want to shake her.

"It makes a huge difference! Gwendolyn is a psycho bitch and it's time to take her down. It's election night. Put down your hot grass water and put on a bra. Or—no, don't wear a bra. But do something with your hair."

Amy shakes her head and takes another sip of her weird tea.

"I'm out, Carla. I'm done."

I fucking *hate* quitters. Unless it's me who is quitting, in which case, get the fuck off my back. I hate when people like Amy quit. Because the world is filled with terrible, talentless idiots like Gwendolyn James who *never* quit, who just roll on through life, never second-guessing their place in the world. Amy can't *quit*. Quitting is for dads and kids with asthma.

"Who in their right mind would vote for me? My kids left me, my husband left me, my *dog* left me? I got fired! I'm a failure as a mother, a wife, and a professional."

I'll admit that she made a compelling argument, but I'm not done yet.

"Amy, I don't know shit about your job. I get my coffee at the gas station and, sometimes, I use a cup I find outside to claim a free refill. I'm not proud of that, but there, it's out there. You might be a failure as a wife, or a . . . whatever you do for a job. But as a mother? Hell no. You're the best mother I've ever fucking seen. No offense, Kiki. Amy, you make your kids eat salad. You compliment them and you mean it. You wait until they're asleep before you get high . . ."

Kiki raises her hand. "Carla, most moms do those things."

"Well, then most moms are fucking awesome. The point is, Amy. The only big fuckup you've made is that you quit trying. Moms don't get to quit. You know why?"

Kiki raises her hand again. "Because we have low self-worth and believe our value as a human is correlated with our willingness to suffer for those we love?"

"What? No. It's because we love our kids. We love those stupid, ungrateful, selfish little sponges, no matter how much of our money, time, energy, and food they take up. We love them so fucking much we'd do anything for them."

Amy rolls her head, cracking her neck audibly. "But I can't *win* the election, Carla!"

For someone who is allegedly smart, Amy is dumb as fuck. No wonder she got fired.

"A-my. This is not about winning. This is about standing up to the heinous bitch who fucked with your little girl. It's not about you winning. It's about the symbolism of you, rising up like Britney Spears post-2007. It's about you saying, 'Yeah, I lost everything, and shaved my head, and I fought someone with an umbrella. But I'm back, bitches. I'm here, and I'm going to secure a residency in Las Vegas and date a bunch of hot young backup dancers,' okay?" This is good stuff. Tony Robbins–level stuff. Dr. Phil–level stuff. I don't even know where it came from, but it keeps pouring out of me.

"Did Britney give up, Amy? Did she? I don't think she did. And if she were here today? I think she'd tell you that you need to stand up and fight. You need to fight on the playground. In the cafeteria. In the parking lot of a Trader Joe's. Because that's what women do, Amy. That's what *moms* do. We protect our young."

Amy is showing signs of life. *I'm getting through to her.* Kiki looks confused. I sometimes forget that she doesn't have a lot of cultural references outside of the Bible and whatever is on the PBS kids app.

"So, Amy. I'm asking you this: Will you come with us to the McKinley auditorium and body-slam this bitch or what?"

Amy nods, chugging the rest of her tea and slamming the mug down.

"Let's fucking do this."

39

PRINCIPAL BURR

I'd forgotten it was election night. I've gotten really good at selective blindness. I can walk through the school all day and not read a single flyer or poster. They all blend together into a cheap sort of wallpaper, and honestly, once you've seen one fifth grader's "Don't Do Drugs" poster, you've seen them all. That assignment makes me so uncomfortable. It's not that I want fifth graders doing drugs—I mean, Amy Mitchell's daughter is a wake-up call for all of us—I just think it's strange to make ten-year-olds sign a pledge saying that they'll *never* do any drugs. Ever? Not even when you're on the cusp of retirement and you find that a few puffs help ease the anxiety provoked by your wife's constant inflow of Amazon boxes? Not even when you're in college, and you're not really sure what it was that you smoked, but you do know that it made you feel like a superhero for at least an hour? Never is a big promise to make. It just seems like we're setting them up for failure.

"Oh, hello, Mr. Burr." The sound of Gwendolyn's voice gives me a physical reaction, like when you walk through someone's fart cloud in a hallway. I was barely out the front door, and she and her henchmoms were in formation on the front step, carrying posters and red, white, and blue bunting.

"How nice of you to offer to help us set up for the election," she simpers. "I do believe that tonight's win will make this the first three-peat victory in McKinley PTA history, is that right?"

She's right. I'd hoped that Amy Mitchell would be able to eke out a victory, or at least shake Gwendolyn's confidence, but it hasn't happened. I'm actually glad Amy hasn't shown up. It would be embarrassing to everyone to watch her lose after the school year she's had. Gwendolyn shoves a box of T-shirts emblazoned with her own signature into my arms.

"Here," she says, "make sure every mom in the crowd is wearing one of these."

THE McKINLEY ELECTION PROCESS IS SIMPLE: INTERESTED candidates are invited onstage to make their candidate statement. It's nothing formal—just a few words—and then the votes are cast. We used to count them by hand, but now they just text in their vote and we know instantly who the winner is. The last two elections have been a landslide. Last year, Gwendolyn got 97 percent of the vote, with 3 percent going to write-in candidates like "Did I do this right?" "How do I vote?" and "Is this working?"

This year, Gwendolyn didn't just bring T-shirts and bun-ting and posters. She brought her own lighting specialist, a pyrotechnics expert (a nice enough guy, named Jed, who as-sured me that indoor fireworks were the hot new thing), and a "glam squad." Her presentation, she reminded me, had been developed in partnership with her friends at TED. Before we took the stage, I saw her checking the crowd nervously. Was she searching for Amy? Had Mitchell gotten to her?

"Burr!" Gwendolyn barks the moment the clock strikes seven o'clock. "It's showtime. Let's go." A few parents are still streaming in—nothing starts on *time* in a school—but Gwen-dolyn gestures to her friends in the back, who slam the doors shut. "*Now*," she growls, and pushes me onto the stage.

40

KIKI

I told Kent that I was going to night church with my friends, and he bought it! He didn't look too pleased, but I reminded him that Bible study helps me feel closer to God, and being closer to God turns me on, and *that* seemed to work. It probably didn't hurt that the kids had already been fed and bathed, and the only thing he had to do was read stories and get them into bed.

"Don't be late," he said, kissing me on the cheek as I left.

I'd only just arrived at Amy's when he first texted me:

KENT: Where are the diapers??

I breathed deeply.

ME: Still in the twins' room.

ME: Right under their changing table.

Twenty minutes later:

KENT: Clara is hungry. Didn't u feed them?
ME: She can have a snack.

Thirty minutes later:

KENT: The twins are crying.
KENT: They want you.
KENT: Kiki??
ME: Poor babies! Tell them I love them and so does Jesus!
KENT: Now Clara is crying.

Carla was right: moms *don't* quit. We just keep going. A few months ago, every single person in our family got the flu at the same time. It was horrifying: as soon as one person was done puking, someone else would start. I puked in the washing machine when I was putting Bernard's sheets in the wash for the third time that day. You would think throwing up in the washing machine is easy, you just turn it on and wash it away. But it doesn't work that way. Little bits and pieces stay in the washer. Kent's undershirts are now a weird green-pink color. I never told him why. And I sometimes find half-digested corn in a pocket. Clara threw up in the bathtub while I was washing puke off her and the twins.

The only person who wasn't sick was Kent, and he spent the weekend at a hotel near his work, because he didn't want to risk being infected. At the time, I thought, *Yeah, that makes a lot of sense.* But looking back, I think, Wait, *does it?* Does it make sense to leave your wife, crawling on her hands and knees through a battleground of bodily fluids, just so you don't have to miss a day of work? It's worth noting that Kent isn't a brain surgeon or a rocket scientist. He works in insurance. Surely in a pinch they can manage a day or two without him.

I'd forgotten entirely about that weekend until this moment. Maybe it's Carla's driving. We've been careening around corners and through red lights, and there doesn't appear to be any safety belts in the backseat. I've been doing my best to stay upright, but I've been rolling around like a marble.

My phone buzzes again. It's my HONYDO app, with a reminder from Kent. He'll need his socks and underwear ironed tonight when I get home. It buzzes again. And he needs his lunch packed.

Carla catches my eye in the rearview mirror. "Everything okay back there, cupcake?" she asks.

My phone rings as Carla takes a hard left, and I slam against the right side of the car.

"Hi, honey!"

In the background, I can hear all four children screaming bloody murder. "Kiki? Kiki!" Kent is panicked.

"Is everything okay?"

"Not *really*. The kids are losing their s-h-i-SHIT! Bernard! Don't *bite*! Kiki, our kid is a biter!"

"Kent, I'm with my friends. You can't show weakness. Just tell them it's time for bed and get them in the routine: books, teeth brushed, bed. Done."

In the background, something falls to the ground. Probably Clara. She's not coordinated enough to climb onto the counters, but she doesn't let that stop her.

"Kiki, I need you home, now." I look in the rearview mirror and see Carla's eyes beaming their confidence into my skull. Amy is looking over her shoulder, giving me an encouraging look. I love these two women. They have my back. Shouldn't my *husband* have my back? I return my attention to my phone, which I hold in front of my face as I breathe in deeply.

"You *need* me home? I need *you* to fucking get your shit together, Kenton. You're a *dad*. Not a babysitter. These are *our* kids. So brush their teeth. Read to them. And get them the fuck to sleep. Because Mama's out for the night. BYE, BITCH!"

I hit the red button just as Carla hit the gas, and we speed through another red light.

MY PARENTS ALWAYS TOLD ME THAT EARLY IS ON TIME AND on time is late and late is unacceptable. Still, rules are rules and Carla is approaching the one-way on Sycamore as if it's a two-way. "Carla. Carla. CARLA!" Amy is screaming in the front seat, but Carla just grits her teeth and takes that forbidden left turn, ignoring the two DO NOT ENTER signs on either side of the road. We have just broken a serious rule of the road, but we've arrived with three minutes to spare, thanks in part to the fact that Carla pulls her car right onto the front lawn instead of checking the parking lot.

There are usually a few other stragglers sneaking in late to any school function, but tonight it's just the three of us, and it appears we have company. Gwendolyn's goons are standing outside the auditorium doors like security guards in Ann Taylor skirt suits.

"Sorry, ladies," one says, and I can tell she is not at all sorry. "Rules are rules."

Carla pushes by her, and, though it is completely unnecessary, kicks the door open.

"I object!" she screams, stumbling forward into the auditorium.

Every head in the room turns to face us, and the silence is replaced by a wave of murmurs. Onstage, Gwendolyn stares down at us with hate in her heart and fire in her eyes. That part might be the lighting. It's very intense.

"Yesssss," I hear someone whisper, and Carla grabs Amy and me by the hand and leads us up the center aisle toward the stage.

"Excuse me, bitches!" Carla screams. "The challenger has arrived!"

41

AMY

Principal Burr looks like someone just woke him up from a twenty-year nap. I'm suddenly very aware of how quiet the room is, and very aware that I should have at least sprayed some dry shampoo in my hair before we left. It feels like it takes a hundred years for us to reach the stage, where Gwendolyn is standing still as a statue, her face frozen in what she probably thinks is a smile.

Principal Burr scrambles back onstage to take the microphone from Gwendolyn.

"A-Amy Mitchell is here, everyone! Just in time for her candidate statement!"

He pushes the microphone into my sweaty, shaking hand. Candidate statement? What is that, a speech? God, I hate speeches. At least when I did one at my party, I had the comfort of drunkenness to calm my nerves. I really wish I'd smoked one of Jane's joints before getting here.

"*Actually*," Gwendolyn snips, leaning into me to speak into the mic, "she's *late* for her statement. We're on an agenda. Maybe next year?"

From below, I hear a voice call out "HELL NO!" Carla has somehow commandeered two front-row seats for her and Kiki, and she's standing on one of them.

"Let her *talk*, G!"

Shouts rise from around the room, and Gwendolyn primly holds up her hands in surrender.

"Okay," she purrs, "I am merely trying to uphold the standards of election decorum. Amy, you have the floor."

My heart is beating so loudly I'm *sure* the microphone can pick up on it.

"Hi," I say, and my voice does that weird froggy thing that happens when you *least* want it to. I cough a little bit. Below, I can feel Kiki beaming love at me from her big eyes.

"Hi, again. I'm Amy Mitchell. For now. I might go back to my maiden name, actually. Yeah, I'm getting divorced. You probably knew that. You know a lot of stuff about me. Or you think you do. Lotsa rumors going around this place, lately."

"Yeah!" Carla shouts.

"A lot of you probably think I'm a pretty bad mom," I continue, "and you know what? You're right. Sometimes, I'm crazy strict. I threw my son's iPad out a car window once because he'd snuck it in the car on a 'no screen day.'"

There's a smattering of laughter, and my shoulders relax by a few millimeters.

"Sometimes, I'm ridiculously lenient. One time? I let that *same kid* stay home because . . . get this . . . his thumb hurt. It was a video game injury."

More laughter.

"Sometimes I say stuff that's so crazy, I can't believe that I'm the one saying it. What works for my daughter never works for my son, and just when I think I have it figured out? They grow up just enough that we're not even playing the same ball game anymore. They're puzzles that I can't figure out. So, the truth is, when it comes to being a mom, I have no fucking clue what I'm doing. And you know what? I don't think anyone does. I think everyone in this room is a bad mom. And you know why? Because it's fucking impossible to be a good mom these days. My mom made it to maybe one soccer game, and I was a varsity all-star! And that was normal! Once, I was *late* for my daughter's soccer game and I got a text from another mom asking if I was planning on arriving or if she should call Child Protective Services."

A groan from the audience. But like, a good one?

"Can we stop that? Can we stop judging one another for like, five minutes, and all just admit that this shit is hard?! It's hard, and it all falls on us. This is the PTA, and we call it the Mom Squad I guess because Dads don't want to be here?"

Two lone male voices call out from the back, announcing their presence.

"That's Kevin and Chase, because of *course* gay dads are the exception. And that's messed up! The expectations for dads are beyond low. The bar is so low for them they can roll out of bed in sweatpants, feed the kids a granola bar on the walk to the bus, and be considered exceptional parents. And the standard for us is—what? Artisanal bake sales? Heck no. HELL no. We need dads to step the hell up. And maybe they would, if we expected them to. If we really shared the duties of parenting children equally."

For a moment I think I'm hallucinating, but I hear applause. Actual applause. The sound of hands contacting one another repeatedly.

"I just want our school to be a place where it's okay to make mistakes. For our kids to know that their value doesn't depend on their being perfect. And neither does *ours*. I want our school to be a place where it's okay to be a bad mom!"

It's quiet. Too quiet. Even Carla won't break this silence.

Suddenly, to my left, Mary McCloud stands up. She looks hesitant. But when she speaks, her voice is clear and confident.

"My kid hasn't had a bath in two weeks!"

"Good job!" I cheer. "What do you think butt wipes are for? Just butts?!"

The crowd laughs, and another mom shouts from the back. "I confiscated my teenager's weed, and then I smoked the shit out of it!"

I laugh. "Hell yeah you did!"

It keeps going, like a game of whack-a-mom—where you never know where the next confession would come from.

"I let my seven-year-old watch *Hellboy*!"

"I can't tell my twins apart!"

"I secretly got my tubes tied in Mexico on spring break, because if I have one more kid, I will absolutely snap!"

"I told my kids that if they're mean to me, I'm going to get cancer and die!"

Each confession is met with roars of applause, even the ones shouted in languages I don't understand. It could have gone on like that all night, but Principal Burr butted in with a one-minute warning. Oh shit. I need a strong finish here.

"The point is this: If you've got the whole motherhood thing down? You probably *should* vote for Gwendolyn. But if you're a bad mom like me and you have no fucking clue what you're doing, and you just want everyone to stop making you feel worse than you already feel about yourself? Vote for me."

42

PRINCIPAL BURR

I'm flabbergasted. I'm astounded. I'm witnessing history, here at McKinley. The numbers speak for themselves, but I still get to say the words.

"McKinley, please meet your new PTA president . . . Amy Mitchell!"

I haven't seen the moms this excited since *Fifty Shades of Grey* came out on video on demand.

Amy is stunned and hugs me like I cast the votes myself (I assure you, I did not).

Then every mom is hugging me, including Jaxon's mom, who holds on a little *too* long. Long enough that I feel like I should tell Jan about it when I get home. She's not going to love knowing that another woman pressed her body against mine for over five seconds, but she's going to love that I have something new to talk about. Something *good*.

43

AMY

I'd stepped onto that stage ready to eat a big slice of humble pie. Ready to just lay down my sword and give up. But something else happened. Right between the woman confessing to us that she tells her kids that church is a "no-kid zone" just to have an hour alone and some woman yelling for a solid minute in what I can only assume was Russian. It was what Oprah calls an "Aha! Moment," when the clouds part and the light-bulb lights and the math problems all make sense and you hit every green light on the way to work. I didn't have anything to own up to or apologize for. I wasn't a bad mom. I'm not a bad mom. And neither are these moms. I'm a normal mom. I'm just a mom. Every woman in that room had gone from nursing a baby (or bottle-feeding and feeling like shit about it because of . . . other moms) to nursing a host of insecurities about her role as a parent. Who do we blame when other people's kids are messed up? The mom. And who do we blame for our problems when we're all grown up? *Our* moms!

When Jane gave my journal back, I spent the night reading through it. I was a very careful recordkeeper as a kid, and the details were astounding and sometimes very, very boring. I realized that I kept track of my own grades to be able to double-check my teacher's calculations at report card time. I idolized my mom for her successful career, and I resented her for not giving me 110 percent of her attention. I wrote a three-page diary entry about how my mom was the Worst Mom Ever, because after coming home from a four-day business trip she didn't want to walk in the front door and immediately drive me to the mall so I could buy a Fiona Apple CD. The first semester of middle school, I made the honor roll. I was thrilled with myself, until my mom pointed out that next semester I could aim for the *High* Honor Roll.

I remember myself as a soccer champion, but that journal led me into a serious nostalgia rabbit hole, and I dug out old yearbooks and notebooks. My fifth-grade behavior report said I shoved Andrew Kelleher's face into the drinking fountain after he beat me in badminton in gym class and chipped his front tooth. My senior yearbook is filled with inscriptions of every time I lost my shit after our team lost a soccer game.

"Hey Amy! Never forget when you kicked the game ball over the train tracks after we lost to Cooper! C/M! LYLAS!"

"Amy, remember when you called the Henry coach a bitch and got a two-game ban? You're crazy. Never change."

All those stories are true, and even though I don't regret

kicking that ball over the train tracks, I'm not proud of how I acted when I lost, or how I acted in general. I took all the things I resented about my mom and did the exact same things to my own girl and resented my mom in the same way that Jane now resents me. And then I perpetuated a whole system of motherhood that is based on competition and comparison. A system that had affected every single woman in that room. It's a mom-shaped snake eating its own tail.

And we are all so, so tired of it. That was enough for me, truly. It was enough to just feel, for a few minutes, like I was enough.

And then the numbers came in. The screen behind me illuminated. It was time to vote. The projector showed the kind of setup you'd see on CNN: on the left side of the screen, a professional headshot of Gwendolyn, pretending to brush the hair out of her eyes while looking just beyond the camera. On the right, a photo of me that must have been pulled from Google Images circa 2009. When was the last time I had bangs? And why was it so pixelated? Under each photo, the election results ticked away in real-time, as moms texted in their votes. It looked high-tech and expensive, like something Gwendolyn would have "donated" to the school to assure her win. But as the numbers rolled in, they only rolled in under *my* photo. It was *my* number climbing and climbing. I was going to win?

Gwendolyn had been looming behind me like a Trump to my Hillary. I had taken the stage with sweaty hands and shaking knees and felt her eyes boring holes in my skull the moment the microphone left her hands.

I don't know when Gwendolyn left the stage or the building. I just know that when the numbers stopped moving, when the very final count came in, I had 95 percent of the vote.

Self-actualization is great and all, but damn, it feels good to win.

44

CARLA

"Excuse me, Mrs. Dunkler?" A deep male voice booms behind me, but I know better than to admit my identity to a stranger. Besides, Amy and Kiki and I are celebrating Amy's historic victory. Kiki had apparently spent the afternoon cutting her junk mail into what I can only assume she meant to be confetti and is throwing handfuls of shredded credit card offers into the air with glee. Amy was mobbed by a bunch of desperate moms ready to pledge their undying loyalty to her, and I am obviously her bodyguard, trying to make sure they couldn't get their sad all over her.

"Mrs. Dunkler?" The voice is attached to a hand, strong and warm, and the hand touches my shoulder. Instinct kicks in, and I dip into a low squat, lunge forward, and thrust my elbow back into my attacker's belly.

"Carla!" Kiki screams. "You killed him!"

I HAVEN'T *KILLED* ANYONE. NOT TONIGHT AT LEAST. BUT I have just knocked the wind out of Mr. Nolan, who is gasping for air on the floor like one of Bernard's betta fish, which we all know he kills on purpose. Even with a limited supply of oxygen, Mr. Nolan is, objectively, a fine piece of meat. A fine piece of meat who needs to learn some fucking manners. "What the fuck." I sigh, offering him my hand and pulling him to his feet. "You can't just creep up behind a woman and expect not to get the shit kicked out of you."

Mr. Nolan coughs, his deep brown eyes welled with involuntary tears. "I needed to talk with you about something," he chokes out.

"Look, we were in kind of a hurry. I'll move my car off the lawn when we're done here, relax."

Mr. Nolan shakes his head.

"No," he struggles to reply, "it's about Jaxon."

THESE PAST FEW WEEKS, I'D FORGOTTEN ABOUT KINDERGAR-ten and Mrs. Fagnani and all the bullshit that kept me from showing up for my kid. I'd let myself think that I fit in here, with Kiki and Amy. I let myself think that where I came from didn't matter, that I could find a place here, the way that Jaxon had. And now this guy was trying to tell me that me and my boy didn't belong. That a little bit of assistance on his summer essay was proof that we were both trash that belonged at Clifton.

MR. NOLAN IS STILL STANDING THERE, RUBBING HIS BELLY.

"Mrs. Dunkler," he asks, "do you have a moment?"

Kiki and Amy have moved on from the scene I'd caused, and are chatting excitedly, holding each other's hands like they're about to do "Ring Around the Rosie."

I cross my arms and crack my neck, getting ready to face the music. I stare Mr. Nolan right in his beautiful eyes. Damn, he's even hotter than his yearbook picture from last year.

"What is it?" I bark, and he digs a piece of paper out of his stupid, handsome shoulder bag.

"I think you need to read this," he croaks. "It's Jaxon's first essay of the year."

"Is there a problem?" I ask him, faking confusion. I knew exactly what Jaxon's essay said. I had written it the night before school started. Besides, I was pretty sure we were going to have an election after-party and talking about school was already ruining my buzz.

Mr. Nolan shakes his head. "Just read it," he says with his gentle smile.

"Fine," I say, snatching the crumpled loose-leaf out of his hand.

What I Did on My Summer Vacation

By Jaxon Dunkler

Other kids might think that my summer was boring. We don't have a lake house we go to, and I didn't go to Six Flags or to Europe or even to Wisconsin. We didn't go anywhere this summer, and that's why it was so great.

My mom is always busy. Ever since I can remember, she's worked really hard. She always feels bad about it, but I really don't mind. I get to eat all the pizza rolls my-self, and I don't have to watch any of those shows where rich women are always arguing at a dinner table. She loves those. My mom probably doesn't know that, but I'm glad she works a lot, because it taught me how to work hard, too.

The only reason I get to play traveling baseball is be-cause my mom works so hard to make sure we can afford the registration fees. It's not much to some families, but it's a lot to our family. She could use that money to get a new car, or to take more karate lessons. But instead, she uses it to make sure I can play baseball, even though she can't come to any games. I think she feels bad about that, too, but the only moms who can sit through four hours of base-ball a night are the moms who don't have to work, or the moms who can work on their laptops when we go into ex-tra innings. My mom can't wax vaginas in the stands. Well, she probably could. I bet the dads would love that.

While Mom was at work, I went outside to practice my pitch. I did sprints up and down the block. I'm a big guy, so it's not easy, and when it was hard, I remembered that as hard as I was working, so was my mom.

This doesn't sound like a fun summer, does it? But the best part about summer is that my mom gets home earlier. Or, maybe not earlier, but that the sun is still out. Sometimes, she'd stop for takeout on the way home, and we'd eat greasy chicken with our fingers, and sit on the front porch. She'd tell me stories about her life growing up, about how she and her mom were always running from

one city to the next because Gramma was *sure* that life
would be better somewhere else. It made me feel lucky
that I've lived in the same little house for so long.

Also, I played a lot of Fortnite. That was cool.

Mr. Nolan is still looking at me when I finish the essay. I
don't bother trying to pretend I'm not crying. My little buddy
wrote *this*?

"He's a good kid, Mrs. Dunkler."

"Ms.—and no shit he's a good kid."

Mr. Nolan opens his shoulder bag again and pulls out a
handkerchief. Not a dirty old Kleenex. A real handkerchief. Is
he a ghost from the past or something? I take it and wipe the
mascara trails from my cheeks.

"Well," he says, looking around us as if anything interesting is happening in the school auditorium on a weeknight, "I
guess I'll see you around?"

Is he . . . nervous? Does he want to take a dunk in the
Dunkler?

I smile at him. "Yeah, I'll be in touch to schedule one of
those after-hours conferences you were talking about."

He blushes.

"So you *did* get my letter."

Shit.

AMY AND KIKI AND I STAY UNTIL THE LAST MOM LEAVES THE
auditorium, sitting in a small circle on the stage I've been
avoiding since Jaxon puked during his kindergarten concert

because he ate too many cheesy gorditas in the car on the way here. It's quiet—really quiet—the kind of quiet that would make you uncomfortable with anybody other than the people who really, truly *get* you.

"Guys?" Kiki whispers. "I'm so glad we're friends."

My first instinct is to say something sarcastic, but I can't. Because I'm glad we're friends, too. And we *are* friends. I'm *friends* with a superhot cool mom and this geeky little weirdo mom. For the past twelve years, I've been a mom, a wife, a divorcée, an overworked and underpaid boss, a daughter . . . and that's it. Have I been a friend? Or had one? When did "friend" fall off my list of titles? It's not like I was totally *friendless*, I had lots of women to hit the club with or grab a drink with. I just didn't have friends like *this*. When you're younger, friends are your everything. And then when you're a mom, friendship goes from being a pillar of life to, I don't know, a random board just nailed onto something else.

Adult friendships are hard. Or, being a friend and an adult is hard. Being a friend and a MOM is hard. I think that's why so many women say their husband is their best friend. Saying that is easier than acknowledging that once we're moms, we're usually forced into friendships with the moms of our kids' friends, who might suck.

But Kiki and Amy are just . . . my people. They are in no way the kind of people I would have picked out of a lineup, but they're the best damn friends I've ever had.

——————

To: Amy Mitchell
From: Tracy
Subject: WHAT HAVE YOU DONE

Amy,

Nobody has heard from Gwendolyn since the election last night. Her calls go straight to voicemail. Given your ostentatious victory last night, it seems very suspicious. As Gwendolyn James's Best Friend, I feel it is my duty to defend her. I will of course file for a re-count with the election committee. But do I need to call the cops??

Xoxo,
Tracy

45

AMY

Gwendolyn James is not missing. I know exactly where she is, and what she's doing. Gwendolyn James is on my couch, wrapped in the quilt my mom had made from Mike's favorite band T-shirts.

CARLA, KIKI, AND I WERE THE LAST TO LEAVE McKINLEY. AF-ter ten PM, the custodial crew started turning off the lights and locking up, and we moved our party of three to the front stairs. It was a crisp night, but my heart was still racing from our victory and I couldn't feel anything but the warm glow of happiness inside me. When had I last felt like that?

"At the risk of sounding like a fucking Lifetime movie," Carla said, fishing in her bag for her keys, "I fucking love the two of you."

"I've loved you since the day we *met*!" Kiki squealed, pulling us both in for a hug.

The car was still parked on the front lawn. There were a few tread marks on the sidewalk, but otherwise, Carla's *Fast & Furious*–style driving hadn't left a mark on McKinley's perfectly manicured landscaping.

Kiki was squeezing into the backseat when I saw two headlights glowing in the parking lot. We weren't alone.

I shut the door on Kiki and leaned down into the passenger side window. "You guys go ahead, I'll get a taxi home."

"Oh, we don't mind waiting AT ALL," yammered Kiki. "I'm perfectly fine staying out as late as we need to."

Carla shot me a knowing look and shifted into reverse, revving her engine. "Later, Aims," she called out, as she powered off the lawn and into the street, Kiki screeching in terror in the backseat.

I WAS THE LAST PERSON THAT GWENDOLYN JAMES WANTED to see. I knew this because that's exactly what she said when she rolled down the window of her Model X (the only SUV she could consciously purchase, and one that happened to also be the most expensive available). For someone who didn't want to see me, she still kept her window rolled down, so I knew she didn't mean it.

For a moment I thought I'd walked up to the wrong car, that maybe there was another blond mom driving a white Model X with a license plate that says GWNJAMES. I'd never seen Gwendolyn look so . . . human. Underneath all the no-makeup makeup, with her pale, blotchy skin exposed? She looked like any other mom who'd had a bad day.

"Did you come to gloat?" She snickered, examining her face in her rearview mirror.

I *had* spent an unhealthy amount of time imagining my next interaction with Gwendolyn. I'd fallen asleep the past few nights running through imaginary conversations where I took Gwendolyn James down a peg or ten, where I looked her in her beautiful sapphire eyes and let her know what a cold, heart-less bitch she was for trying to ruin Jane's life. In these fanta-sies, Gwendolyn would remain aloof and frozen, completely shocked at my audacity. She wouldn't blink an eye, but I'd know that even getting a word in was a win. Even tonight, as the results were tallied, I'd thought about how great it would be to rub this victory right in her unlined, blemish-free face.

Gwendolyn turned from her reflection and looked me in the eye. One eyelash extension hung from the corner of her right eye. *I knew they weren't real.* A day ago, I'd have taken this information and cataloged it as Things to Gleefully Tell Carla and Kiki Later.

"I came to see if you were okay," I said, surprising myself. For all the time I spent imagining rubbing this victory in her smug face, I actually meant what I was saying.

Gwendolyn laughed. "I'm *fine*. It's allergy season, and I don't have my essential oils with me, so—"

I slowly reached my hand in through her car window and up to that loose eyelash extension. I felt like I was sticking my hand into a lion's cage, but Gwendolyn stayed there, still, as I brushed that eyelash extension from the corner of her eye. It clung to my pointer finger, which I offered gently to Gwendo-lyn. She looked at me like I had lost my mind.

"Make a *wish*!" I encouraged her. "Didn't your mom teach you to do that when you lose an eyelash?"

To be perfectly frank, I wasn't sure if the wish rules in-cluded eyelash *extensions*, but I was trying to be nice. I ex-pected to be thoroughly berated, but instead, she laughed, closed her eyes, and blew the eyelash extension from the tip of my finger before she blinked her eyes open.

"Nope. You're still here."

There's the Gwendolyn I was looking for! My blood pres-sure spiked, and my brain switched on. What was the thing I was going to say to her? The thing that was going to fully put her in her place? I was gearing up to lose my shit when Gwen-dolyn beat me to it.

"You know what, Amy?" she said through clenched teeth. "To answer your original question . . . no, I am not okay. Not even close. This"—she gestured toward McKinley, as if it were her kingdom, which . . . I guess it kind of is—"this was the last good thing I had in my life. And now that's gone, too."

My eyes rolled so hard they nearly dislocated themselves.

"Really, Gwendolyn? That's the last good thing in your life? Your life is PERFECT. Do you even follow yourself on Instagram? This is one stupid little election, you've got like, three boats!"

"I have four boats," she corrected me, "and who gives a shit? Now get in." I got in before she could change her mind. It was freezing out, and I instantly relaxed into her heated seats.

THERE'S SOMETHING ABOUT A CAR RIDE THAT MAKES IT EAS-
ier to share your deepest, darkest secrets with someone. Maybe
it's the proximity and the lack of eye contact? The fact that the
doors are locked, and that the conversation can only last until
your destination is reached?

I barely had time to buckle my seatbelt when Gwendolyn
unloaded on me.

"You know, Amy. I really did like your speech tonight.
You made a lot of really salient points."

I did? I mean, hell yeah I did, I won the election!

"It's hard to be a mom," she said. "It's hard for me,
too, Amy."

I know she's right. I know that not everything that shines
on Instagram is going to be gold. But what I don't know is
why she's telling me this.

"Don't you wonder how I found out about you and Mike?"
she asked, and I shook my head.

"I don't know, I just figured that your little gossipmongers
told you."

"Where do you think *my* husband is, Amy? He's shacked
up in the same hotel as Mike."

That surprised me. Her husband—and I have no idea what
his name is because she always refers to him as "my husband"
as if that's what is printed on his birth certificate—seemed as
perfect as the rest of her life.

"Yeah, that's right. He's in love with his high school girlfriend. Isn't that cute? And all of the money he invested in his
Northern California weed farms is going to finance their new
life together 'off the grid' whatever the *fuck* that means."

"Okay, that is not good," I said, trying not to sound freaked out. Could it possibly be that Gwendolyn and I were more alike than we were different? Could this be a goddamn *lesson* for *me*? We were on my block, finally. And even though I've envied Gwendolyn's walk-in pantry and her high-end seasonal décor, I had a full and new appreciation for my own cozy neighborhood. I loved the bikes lying in every front yard, and the sagging front porches that are decorated year-round with Christmas lights. My own flickering porch light, which I've been meaning to replace for years, was now a beacon of hope in this bizarre conversation in my enemy's car.

Gwendolyn silently pulled into my driveway, her car proudly announcing to us that we had arrived at our destination. I could tell Gwendolyn wasn't done talking, that I uncorked something inside her that wasn't ready to stop flowing. So even though I just wanted to go inside, put on some sweatpants, and fall asleep watching Netflix, I did something I never thought I'd do.

I invited Gwendolyn James into my home.

"CAN I ASK WHERE YOU GOT THIS?" GWENDOLYN SAYS, SINK-ing into the worn cushions and pulling one of my old afghans over herself. "Please don't tell me it's custom, I have to have one just like it."

"It's from a little shop called IKEA," I say like a TV host. "You might be able to get them to make one for you, too."

"No kidding?" She sighs, rubbing the sleep from her eyes.

Gwendolyn is wearing one of Mike's hoodies and a pair of

my old sweatpants, her blond hair piled into a messy bun on top of her head. We've spent the better part of the night sitting on opposite sides of the couch, our legs tucked under a pile of throw blankets and pillows, drinking some herbal tea that I'm sure she was judging for not being artisanal.

For all the revenge fantasies I played out in my head, none of them involved Gwendolyn James weeping on my couch about her life, begging my forgiveness for what she'd done to Jane. None of them involved me tucking Gwendolyn in on my beat-up IKEA couch after she'd cried herself to sleep. And none of them involved me gently shaking her awake the next morning so she could provide proof of life to the other McKinley moms.

Gwendolyn picks up her phone and scrolls through her notifications.

"Christ," she says, sighing and patting the space on the couch next to her. "Come here, Mitchell."

I settle in, handing Gwendolyn her coffee, and she lifts her phone up, tilting her head toward mine. Our sleep-lined faces fill her screen, and Gwendolyn smiles.

"Say 'bad moms'!" she whispers, and pushes the red button.

PART III
WINTER

46

AMY

Aside from the recent delivery of a small cardboard box filled with framed photos, half-used pens, and about two dozen lipsticks and lip glosses that had been at my desk during my time at CoCo, I haven't thought of my old job since I was fired/quit. I have been very busy embracing my new life as an unemployed single mom. Mike and I are in mediation, and we all do family therapy together, so the kids are learning how to identify and process their feelings, which, it turns out, is something that Mike and I also need to learn. Jane asked for her own (leather-bound, monogrammed, college-ruled) journal for Christmas, and I gave her four, because I know she's going to fill them. I swear I don't read them while she's at Mike's apartment (okay, I sometimes do).

I'm not going to act like divorce was the answer to all my problems and now life is *perfect*. Sometimes I miss Mike, and the encyclopedic way he knows me. But that's just sometimes. Mostly, my life involves exciting things like comparing the price per unit of the generic vs. brand-name toilet paper at Target. That's where I am, stocking up on two-ply, when my phone rings.

Dale? Obviously a butt dial.

I answer anyway.

"Hello?" It isn't silence, or the telltale rustling of a butt dial; it's pandemonium, like when you call Kiki right before naptime.

"Dale? DALE."

"Amy! Oh, Amy, thank God. I need you to come back." His voice is desperate, and when he catches his breath, I listen to at least twenty straight minutes of apologies.

BY THE TIME I REACH THE CHECKOUT LINE, I AM THE PROUD new CMO of Coffee Collective, making enough money to pay the mortgage on my own, and with a schedule that includes time for me to be a mom, and a person. Speaking of which, I *am* still a person, aren't I?

ME: Have you ever slept with a Boss?

JESSE: Like, my own boss? Have you seen him?

JESSE: Do you want to?

ME: No, idiot. We've got 2 hours till pickup.

JESSE: I don't know, I have some pretty cool meetings this afternoon . . .

JESSE: YES. YES. YES.

To: McKinley PTA
From: Amy Mitchell
CC: Principal Burr; McKinley Staff
Subject: WHOOPSY!

Hey there,

Amy Mitchell here, reporting for duty. Sorry I have been MIA. I tried to log in to this email address using my usual password (my dog's name and my birthday, please don't steal my identity), but I had my birthday wrong. My OWN BIRTHDAY. I got locked out like a doofus and then the holidays happened, and things got a little away from me. Anyway, shoutout to the parents and teachers who still figured out how to make the concert happen and how to arrange a non-denominational solstice gift exchange. Turns out you might not *need* me, but too bad because I'm back and ready to associate the FUDGE out of our parents and teachers!

Do you regret electing me yet?

To: McKinley PTA
From: Mike Mitchell
Subject: RE: WHOOPSY!

I went to the wrong school for pickup yesterday. I waited for 20 minutes outside a school our kids have never even attended before I realized where I was. So, I think you're pretty great.

To: Mike Mitchell
From: Amy Mitchell
Subject: RE: RE: WHOOPSY!

Mike! You REPLIED ALL!

To: McKinley PTA
From: Jan McManus
Subject: RE: RE: RE: WHOOPSY!

I forgot my son's name last night. I called him Jack (my husband), Boomer (our dog), Lindsay (his sister), and then . . . just ran out of options and stared at him, blankly.

To: McKinley PTA
From: Carl Thorpe
Subject: RE: RE: RE: RE: WHOOPSY!

My kids ate their cereal with coffee creamer today because we ran out of milk.

To: McKinley PTA
From: Kent
Subject: RE: RE: RE: RE: RE: WHOOPSY!

I threatened to throw all the LEGOs in the recycling this morning.

To: McKinley PTA
From: Amy Mitchell
Subject: RE: RE: RE: RE: RE: RE: WHOOPSY!

Okay! Sounds like we're all on the same page here. I am honored to be your deeply flawed leader. I am also relieved to know that we are a band of fools just doing our best, and I'm hoping we can all figure out this parenting thing together.

I want to start by saying, if you don't have time to give to the PTA, THAT IS OKAY! This is a completely optional part of parenthood, and if the only thing you can handle right now is making sure your kid gets to school, well, okay. Because sometimes even that is hard (anyone else have a child that basically morphs into a sloth as soon as it's time to get in the car?).

And if you want to spend all your time helping? GREAT! Get in where you fit in, give what you can, and don't stress too much. Our kids are going to be fine whether or not we help them launch a rocket into space, and it's okay if their pizza rolls aren't organic.

If you have questions or comments, let me know. I'm only checking this email address on Thursdays, so I'll get back to you then.

Xo,
Amy Mitchell

GWENDOLYN JAMES STYLE

Farewell, Friends!

Beautiful Readers:

Thank you for your many years of support here at Gwendolyn James Style. I've so loved walking the journey of motherhood alongside all of you. Alas, all good things must come to an end, and that includes my blogging career.

I'm going to be spending some time offline, reconnecting with my true essence and reassessing my priorities. If you're looking for a new source of inspiration, follow my friend Oska over at her brand-new blog.

In Love and Light and Great Style,
Gwendolyn James

PART IV
SPRING

47

CARLA

I packed for a weekend away. You never know how long a baseball game is going to take, or where the weather will go in the Midwest. I bought one of those foldy chairs that the other moms are always sitting in, one with a little canopy above it in case it rains or if it's too sunny. It has an oversize cup holder, too, so it'll fit my giant gas station soda (or a forty if it turns into that kinda night).

I found a cooler in the back of the garage, and once I wiped all the spider eggs off it and gave it a rinse in the shower, it was good as . . . not new, but as good as anything you could find on the side of the road. I packed three red Gatorades, two Diet Mountain Dews, and some of those baby carrots that look like orange amputated fingers. You know, some healthy shit. I also got a few beef and cheddars because protein is a necessary part of any kid's diet and if Jaxon sweats a lot, he might need some extra sodium.

IT TOOK FORTY-EIGHT MINUTES TO GET TO THE FIELD. I crawled through traffic, watching the clock tick closer and closer to game time. Who were all these fuckers in their cars at five PM and why were they driving the exact same direction as me? I had forgotten about this part. Baseball isn't just a few hours watching a bunch of kids stand around a big field of dirt and grass grabbing at their nuts; it's all that *after* a long-ass drive to some godforsaken suburb that has a law against open containers in public parks.

The minute Jaxon was old enough to ride the team bus, I shoved him on it and claimed that drive time as Carla Time. It was almost ten extra hours a week to do whatever the hell I felt like, and you know what I never felt like? Sitting through several hours of a sport where basically nothing happens.

Tonight is a surprise for Jaxon. My mom was *always* promising to show up to shit. Then I'd sit there like a dipshit looking through the crowd for her like she'd actually *show*. I've been under-promising and under-delivering to Jaxon his whole life, but now I'm trying to under-promise and *over*-deliver. This morning, I'd seen him off to school like I always do. Well, sort of like I always do. We didn't go to the Arby's drive-thru, and we weren't running late. I'd gotten up early to wake him up, and we'd eaten breakfast together. I packed him a lunch— Kiki printed out a bunch of shit from the Internet about kale, so I jammed a bunch of it in a sandwich—and I dropped him off ten minutes before the bell rang. It's weird, but weird is kinda normal for us now.

It's been a weird couple of months. And not just for us. At drop-off, nearly every mom I see is still in her pajamas, drinking coffee from a regular mug, her greasy hair in a messy bun. But there aren't as many moms as usual. There are tons of *dads*, bewildered and asking one another for directions to their kids' classrooms, negotiating tantrums, wrestling little ones out of their car seats, and generally looking like they could puke at any minute. Now I can barely even pick Hot Jesse out of the crowd, because there are so many men wearing Elsa backpacks wandering the sidewalks. It's been awesome.

THE OTHER BASEBALL MOMS ARE USUALLY HERE ABOUT forty minutes early, before the team even arrives. They use that time to manicure the field (I think that means cleaning up any cigarette butts left behind by the beer league softball teams), to set up the "hydration station" for the players (apparently *water* isn't descriptive enough), and to set up their own little pad for helicopter parenting. Dads arrive somewhere between the first and third innings, to find their seats ready and waiting, with an array of snacks and beverages for them to choose from.

Weirdly, *I'm* the first mom to arrive, just ten minutes before game time. Am I even at the right place? I choose the perfect spot to watch the game: close enough to our team's bench to look like I give a shit about team spirit and far enough away that the other parents can't easily engage me in conversation. The team is winding down warm-ups (a lot of standing around, with small bits of running and catching in between) when I finish setting up my little Dunklerville. I'm just about to crack my first Diet Mountain Dew of the night when Jaxon comes barreling over, grinning like a golden retriever.

"You're here?!" he screams, throwing his arms around me so hard I hear my back pop a little bit. "Are you staying the whole game?"

Uh, look around you, kid. I could stay the entire week if it comes to extra innings. "Yeah, of course I am," I say, squeezing him back. "Duh, I fucking love you, ya dummy."

He is still hugging me when the whistle blows.

"Dunkler!" his coach shouts. "Get over here, it's game time!"

I watch Jaxon jog back over to the bench for a couple hours of standing around. God, I wish I'd brought something harder than Mountain Dew. To my left, I can see a pair of khaki legs about to step into my view and I swear to *God above* if I came all this way just to get in a physical altercation—

"Excuse me? Ms. Dunkler?" It's Mr. Nolan. He's wearing a T-shirt and a baseball hat and I gotta say, it's pretty hot.

"What's up, Nolan?" I say, trying to be breezy and casual. "You gonna take a seat or what?"

I scoot over to make room for him, but he laughs.

"I'm the assistant coach. I guess we'll have to schedule a one-on-one after the game?" He squats down next to me, and his knees don't even crack. "In case I'm not being clear," he says, looking right into my eyes, "in three weeks I will no longer be Jaxon's teacher and I would like to take you on a date."

"Hell yeah," I say, and watch his cute ass jog over to the bench.

48

KIKI

My HNYDO app is long gone from my phone. Kent and I had a long talk after the election, and he agreed to revisit the breakdown of work duties in our home. We used some of the same analysis tools he uses at work and, it turns out, all my unpaid labor was worth more than Kenton's yearly salary, even with bonuses! He's been folding his own socks and packing lunches ever since. Plus, I take every Saturday morning off to get a special coffee with the girls. That's what I call Amy and Carla now. Isn't that cute?

"OH MY GOD, DID YOU GET FIRED?!"

Kent arrives at exactly 5:36 every single day, 5:34 if he hits green lights on Douglas Avenue. He does not, ever, under any circumstances, come home at 1:27 PM. There is just one possible explanation: he's lost his job, and now we're going to lose our house, our minivan, and all our dreams. On the upside, if we end up living in a two-bedroom apartment, I'll at least have less space to clean. And if the kids all share a bed, that's a lot less laundry, too. It's been thirty seconds since Kent walked in the door and I've already settled into our new way of life, taking a night job to make ends meet while Kent struggles to find gainful employment during the day, serving the kids regular milk instead of organic.

Kent hangs his coat on his special hanger in our coat closet and puts on his indoor shoes, just like Mister Rogers always did. "I just wanted to come home and see my beautiful wife and my darling children," he says. "Where are they?"

"They're *napping*, Kenton. You know the schedule."

Kent smiles at me, the kind of smile he uses only on Friday nights. He can't be serious. It's daylight, and as an unspoken rule we only ever have sex in total darkness.

Kent is totally serious. He is kiss-me-on-the-lips serious. He pulls my sweatshirt over my head and runs his hands down my body, unhooking my nursing bra—*why am I still wearing this???*—and grabbing my boobs like he used to in college. I step back, just to make sure that this *is* Kent and not some sort of sexy intruder.

"I canceled my afternoon meetings," he explains. "My team can handle a few hours on their own. Plus, I thought you might like the afternoon off from kid duty."

I would absolutely like the afternoon off from kid duty, but this is also the sexiest thing I've ever heard in my gosh-darn life.

"I'd love the afternoon off," I say in a voice that I hope sounds sexy, "but first, I'd like to spend some time on . . . you." That's sexy, right?

Kent smiles and pulls me closer, kissing me on the mouth *with tongue*. We fumble our way to the couch, where Kent knocks off the layer of toys with one sexy sweep of his hand, pulling me down on top of him. Instinctively, I grind my hips into him. Usually, it's like rubbing myself against a half-filled water balloon. But, this time, there's something hard there. Like, actually hard. Like, a hard penis? Kent moans, breaking our other unspoken rule that we have sex very, very quietly. I unbutton his wrinkle-resistant oxford and pull his crisp white undershirt over his head. I'm just about to stand up and fold them before we really get down to business, but Kent stops me.

"Who cares?" he whispers, sliding his thumbs under the band of my Costco underpants.

I sigh. Groan? I'm about to have sex in the light of day. This is now my ultimate, number one fantasy, way ahead of me getting hit by a car and experiencing some light paralysis.

"Kiki?" Kent says, pulling down my yoga pants. "In case it's not clear? I want to clearly express that I appreciate you as a partner."

"That's great, honey," I reply, pushing my hips up to meet his, "but naptime's almost over so let's get this show on the road."

49

THE BAD MOMS PLEDGE

I, _____, agree to the following terms and conditions of Motherhood, which are inevitable and irrevocable. This pledge is not legally binding, but it is *karmically* binding. Probably.

We run late. Sometimes very late. Look, if we say we're on the way we haven't left the house yet and that *has* to be okay, because getting out of the house is hard enough on your own but when your kid forgets his backpack *every single day*? We're trying here.

We let teachers teach and coaches coach. If you're thinking about being a dipwad about this . . . don't.

Childhood is a series of failures meant to prepare our children for life. We let our kids fail, and we let them pick themselves back up.

Motherhood is a no-judgment zone, and we hereby reserve all judgment for people participating in reality TV. Joking! We judge each other all the time because we're still struggling to de-program ourselves from generations of patriarchy! But we judge ourselves most harshly, and we gotta cut that crap out, too.

On our worst days, we are sure we have no idea what we're doing. Guess what? We don't! But our kids probably don't know that. They love us anyway, even though they've spent most of their lives with the same view of us as a front-facing phone camera we didn't know was on.

We're not just moms. We're Cool Moms and Earth Moms and Attachment Moms and Detachment Moms. We're Weird Moms and Old Moms and Young Moms and Single Moms. We're Gluten-Free Moms and Short Moms and Funny Moms and Gay Moms and Tall Moms and Sleepy Moms.

We are the forgetful Tooth Fairy, the life-makers and gift-givers. We're the owie-kissers and the snack providers and the butt-wipers. Some days, we're a walking Kleenex.

We're Bad Moms. Which is the only damn kind of mom worth being.

Signature and Date _____

AUTHOR'S NOTE

True story: I watched the *Bad Moms* movie on a snowy November night in 2016. I was already a mom and a step-mom, and I was pregnant with my youngest. I laughed so hard at these hilarious female characters that I went into labor. A few years later, I was asked to adapt that same movie into a book. The point is: sometimes dreams come true before you even dream them!

ACKNOWLEDGMENTS

I owe some pretty big thanks to Jess Regel and Michelle Weiner and Cait Hoyt and Carrie Thornton. Jeanie Lee, you are a fantastically patient person!

Scott Moore and Jon Lucas are two of the funniest, most generous people I've ever worked with. Thanks, dudes. Hannah Meacock Ross is my Motherhood Role Model.

My husband, Matthew, does most of the parenting in our household, and I'm very grateful for that, especially because, like Kiki, he does fold my underwear neatly.

I have never met Kathryn Hahn or Kristen Bell or Mila Kunis, but I held their performances in my mind as I wrote, and now I believe that we are close personal friends (we are . . . not . . . yet?).

I wouldn't get to be a mom without my kids, who forgive me all my mistakes. Or at least are waiting until their thirties to recap my shortcomings. I love all of you so much, and I love one of you more than the others, but you'll find out who that is at my will reading.

ABOUT THE AUTHOR

Nora McInerny is the author of *It's Okay to Laugh* and *No Happy Endings*, the host of the *Terrible, Thanks for Asking* podcast, cofounder of the Hot Young Widows Club, and the founder of Still Kickin. She's proud to be a Bad Mom.